SWAMP SANTA

JANA DELEON

Miss Fortune Series Information

If you've never read a Miss Fortune mystery, you can start with LOUISIANA LONGSHOT, the first book in the series. If you prefer to start with this book, here are a few things you need to know.

Fortune Redding – a CIA assassin with a price on her head from one of the world's most deadly arms dealers. Because her boss suspects that a leak at the CIA blew her cover, he sends her to hide out in Sinful, Louisiana, posing as his niece, a librarian and ex–beauty queen named Sandy-Sue Morrow. The situation was resolved in Change of Fortune and Fortune is now a full-time resident of Sinful and has opened her own detective agency.

Ida Belle and Gertie – served in the military in Vietnam as spies, but no one in the town is aware of that fact except Fortune and Deputy LeBlanc.

Sinful Ladies Society – local group founded by Ida Belle, Gertie, and deceased member Marge. In order to gain membership, women must never have married or if widowed, their husband must have been deceased for at least ten years.

Sinful Ladies Cough Syrup – sold as an herbal medicine in Sinful, which is dry, but it's actually moonshine manufactured by the Sinful Ladies Society.

CHAPTER ONE

IDA BELLE IMPATIENTLY HONKED THE HORN FOR THE TENTH time.

"What the heck is keeping that woman?" she asked. "We have to beat Celia to the school."

We were sitting in Gertie's driveway, waiting for her to emerge so we could head to the middle school auditorium for the Christmas gala. It sounded fancy but basically, it was a night of performances by schoolkids and a re-creation of the manger scene by the adults, then food and pictures with Santa. Since no denomination could claim ownership of Christmas, the Baptist and Catholic churches worked on a joint production. Plus, neither could find enough volunteers or live animals to manage it alone.

Ida Belle was in charge of the Baptists. Her nemesis, Celia Arceneaux, wrangled the Catholics. Hence the reason for all the horn honking. Ida Belle wasn't about to let Celia outdo her at anything, not even arriving at the school.

"That woman better not be trying on that sexy elf costume again," Ida Belle said. "I almost had a heart attack when I walked in on her with it on the other day."

"Maybe you should knock and yell out for decency before you go into her bedroom," I said.

"She was in the kitchen—cooking a casserole. I couldn't even stay for dinner. Just thinking about what those ingredients had seen..."

I grinned. "Well, at least she plays a wise man in the show. Can't make that sexy."

Ida Belle shot me a worried glance. "One year, she wrapped the robe around her like a toga. Half her thigh was showing, which means all of her .45 was in full view. It took three of us to unwrap it she had it twisted around so tight."

"Why was she strapping a .45 for the Christmas gala?"

"She claimed it was in case any of the animals got out of line."

"Was she referring only to the four-legged kind?"

"Ha! Good question. I confiscated the gun so we didn't have to find out."

I nodded. Since a wise man wouldn't carry a huge handbag, they were probably safe after that.

Finally, the door opened and Gertie stepped out. But she wasn't alone. Perched on her robed shoulder was Francis, her parrot.

"What the heck is she doing with that bird?" Ida Belle asked.

"It looks like she's added an accessory to her costume."

Gertie climbed inside the SUV and we both turned to stare.

"You cannot bring that bird to the show," Ida Belle said.

Francis let out a wolf whistle. "Pretty ladies alert," he said.

"You have to admit, he *is* good for the ego," I said.

"This is a religious performance," Ida Belle said. "Not a reality show. There is no role for ego."

I gave Gertie a shrug. "I tried."

"There's all kinds of animals in the show," Gertie said. "I don't see why I can't bring Francis."

"There are farm animals in the show," Ida Belle said. "A cow, a sheep, a goat...and they add to the presentation. They don't distract."

"What about that year the cow went into labor and plopped out that calf, right there next to the manger?" Gertie asked.

"Fred should never have brought a pregnant cow," Ida Belle agreed.

"Seems like a live birth would have been somewhat appropriate," I said.

"We got a lot of complaints from parents after that one," Ida Belle said. "Apparently, some of them had convinced their children that calves arrived by really big storks."

"The hazard of using live animals, I suppose," I said.

"Aside from that," Gertie said, "the most exciting thing one of those farm animals has done is poop. Until you reach a certain age, you don't get excited about a poop."

"That's not the point," Ida Belle said. "A parrot doesn't fit into the narrative."

"Why not?" Gertie asked.

"Because you're a king from the Orient," Ida Belle said. "Not South America."

"That Orient thing is legend, not fact," Gertie argued. "Maybe a king did visit Jesus from South America."

"Really?" Ida Belle said. "And just how did he get there?"

"You really should watch *Ancient Aliens*," Gertie said. "Hey, maybe next year we can work ET into the production. That would be way cool."

Ida Belle threw her hands in the air. "I give up. Keep the bird, but I take no responsibility for any nonsense he spouts off in front of the whole danged town."

"If he talks too much, I'll give him a grape," Gertie said. "That always shuts him up."

"As soon as we get to the school, I'm going to start a betting pool on when he breaks out singing," I said.

Ida Belle frowned at me. "You are not helping."

"I'll let you have first pick at a slot," I said.

"Maybe you're helping a little." She backed out of the driveway, threw the SUV in Drive, and took off, obviously still intent on beating Celia to the school.

"Did you have the Sinful Ladies meeting last night?" I asked, changing the subject.

Ida Belle was a founding member and the leader of the women's group that had been running Sinful behind the scenes for decades. But her recent engagement had left the group with a dilemma. Married women weren't allowed in unless they'd been widowed for a minimum of ten years. If Ida Belle went through with tying the knot with Walter, then she would no longer be eligible for her own group. That issue had been a hot matter of debate among the Sinful Ladies ever since Walter announced their engagement at Thanksgiving.

"We finally voted last night," Gertie said.

"And?" I'd been waiting to hear the outcome since the moment I learned that Ida Belle had finally said yes to Walter. This was huge. If Ida Belle had to step down from the Sinful Ladies, the universe would be out of balance. Sinful might topple into the Gulf.

"We decided to allow her to remain a member and keep her position as president," Gertie said. "And we're starting a prayer chain for Walter."

I let out a breath of relief. "That sounds reasonable."

"The reality is, no one wanted Ida Belle to step down, much less out," Gertie said. "And after seven...er, a lot of years

4

of doing exactly as she pleased, we didn't figure Walter would be able to make a scratch in her armor."

"So your stance is that past a certain point, a woman can't be influenced by a man," I said.

Gertie shook her head. "Our stance is that *Ida Belle* can't be influenced by a man, but then I could have told them that in kindergarten."

"Got that right," Ida Belle said.

"He finally convinced you to get married," I pointed out. "I'd say that's huge."

"He didn't convince me," Ida Belle said. "I just finally decided it was time."

I grinned. "So when do we start wedding planning? Ally has been showing me pictures in bridal magazines for weeks. If you don't let her help, I think she might explode."

"Tell her to keep those magazines to herself," Gertie said. "I already tried that route, and *someone* suggested I might need surgical help getting them removed if I showed her one more picture."

I shook my head. "Look, I get that you're not into the girlie stuff and you're the furthest thing from the bridezilla mentality that could possibly exist, but this is an exciting thing. Especially for those who've been around for the rejections all those years. You can't expect to finally agree to marry Walter and not have some hoopla surrounding you."

"And I suppose when you marry Carter, you'll have no problem with people shoving dress and cake photos at you all day long?" Ida Belle asked.

"First off, cake is never a problem," I said. "And if Carter and I ever take that step, then I fully expect that it will come with some things that I am supposed to make a big deal over but couldn't care less about. I'll look at it as doing everyone else a favor."

Ida Belle grimaced. "I don't want a big deal. All that crap—frilly dresses and flowers and cakes with icing that's too thick and too sweet—that's not me."

"Well, you can't get married in your bass boat wearing camo," Gertie said.

"Says who?" Ida Belle asked.

"Hey, instead of bouquets, we can all hold pistols," I said.

"You are not helping," Gertie said. "Can't you just this one time find your inner girl?"

"We could wrap the firearms in pink streamers," I said.

"Hide the firearms in the wall," Francis said. "The DEA is on the take."

I glanced at the bird and frowned. "I'm surprised the DEA didn't whack that bird."

"You should hear what he has to say about the mayor over there," Gertie said. "When he gets going, he sounds like a TMZ broadcast."

"You better hope he doesn't TMZ it during the gala," Ida Belle said. "This *is* a family event."

"Which is why I brought Francis," Gertie said. "The kids will love him."

"You think?" I asked. "I thought after the show there was that whole sit-on-Santa-Claus thing. I figured all the kids would be fidgeting until the show was over, just waiting to get in their list of toys."

"Santa is definitely a big draw," Gertie said. "Rollie Long has been Santa for a coon's age. He's awesome."

"I keep hearing that expression," I said. "Do raccoons have a long life expectancy?"

"Not around Sinful," Ida Belle said.

Gertie nodded. "Good eating."

"Yuck," I said. "I'm going to pass. As long as they're not in my attic, I'm on the live-and-let-live train."

6

Ida Belle made a hard right and pulled into the parking lot. I spotted Celia's car just ahead of us.

"Crap!" Ida Belle said and floored it. "Fortune, get ready to run for that door."

"And do what? Guard it until you get there?"

She pulled a key from her pocket and handed it to me. "As long as my key unlocks the door first, I win."

Celia had the back door open on her car, probably about to remove some supplies, when she heard Ida Belle's SUV roaring into the parking lot. She slammed the door shut and took off for the school at a dead run. It wouldn't have been a challenge for me, as Celia could hardly beat me in a foot race, except that she had the advantage of being much closer to the door.

"She's going to beat us," Gertie said as Celia made it to the sidewalk and kept huffing.

"We'll see about that," Ida Belle said and headed straight for the curb.

The SUV bumped over the curb and onto the school lawn so fast that I was glad, once again, that I'd fastened my seat belt. Gertie still hadn't learned her lesson on that one and flew up, hitting her head on the top of the vehicle. Francis, sensing impending doom, abandoned his perch and flew right for the steering wheel, where he totally blocked Ida Belle's view.

"Hard right and brake!" I yelled as Celia came into view.

Ida Belle cut the wheel to the right, flinging Francis off his newly adopted perch and into my lap. Celia tried to stop, but momentum had the advantage. She ran smack into the fender of the SUV with a hit that would have made an NFL linebacker proud.

"You better not have dented my baby!" Ida Belle yelled.

I grabbed the agitated bird and tossed him in the back seat, then flung open the door, jumped out, and ran. No sense

7

losing now. I had unlocked the school door and was standing there like a butler when Celia finally limped up, glaring at me.

"I'm going to have that woman arrested," Celia said. "She tried to run me over."

"If she'd wanted to run you over, it would have already happened," I said. "There was a problem with the bird. It was all an accident."

Ida Belle and Gertie strolled up, grinning as if they didn't have a care in the world.

"It's always an accident with you people," Celia fumed. "But I find it strange that your accidents always tend to fall out on me."

"Not at all," Gertie said. "We inconvenience and otherwise assault others on a routine basis. But it's never intentional."

I coughed.

"Okay," Gertie said. "Sometimes it's intentional. But that's only the bad guys."

"We're not the bad guys," Francis said, and Celia jumped back, her eyes wide.

"That thing is real?" she asked.

"Of course he's real," Gertie said. "Why would I walk around with a stuffed parrot on my shoulder?"

"I don't know why you'd walk around with a real one," Celia said. "You're trying to ruin the show, aren't you? You ruin everything."

"I make things interesting," Gertie said.

"Ladies...and Celia," Ida Belle said. "We have work to do." She strode past me and headed into the school, Gertie right behind her.

I just grinned at the still-sputtering Celia and headed inside as well, letting the door close in Celia's face.

"I should have a more charitable spirit given that it's Christmas," I said.

Gertie waved a hand in dismissal. "That woman would find a flaw with Jesus himself if he showed up."

Francis broke into a rendition of *Jesus Loves Me* and I laughed. I had a feeling this was going to be one heck of a show.

———

CARTER AND I BROKE INTO POLITE APPLAUSE ALONG WITH the rest of the audience as a group of elementary school students ran off stage. They'd just finished singing a medley of favorite children's Christmas tunes with their accompanying string quartet, also made up of elementary school students who had just begun to learn how to play.

I pulled the cotton out of my ears and smiled as Carter did the same.

"I'm glad you came prepared," I whispered. "That quartet sounded like cats in heat."

"I think cats in heat are probably more in tune," he said and smiled. "If they stick with it, by the time they get to high school, they're much better. Of course, we've only had one high school quartet in the show in the past ten years."

"I guess most don't stick with it."

"As a former cat in heat player, I can tell you that it's a lot harder than it looks."

I laughed and got shushed by the lady behind me.

"It's time for the big finale," Carter said.

That meant the adults were on. Well, the adults and Gertie. During setup and practice, there had been some objections to Francis taking part in the show, but it was only Celia's group that complained. Everyone else thought the bird was a cool addition to the otherwise boring farm animals that took part. It wasn't as though you could count on a live birth every year.

The music began and the shepherds walked onstage with their sheep. It pleased me to no end to see that Celia and her crew were relegated to playing the shepherds while Gertie got to play one of the wise men. I imagined that irritated the heck out of Celia, but Ida Belle had explained to me that all slots were allocated based on group vote. Apparently, Celia didn't have enough votes to get a better role.

Once the shepherds and sheep were in place, Joseph and Mary entered. I was impressed that Mary was actually riding on the back of a donkey. Sinful really did go all out. The story progressed from the arrival to the inn being full and to the birth of Jesus. That part was glossed over a bit with the baby magically appearing after a bright glow enveloped the stage.

"Nice cover," I whispered.

Carter grinned.

There was a song break after the birth and the audience sang along to *O Holy Night*. While the robust but rather off-key rendition was performed, the cow took an opportunity to deposit its most recent meal onto the stage. The shepherds, who were positioned next to the cow, lifted their robes to cover their noses and I coughed, trying not to laugh out loud. I could feel Carter shaking beside me but didn't dare look at his face, or I knew I wouldn't be able to hold it in.

Then came the time for the three kings to enter. They walked onto the stage at the same time, their steps in unison. Each carried their offering for baby Jesus in their hands, but only one had a live parrot on her shoulder. A general murmur passed over the crowd and I was sure Gertie had succeeded in confusing everyone in attendance.

Except for me and Carter, of course.

I already knew about Francis being part of the show and

nothing Gertie did confused Carter. His policy where she was concerned was to always expect the unexpected. His policy was also that unless he was on duty, it was an opportunity to catch a moment on film. He pulled out his phone and started filming. I noticed a lot of other people around us doing the same.

The first king stepped forward and started his lines about his offering of gold.

"Melt the gold," Francis said. "Trade it for the guns."

The audience chuckled and one man called out, "Got that right!" Gertie popped a grape in the bird's mouth. That kept him quiet long enough for the second wise man to present his gift. But when Gertie stepped forward, Francis had finished the grape and was ready to chat.

"You're smoking hot," Francis said, looking at Mary.

The chuckles turned to outright laughter and I didn't even bother with the cough cover any longer. Everyone who hadn't pulled out their cell phone before had it out now. Pastor Don, who was the official director, of sorts, waved from the edge of the curtain, probably gesturing for Gertie to get on with her lines.

Gertie knelt down in front of the manger and held out her offering. "I present to the Lord Jesus, frankincense."

"Frank Sinatra is dreamy," Francis said. "Frank Moretti will do the hit."

Joseph reached out to take the gift and I could see his whole body was shaking as he did it. Mary had lifted baby Jesus up until he was almost covering her face.

"Will you shut that bird up?" Celia said. "He's ruining everything."

"Why don't you shut up, Celia?" a woman shouted.

"Celia Arceneaux is the Antichrist," Francis said.

The entire auditorium erupted, no longer making any

effort to contain themselves. The noise startled Francis and he took off from Gertie's shoulder, but his leg leash only allowed him to fly as far as the goat. He landed on the goat's head and started belting out *Away in a Manger*. The startled goat bleated and jumped on top of the hay bale that the cow was currently munching on.

The cow was not impressed with the goat or the singing bird and kicked one of the supports holding up the stable, which sent the entire thing toppling onto Mary and Joseph. Mary involuntarily flung baby Jesus—who, thank God, was a prop—and it hit the donkey right between the eyes. The donkey spun around and took off, dragging the shepherd who'd been charged with holding him. The sheep assumed that the donkey was running for a reason and took off after him, knocking the shepherds down as they scrambled.

And sending Celia face-first into the cow poop.

Some of the audience scrambled onto the stage to lift the barn off Mary and Joseph. Others attempted to corral the panicked animals. Carter, apparently feeling that it was his place as law enforcement to help out, shoved his phone into my hand.

"Keep recording," he said. "This is the most awesome Christmas show ever."

He headed for the stage and as I watched the drama unfold, Ida Belle sidled up to me, shaking her head.

"I told you that bird was going to be trouble," she said.

"Yeah, but it's hilarious." I pointed to Celia, who'd just managed to get upright, then as she took one step, slipped on the poop and fell right back in it.

"She's going to throw her back out if she keeps that up," Ida Belle said.

"I notice her crew didn't stick around to help."

"There are limits to what one will do for Celia. Cow poop is probably one of those lines."

"Look! Gertie nabbed Francis."

Gertie had finally managed to reel in the wandering bird and plopped him back on her shoulder. Then she walked to the edge of the stage, grinned, and took a bow.

The applause was thunderous.

All the kids and more than a few adults rushed toward the stage to get a better look at the bird that stole Christmas.

"Santa is going to be a real snoozefest after this," I said.

I couldn't have been more wrong.

CHAPTER TWO

THE CAFETERIA HAD BEEN TRANSFORMED FROM A PLACE where lunches of questionable content were served to children who would have preferred frozen chicken fingers and into a winter wonderland. It was really quite the accomplishment. I knew that from firsthand experience as I'd been on the decorating committee—thanks to Gertic—and had spent the last three days erecting false storefronts, hauling in a million elves, dancing polar bears, and packages, and making sure fake snow was underneath the whole shooting match. Fake snow with glitter so that it sparkled. No matter how many times I showered, I couldn't get all the glitter off. I had resolved myself to looking like a stripper until I had time to do a large-scale exfoliation.

Snowflakes hung from the ceiling and projectors added to the display by showing flurries on the ceiling, creating the effect of a snowstorm. It was actually really pretty. And with all the colorful buildings that created the fake village, it was very festive. A giant Christmas tree stood off to the side, with bags of candy and cookies hanging on the branches. Each child would receive a bag and the decorating committee had already laid claims to any leftovers, especially as Ally had donated the cookies.

But the big draw was Santa's platform. It was covered in fake snow and had giant candy canes across the back. In the center was a massive red chair with gold trim. There was a section to form a line in front of the platform, created with red-and-white streamers, and the kids were already running for their spots. Santa, in all his glory, was perched in his chair, looking every bit the part.

Except that he was asleep. Or drunk.

He was slumped slightly to the side, his head resting against the curved side panel of the chair. To be fair, I'd given the chair a test run while decorating. It was padded with memory foam and super comfortable. If I'd had the opportunity, I might have taken a nap in it as well. At least, I hoped he was taking a nap. Drunk Santa wasn't a good look for a Christmas event.

Someone had apparently notified Ida Belle of the issue and she ducked under a streamer and headed for the platform. She leaned over to whisper to Santa then straightened up and motioned to me.

"Fortune, can you please help me adjust the chair?" she asked.

I frowned. The chair wasn't adjustable. It was molded plastic and the only way to change it would be fire or a chain saw. But even though her expression was pleasant and her tone was normal, there was a slight edge to it. And I'd seen her stiffen slightly when she'd bent over.

Crap. Drunk Santa.

I ducked under the streamer, trying to figure out how we were going to get him out of the cafeteria without the kids catching on. Then we had to strip him down without risking a sexual harassment lawsuit, so that someone who wasn't drinking could fill in. Then we had to find someone who wasn't drinking. That last one might be the clincher.

I stepped onto the platform and next to Ida Belle.

"Drunk?" I whispered.

She shook her head. "Dead."

I stared. Death was one of those things we had no contingency plan for.

"You're sure?"

"No pulse."

I reached out and felt his neck, careful to position my body so that no one behind me could see what I was doing. Yep, he was dead. But he was still warm.

Before Ida Belle could say a word, I pulled the man out of the chair and dropped him onto the platform. People gasped and several of the kids screamed that I was killing Santa. I tore open the suit, yanked away the padding, and started performing CPR. Ida Belle dropped next to me and delivered the breaths.

The noise level in the room went through the roof and a young man I recognized as Brett, one of the local paramedics, jumped up onto the platform. He checked Santa's vitals then took over for me.

"I called 911 as soon as I saw you drop him on the platform," he said as he pushed.

"I'm glad you didn't think I was assaulting Santa," I said, checking again for a pulse and finding none.

"You were CIA," he said. "You guys don't do anything and leave witnesses."

Carter came running onto the platform and knelt down. "What happened?"

"Ida Belle found him this way," I said. "I started CPR. Brett called 911 and took over for me."

Brett gave Carter a nod. "He's still warm but there's no response. We need a defibrillator."

"I don't think it will do any good," Ida Belle said. "He's been in that same position in the chair since I walked into the cafeteria. And that was at least five minutes ago. I thought he was napping and would wake up when people started filing in. By the time the ambulance gets here, he will be too far gone, and that's assuming he arrested right before we arrived."

Brett removed his hands from the man's chest, sat back on his heels, and sighed. He knew the score better than anyone. Even if there was a slight chance he could get the heart pumping again, the brain had been without oxygen for too long. The damage would be severe.

"That's why you didn't start CPR yourself," I said to Ida Belle. "Well, crap. I probably just scarred a whole generation of Sinful youth for life."

"You tried to save him," Ida Belle said. "I think that's the side of things that parents will be pushing."

Gertie stepped up next to Carter and stared down at the disassembled Santa, tears in her eyes. "At least Rollie went out doing something he loved. This was his favorite day of the year."

"Hunting season opens," Francis said.

"Okay, second favorite," Gertie said.

So far, the crowd had remained behind the streamers. But the quiet that had descended over them when we were administering CPR had grown to a murmur, and now people were softly crying.

"I need to do something," Ida Belle said, and for the first time that I can remember, she looked completely lost.

"I got this," I said and rose to face the crowd. "I'm so sorry, kids, but the weather leaving the North Pole was rough and Santa has a little motion sickness. You know, like when you go out on your boat and the waves are really big and it hurts your stomach."

Some of the kids stopped crying and several nodded. Good. I had them.

"The paramedics are on their way to pick Santa up and then doctors will get him all better in time to deliver presents on Christmas Eve. In the meantime, you're going to tell Francis the parrot what you want, and he'll make sure Santa gets a list when he's better. How does that sound?"

I saw a lot of nodding and a couple smiles. Parents looked ready to pass out in relief.

"We'll get Gertie and Francis a place near the Christmas tree. In the meantime, help yourself to some punch and sweets."

The parents, cluing in that we needed them to move the kids away before they saw more than I could erase by dangling a visit with a parrot in front of them, began to usher their kids toward the food table.

Gertie looked at me wearing a slightly stunned expression. "That was great."

"Exceptional," Ida Belle said. "Thank you. I completely blanked but you covered that so well."

"Well, I might have had some experience in that area," I said.

"You've witnessed more than one dead Santa?" Gertie said. "That has to be some kind of record."

I frowned and Carter glanced at me before responding.

"I think she means distracting children from death," Carter said.

Gertie's and Ida Belle's expressions cleared in understanding.

"Oh," Gertie said. "Sorry. I didn't think..."

"Hey, I never had a parrot to work with," I said. "This one was easy."

Ida Belle nodded. "It will certainly help make up for the lack of Santa. Let's get those streamers moved. Good call choosing the Christmas tree."

The tree was at the opposite end of the cafeteria from Santa, which is exactly why I'd picked it. The farther away we could move the crowd the better.

"I guess I better call Rollie's son," Carter said, and sighed. "You don't know how much I hate making this kind of call, especially right before Christmas."

Gertie had been staring down at Rollie and was now frowning. "Maybe you best hold off on that just yet."

"I'm sorry, Ms. Hebert," Brett said, "but there's nothing the paramedics can do."

"It's not that," Gertie said. "It's that mole peeking out of his fake mustache."

Ida Belle turned around and stared.

"What about it?" I asked, not understanding why a mole mattered since the man was dead.

Carter cursed. "Rollie doesn't have a mole."

"Then who the heck is this?" I asked.

Carter leaned over and pulled off the hat and glasses and completely removed the beard. He looked up at us and shook his head.

"I have no idea."

IDA BELLE AND I MANAGED TO GET THE KIDS ORGANIZED for a visit with Francis, and Ally worked overtime pushing baked goods and punch at everyone. Between the fiasco of a show, Santa getting CPR, the sweets, and all of them getting to pass on their Christmas wishes to a talking bird, I figured their parents were never going to get them to sleep. It was excitement overload.

I had to admit, I was beyond antsy myself. Immediately after discovering that Rollie was not our deceased Saint Nick, Carter had checked Santa's pockets but come up empty. Then he'd placed a quick call to Rollie to see if he could explain what was going on. After receiving no answer, he'd torn out for Rollie's house. Other than a brief text some time later to say that Rollie was all right, we'd been in the cafeteria for hours with all those unanswered questions eating us alive.

"I'm going to explode if we don't find out something soon," Gertie said as we crawled into Ida Belle's SUV.

"You and me both," I said.

"The explosives are under the couch," Francis said.

Ida Belle and I both looked at Gertie.

"Not *my* explosives," she said. "You don't ever keep your weapons near the front door. That's the most likely point of entry for the bad guys. Then you wouldn't have time to access your goodies."

I really hoped that dynamite wasn't Gertie's go-to choice in the case of a robbery or home invasion, but I was too tired to pursue the topic.

Ida Belle let out a long-suffering sigh. "Why can't this town manage a holiday without a death?"

"There *has* been a run on holiday corpses this year," Gertie agreed. "But hey, at least we don't know this one and it was a heart attack, so there's that."

"Exactly," I said. "But who convinced Rollie to let him take his place? And why? I can't come up with a single good reason. At least not anything that doesn't belong in a dark thriller story. And if there *was* a good reason, then why didn't Rollie let you know?"

Gertie frowned. "It *is* weird. I'll give you that."

"I don't like it," Ida Belle said. "Something about it *feels* like a dark thriller story."

"I agree," Gertie said. "I'll be glad when we know something. Anything."

"I'm sure Carter will come by as soon as he can," I said. "That could be ten minutes from now or tomorrow, for all we know. But if you guys want to camp out with me for the duration, I have a crap ton of food and my new reclining couch was delivered this morning."

"Definitely."

"Sounds like a plan."

"I need to take a huge crap."

All three responded at once and Ida Belle gave the bird a hard stare.

"If that bird craps on my seat, you'll be paying for cleanup," she said.

Gertie waved a hand in dismissal. "He's just repeating things he's heard."

"Not helping," Ida Belle said.

"He didn't hear it from me," Gertie said. "Good Lord, I don't walk around my house talking out loud about bathroom business."

"We should drop off Francis before we go to my place," I said. "I don't think he and Merlin can be friends."

"Probably a good idea," Gertie said. "My shoulder's starting to ache anyway. He gets really heavy after a while. And he did have all those grapes…"

Ida Belle shot her a dirty look, then glanced over at me. "So tell us more about this bevy of food you have?"

"Between Ally and Gertie baking for this holiday, I have at least sixty pounds of body weight on my kitchen counter," I said. "I can't eat it all. Friends don't let friends go up a pants size over the holidays."

Gertie laughed. "You have so much to learn about Southern living. Most people have winter clothes and summer clothes. Southerners also have everyday pants and holiday pants. Of course, now that you can get most everything with spandex in it, it makes things a lot easier."

"I refuse to give in to the spandex craze," Ida Belle said.

Gertie rolled her eyes. "You refuse to wear shorts unless we're in a different state."

"Well, I for one am glad that spandex is a part of everyday life for me," I said. "Without yoga pants, I'd probably have to just bop about in underwear."

"There's just as many people in Sinful who wouldn't complain about that as would," Ida Belle said. "The danger, of course, is starting a trend. We don't want to see just any panty-clad butt strolling down Main Street."

"We've all seen Celia's a million times now," Gertie said. "I don't think it can get worse than that."

"Famous last words," Ida Belle said as she pulled into Gertie's drive.

Thirty minutes later, we'd all showered and changed and were sitting in my kitchen, drinking wine and sampling goodies from ten different containers.

"We really should have some protein with all this sugar and carbs," Ida Belle said.

"I have Greek yogurt," I said.

"Oh, bring that out," Gertie said. "I can dip the chocolate-covered strawberries in it. Then I've got all the food groups represented."

"You don't have vegetables," Ida Belle said.

"I do if I eat the leaves," Gertie said.

I considered it a somewhat reasonable compromise but Ida

Belle didn't look convinced. Ten minutes later, she had my grill fired up and chicken cooking. Despite the fact that it was December and 10:00 p.m., it was still seventy degrees outside, which I'd been informed by Gertie was either light jacket or thick T-shirt weather, depending on your hormonal level. I opted for the T-shirt route and we toted wine out to the lawn chairs. Merlin, who'd been pursuing a rather wily lizard when we'd come outside, had opted for the easy and guaranteed meal route and now waited patiently next to the grill.

"So tell me about Rollie," I said, figuring who he was had to play into this whole scenario somehow.

"Not a whole lot to tell," Gertie said. "He's midsixties and has a build that's perfect for the Santa suit, which is how he got tapped for the role years ago. His family has been here three generations, although he's the last one left in Sinful. His parents died years back and his wife maybe five years ago. Cancer. They had one son who never really fit into small-town life, even as a kid. He's a programmer in Silicon Valley."

"Is Rollie trouble?" I asked.

"Not by Sinful standards," Ida Belle said. "He likes his drink but does it at home or while fishing. He's hunted out of season and probably poached a gator or two, but that's it."

"What does he do for a living?" I asked.

"He's retired now," Gertie said. "But he was an electrical engineer. He's the brainy type and quiet. Mostly always been a loner, really."

Ida Belle nodded. "But not in a Unabomber way. He's just a typical geeky introvert. He's always been nice, though, and he's really good with kids...another reason he's kept the Santa role for so long."

Even more strange. A retired, introverted engineer with no bad habits, other than the usual Sinful ones, didn't exactly fit the role of intrigue he had been cast into.

"And you guys really didn't recognize Santa?" I said, still struggling to come up with an explanation for the imposter.

They both shook their heads.

"That's odd," I said. "I mean *really* odd. Because both of you remember people you haven't seen in years or people you've only met once. So if his face doesn't even cause a twitch, that means it's likely you've never seen him before."

"Probably not," Ida Belle agreed.

"But he knew enough about Sinful to know about the Christmas show and that Rollie always played Santa," I said.

They both frowned.

"I hadn't thought about it in that perspective," Ida Belle said. "But you're right."

"Do you have anything online?" I asked. "Social media? Blog? Anything that gives dates and times, maybe pictures and names of past participants?"

"It's on the Baptist church website," Gertie said. "There's always a page dedicated to the event, with a description of everything planned and approximate starting times. There's always a thanks to the volunteers and pictures of past events, of course."

"But does anything identify Rollie as Santa?" I asked.

"Not on our site," Gertie said. "But the Catholic church probably has one, and that's where Rollie attends."

"Rollie hasn't attended church since he was young enough that his mom could make him," Ida Belle said. "But Gertie's right. I suppose he's still a member."

I pulled out my cell phone and looked up the Catholic church website, then navigated to the page about the Christmas show. I scrolled down the page and located a picture of Santa with a child on his lap. I read the caption.

"'Church member Rollie Long always does a great job fulfilling the role of Santa.'"

"Well, there you go," Ida Belle said. "Everything someone needed to know right there on the internet. I miss the days when you had to live with a person to know anything about them."

"It does make stalking a bit easier," I said. "And robbery. People can't seem to keep from advertising on social media when their houses are empty."

"You won't catch me advertising my business on those sites," Ida Belle said. "If someone cares what I had for dinner, that person needs a hobby."

"I'm all over social media," Gertie said.

"Courtesy of your ability to make a scene and a million people with smartphones," Ida Belle said.

Gertie nodded. "Francis and I are totally trending on YouTube right now."

"Our society is doomed," Ida Belle said.

"I'd have to agree with that." Carter's voice sounded behind us and we all turned around to look as he approached. "Please tell me there's enough of whatever that is cooking for me?"

"I think we can make do for Sinful's most dedicated law enforcement officer," Ida Belle said as she checked her watch. "In fact, it's time to take the chicken off the grill."

"Baked beans should be ready," Gertie said. "And the kitchen counter looks like a bakery exploded."

"I couldn't be more grateful," Carter said.

"Grateful enough to tell us about the investigation?" Gertie asked.

"What I know won't take us through one serving of baked beans," Carter said.

"It's got to be more than we know now," Gertie said. "And probably a sight better than the crazy theories we've been rolling around."

"I wouldn't be so sure," he said.

We headed into the house with the chicken, Gertie served up the baked beans, I grabbed more drinks, and we ate silently.

"Jeez Louise," he said finally. "It's quieter than prayer time at church in here."

"That's because people are snoring in church," Gertie said. "We've just been waiting for you to come up for air and tell us what happened with Rollie."

Carter nodded. "I'll tell you but I don't think it's going to help with the crazy theory part of the night. Someone knocked on Rollie's door this evening and when he opened it, the guy punched him in the face then added a couple more blows to the mix. Next thing Rollie remembers is waking up in the dark and tied up. He was still locked in his living room closet when I arrived. He heard me knocking and started yelling."

Gertie gasped. "Good Lord! Is he all right?"

"He's got a shiner and his jaw is going to hurt for a while," Carter said. "He's got some rope burns on his wrists and given his general physical conditioning, I don't imagine his back is going to be happy about being slumped over and bundled up in that closet. But otherwise, he'll be fine."

"Who hit him?" Ida Belle asked.

"Fake Santa," Carter said.

"He knows who Fake Santa is?" I asked.

"Not a clue," Carter said. "But I had the paramedics snap a picture for me and Rollie recognized him as the man who attacked him."

"What the heck is going on?" Ida Belle asked. "This is over-the-top, even for Sinful."

Carter nodded. "I can honestly say I have absolutely no idea. I can't even work up a far-fetched guess."

"Maybe you'll find out when the medical examiner comes up with an identity," I said.

"You don't know how badly I'm praying that Fake Santa's prints are on file," Carter said. "I mean, he's dead so it's not like I'll be arresting him for assaulting Rollie, but the whole thing stinks. Who attacks a man so he can pose as Santa?"

"I'm not sure I want to know the answer," Ida Belle said.

"I'm pretty sure I don't either," Carter said, "but I have to try."

I nodded. I understood all the possible implications, and the fact that it took place during an event focused mostly on children made it that much more insidious. I wanted to know what was going on as much as Carter did and I was certain that as soon as word got around that Rollie wasn't the dead guy, Sinful residents were going to be clamoring for answers. The whole thing had the potential to be a huge nightmare for Carter.

"If there's anything we can do, let us know," I said.

Carter looked at Ida Belle and Gertie. "You guys are sure you didn't recognize him?"

"Not at all," Ida Belle said. "We were just discussing that earlier. If Gertie or I had seen him before, we'd remember. We might not remember who or where but we would have known if we'd seen his face."

Gertie nodded. "I've never seen him before. I'm certain of that."

Carter sighed and started to speak, then his cell phone rang. He pulled it out and answered.

I could hear muffled talking on the other end but couldn't make out the words. But only seconds after the man started speaking, Carter stiffened and I saw his jaw flex.

"You're certain?" he asked, then paused. "On it!"

He jumped up from the table as soon as he hung up the phone. "We have to get Ida Belle to the hospital now!"

He moved beside her and grabbed her shoulder, tugging her up from her chair.

"What the hell are you doing?" Ida Belle asked as I stared, completely confused.

"Santa was poisoned," Carter said. "Cyanide. And you gave him mouth-to-mouth."

CHAPTER THREE

IDA BELLE STARED, HER EYES WIDE. "I THOUGHT HE SMELLED like almonds because he'd been eating the cookies."

"Holy crap!" Gertie said and scrambled out of her chair. "Someone call 911!"

"That will take too long," I said. "Let's go. I'll drive Ida Belle's race car. Carter, you lead. Lights on, please."

Ida Belle didn't utter a single word of protest as I hurried her out the door and into the passenger seat. Gertie was pale and clearly panicked as she jumped into the back seat and leaned forward, studying Ida Belle's face, apparently waiting for her to fall out in the floorboard.

"Stop breathing on me," Ida Belle said, and waved a hand at Gertie. "I'm fine."

But I could tell by her tone that she was as worried as I was. I backed out of the drive and took off after Carter, who had the emergency light on his dash flashing as he tore through town for the highway.

"Let's not panic," I said, trying to recall what I knew about cyanide poisoning. "Any headache, dizziness, abdominal pain?"

"Sure," Ida Belle said. "All those sweets gave me a stomachache. Your driving is giving me a headache. And Gertie's breath is making me dizzy."

Gertie sat back. "She's fine."

I wasn't ready to launch into full-on alarm mode but I was still glad Carter was breaking every traffic law on the books. Given how long it had been since she was exposed, there was a good chance that Ida Belle hadn't ingested any of the poison, but it was always better to be safe. And no way was I taking chances with Ida Belle.

"Should we call Walter?" I asked.

"Hell no!" Ida Belle said. "He'll probably drive himself into a ditch trying to get to the hospital and for what? So all of you can sit around and wait for doctors to tell you there's not a darn thing wrong with me?"

I glanced in the rearview mirror at Gertie, who held up her cell phone. A second later, I heard her punching the buttons.

"Are you sending a text?" Ida Belle turned around and snatched the phone from Gertie's hand.

"Nope," Gertie said. "I *sent* a text."

Ida Belle tossed the phone back at her. "That does it. I'm returning your Christmas gift."

"I'll take it," I said. I had helped Ida Belle pick out the riflescope and knew it was top-notch.

"You told me to send it," Gertie accused.

"I never said a word," I said.

"You wanted me to," Gertie said. "I could tell by your look."

"I'm going to keep your gift for myself," Ida Belle said.

"Give us a break," I said. "You know if Carter hasn't already called, he will as soon as he stops his Dale Earnhardt routine."

No way was Carter escorting Ida Belle to the hospital and then not letting his uncle know that the woman he was now engaged to might have been poisoned. That was a level of aggravation that he didn't need.

"Fine," Ida Belle said. "You can have your gifts, but I'm returning Carter's. This is all unnecessary."

"If it were me or Gertie, would you be saying the same thing?" I asked.

"Busted," Gertie said.

Ida Belle sighed. "I'll get checked out. But I'm telling you, I'm good. I don't have any symptoms and I haven't since I gave him mouth-to-mouth."

"You looked a little worried back in Fortune's kitchen," Gertie said.

"Well, of course I was worried," Ida Belle said. "I'd just been told I might have been poisoned, but once I had time to process it, I realized that I haven't had any side effects."

"Look at it as doing Carter a favor," I said. "If it got out that you could have been exposed to cyanide as part of a murder investigation, and he didn't insist that you get checked out, it wouldn't look good for him."

"That's true," Ida Belle agreed. "But I still think everyone could have waited until tomorrow to tell Walter about this."

"Not if we all want to continue living in Sinful," Gertie said. "Walter is a peaceful man, but I have a feeling that when it comes to you, he could get Old Testament."

Ida Belle frowned. "This is all my fault. If I hadn't agreed to marry him, no one would feel obligated to put him in the loop. And this kind of thing is exactly why I've said no for so many years."

"It will be okay," I said, understanding her dilemma. "Walter has known you your entire life. He's hardly going to fall apart when something bad happens."

Gertie nodded. "If he did, the man would be practically numb by now."

We pulled into the emergency room drive and Carter rushed inside, calling for help. An orderly hurried out with a gurney and Ida Belle climbed out of the SUV and glared at him.

"Until I'm dead, I'm not taking a ride on one of those things," Ida Belle said.

The orderly, apparently used to a variety of denial and bad manners, simply nodded and waved his hand at the door. "Come with me and I'll get you in a room."

Carter was talking to a doctor as they walked by and Ida Belle shot him a dirty look.

"I got a call from the ME," the doctor said as Gertie and I stepped up. "Has she had any symptoms?"

"No," I said. "And we've been with her since she administered mouth-to-mouth."

The doctor nodded. "That's good. I'll run some tests but if she's not presenting with any side effects, she either didn't ingest or inhale any of the poison or didn't process enough to cause problems. But we'll make sure."

"Thank you," Carter said, and looked at us as the doctor walked away. "This will probably take a while. I'm going to make a coffee run. Orders?"

"I can do it," I said.

"That's all right," he said. "I'm already in the mode."

Gertie and I told him what we wanted and he headed out. Five minutes later, Walter rushed in the ER wearing striped pajamas like you saw in the movies and started demanding answers from the nurse at the desk. Then it hit me why Carter had offered to do the coffee run.

"That was sneaky," I said to Gertie. "He left us to deal with Walter."

"I don't know whether to be irritated at his scheming or admire his cleverness."

"Let's see how bad a reaming we get, then we can decide."

I stood up and hurried over to a clearly distraught Walter and touched his arm. He whirled around and looked relieved to see me standing there.

"What's going on?" he said. "This nurse won't tell me anything."

"That's because she doesn't know anything," I said, and guided him over to a couch to sit. I explained everything that had happened, making sure I stressed what the doctor had said and that Ida Belle had never experienced any symptoms.

His shoulders slumped in relief. "When Carter called me, I about had a heart attack. Then I got that text from Gertie and I knew it was serious. You three don't tattle on one another."

Gertie shot me a guilty look.

"Well...given the status change in your relationship, we didn't feel it would be right to wait until tomorrow," I said.

"Oh, I see," Walter said. "So if she'd said no to my proposal, I'd still be none the wiser."

"Yeah, pretty much," Gertie said.

He raised one eyebrow. "Really? So what you're saying is you wouldn't have told me because you're more afraid to face me than Ida Belle?"

"No," Gertie said. "Ida Belle scares the heck out of us. We wouldn't have told you because we *like* you more than Ida Belle. No sense worrying about that woman if there's no cause."

His lower lip trembled and finally he smiled. It wasn't a huge smile, but at least he wasn't as stressed as when he ran in.

"You're sure she's all right?" he asked.

"I think so," I said. "You know me. If I thought Ida Belle was in any physical danger, I'd be standing in the ER with a gun on the doctor."

Walter looked satisfied. "So I guess we just sit and wait."

"You can take a nap if you'd like," Gertie said. "You're already dressed for it."

Walter looked down at his clothes, apparently just now realizing he'd run out wearing his pajamas and no shoes.

"Good Lord!" he said. "I've lost all sense of propriety. What are people going to think?"

"I think it's cute," I said. "Ida Belle thinks we're all a pain in the butt. No one else matters. And is propriety really a thing in Sinful?"

Walter's ears reddened when I said he was cute and he stared down at his bare feet.

"Come on," I said. "Let's figure out which chairs are the most comfortable and stake them out. We'll leave the hardest one for Carter since he took off out of here for coffee, I'm guessing so he wouldn't be the one facing you."

Walter shook his head. "I haven't heard the boy sound that scared since he shot a hole in my boat."

"He probably feels responsible since he didn't insist Ida Belle go to the hospital right away," Gertie said.

"Why on earth would he?" I said. "We thought the guy died of a heart attack. How were we supposed to know he was poisoned? And short of arresting and hog-tying her, Carter would have never gotten Ida Belle to go to the hospital. We barely got her here after she found out she'd been exposed to cyanide."

"That woman takes stubborn to a whole new level," Walter said. "Since we'll be sitting here a while, why don't you tell me what's going on with this Santa business."

"The only part you don't know is about Rollie," I said, and told him what had happened to the regular Santa. "That's all we know. Or all Carter's telling us. We wouldn't have gotten cause of death if Ida Belle hadn't been exposed. You know his policy."

"I do, and I happen to agree with it," Walter said. "You three do some good work but you also put yourself in some dangerous situations. It's not just Ida Belle I care about, you know."

I reached over and squeezed his hand. "You're a good man. And Ida Belle is lucky to have you."

"Got that right," Gertie said. "It takes a special kind of person to put up with her for decades on end. I would know."

"You're one to talk," Walter said. "That bird of yours stole the show tonight. Well, maybe a better phrase would be took down the show. You know Celia went straight from the stage to the sheriff's department wanting to file charges against Gertie for assault. Myrtle took one whiff and marched her back outside onto the sidewalk and had Deputy Breaux put Mentholatum up his nose before he went out to listen to her complaint."

"But Gertie never touched her," I said. "And technically, the sheep she was supposed to be watching assaulted her."

"The truth never mattered much to Celia," Walter said. "Especially not if she's the butt of the joke and Ida Belle and Gertie are laughing on the other end of things."

"So what did Deputy Breaux do?" Gertie asked.

Walter grinned. "He told her there was no way he could take her complaint without passing out and said she could either go home and shower and come back or he'd be happy to hose her down behind the building."

"Go Deputy Breaux," I said.

"She ranted, of course," Walter said, "threatening to get him fired and all, which everyone knows isn't happening as long as Lee is sheriff and Carter is really running things. Finally, Deputy Breaux got tired of listening to her—or smelling her—and went inside and locked the door."

"Did she ever come back?" I asked.

"Not that I'm aware of," Walter said. "But tomorrow's a whole other day."

I nodded, wondering what tomorrow would bring. Today had been stuffed rather full. Christmas shows, panicked barn animals, assault, unknown identity, murdered Santas, ER visits...

But at least things were never dull.

———

GIVEN THE AMOUNT OF SWEETS AND WINE CONSUMED THE night before, I'd planned on falling into bed and going into a light coma. Unfortunately, the late-night hospital visit and subsequent coffee ingestion had overridden the carbs and sugar fest and it was 4:00 a.m. before I crawled into bed. We'd waited for hours for the doctor to come back with test results. He'd finally stepped up the pace when Ida Belle simply got off the bed and walked out of the ER. He'd caught up with her in the lobby, but all requests for her to remain overnight fell on deaf ears.

The doctor finally admitted that it was just a precaution— and probably one he was taking because her situation was directly tied to a murder—and agreed to discharge her. Ida Belle had told him what he could do with his precaution and his discharge and stomped out the front door. She'd continued to express her displeasure by threatening to shoot anyone who tried to stay with her overnight. None of us were willing to test her on that one, so I dropped off Gertie, then drove to my house and turned over her vehicle. She barely waved before driving away.

Despite all the coffee and the million unanswered questions I'd come up with while waiting at the hospital, I fell asleep quickly and stayed that way for a good long time. It was after 8:00 a.m. when I finally awakened. Merlin was standing in the bed next to me, staring right into my face when I opened my eyes. I jumped up, startling him, and he peeled out across my head to make his escape. I yelled all kinds of threats as he fled the room, but I knew when I walked downstairs, he'd be sitting in front of the pantry, glaring at me because I was an hour late with his breakfast.

And because I would be sporting stinging claw marks on my head the rest of the week, I decided to take my time getting dressed. When I finally made it to the kitchen, he'd knocked every can of cat food off the shelf and was standing in the middle of them, giving me a look that could kill. If cats had opposable thumbs, I was convinced they wouldn't tolerate humans.

I made him even madder by taking time to put on my coffee first and didn't even hear Gertie come in over the sounds of his wailing.

"You should never antagonize a cat," Gertie said as she stepped into the kitchen. "Have you smelled cat pee? I mean, up close and personal, like on your pillow or your new reclining couch?"

Aside from the litter box, which I cleaned daily and had those deodorizers, the answer was not really. But if the woman who'd kept an alligator in her bathtub was issuing a warning about animals, I figured I better listen. I grabbed a can and served up Merlin's breakfast. He took a sniff, then walked off.

Butthole.

"Even without making a sound, he always manages to have the last word," I said.

"Why do you think I don't have a cat?" Gertie said. "I don't need the competition. I've got enough stubborn and crazy going on with just myself."

"Speaking of which, have you talked to Ida Belle this morning?"

"I called her grumpy butt as soon as I got up. She was waxing her SUV and said we better not try to treat her like one of those old, sick women or she'd give our Christmas gifts to Celia."

"Ouch. She's really peeved about this."

"Ida Belle loathes hospitals and can't stand people fussing over her when something is wrong. Given that she spent a good portion of the night in the ER, with all of us lurking in the lobby, and she's right as rain, she's really hacked. Not at us, really, but more at the situation."

"I get that. Maybe waxing her SUV will burn off her aggravation."

Gertie nodded. "Sooner or later, she'll be over here wanting to hash everything out. It is a murder, after all, and a particularly nasty one as someone chose to do it in the middle of our Christmas celebration."

"I've been waiting all night to ask my questions, so I guess waiting a little longer won't kill me. Is there any particular reason you stopped by?"

"Can't a friend just pay a visit?"

"Some friends, yes. But your visits usually come with additional requirements."

"Well, I know you said you weren't going to decorate since the big Christmas Day gathering will be at Emmaline's house, but I was hoping I could change your mind. I've got more tree decorations than any ten people can use so I hauled some more out of storage and brought them over."

"What are we going to decorate? The couch?"

"No. I had an old artificial tree as well. I used to put it on the landing upstairs but I'm too lazy to carry all that mess up there anymore. Plus, I'm having enough trouble keeping

Francis out of the downstairs tree. I don't need him venturing to the second floor."

I'd really hoped to avoid the whole decorating thing. The truth was, I hadn't decorated a Christmas tree since my mother died. Carter's mom, Emmaline, had put up a tree in his house and decorated it while he was at work, so I'd gotten out of helping there. And I'd insisted that I didn't need to spend the money on buying a bunch of decor for my own house since Emmaline always hosted Christmas at her place.

But Gertie's hopeful look broke me down. Maybe it was time for new traditions, and decorating a Christmas tree with one of my best friends was definitely the kind of thing I needed to adopt.

"What the heck," I said. "Let's go take a look and figure out the best place to put it, or maybe you can just tell me where Marge put hers."

Gertie laughed. "You bought her house with everything she owned in it. Have you come across a Christmas tree? Or any decorations?"

"Now that you mention it, I guess I haven't."

After I officially bought the house, Ida Belle and Gertie had helped me go through everything and get it sorted into things I would keep, things I would donate, and things that belonged in a landfill. We'd hauled a lot of stuff to local charities but I couldn't recall a single Christmas decoration among them.

"So what gives?" I asked. "Marge didn't like Christmas?"

"She loved Christmas. Not as much as hunting season, of course. Marge just wasn't into frills. You see how her house was decorated. Functional sparse is what I always called it. One year, I put a wreath on her door. She used it for target practice."

"That *does* send a message. I can't promise I won't shoot anything, but if I do, it won't be intentional."

"Can't ask for more than that. Let's go unload my car. I might have gone overboard."

Since Gertie usually thinks her over-the-top antics are completely normal, I was more than a little worried about what 'overboard' in the Christmas decor arena looked like. Apparently, it took the form of twelve storage containers shoved into an ancient Cadillac. The tree was strapped to the top. If I hadn't seen it myself, I wouldn't have believed it possible.

An hour and four hundred and sixty-two cuss words later, we finally had the tree erected, all the lights working, and were making a dent in hanging ornaments. I had to admit that it looked kind of pretty tucked against my staircase. We finished up the ornaments and Gertie held up some bags.

"Tinsel or no?" she asked. "It's a mess to clean up but it's pretty and sparkly."

"Why not? I've got time on my hands. A little cleaning won't kill me."

Gertie handed me a box and we started sprinkling tinsel on the tree. "I really think you'll start seeing business after the holidays. Most people pretty much put things on hold between Thanksgiving and New Year, then they hurry to play catch-up on all the things they were putting off."

I nodded. "I figured as much. And it's okay to have some downtime. I've been taking some online courses on crime scene investigation and forensics. Really cool stuff. And I've been enjoying relaxing more with you guys and Ally and Carter."

"It would be more relaxing if dead bodies didn't keep popping up," Gertie said.

"True. But at least this last one wasn't a Sinful resident."

"I'm not sure if that makes me feel better or worse, given the circumstances."

I sighed. "Yeah. I'm kind of with you on that one. I hope the ME identifies the guy soon and we get some sort of plausible reason for him doing what he did."

"But what kind of plausible reason could there be?"

"I have absolutely no idea."

"Me either."

"You want a soda?"

"Yes, please. I think those boxes had ten pounds of dust on them. We're going to have to do a good clean in here when we're finished with the tree."

I headed to the kitchen and snagged some sodas and heard a familiar cry at the back door. Apparently Merlin was done with his morning trek and ready to come in and take his all-day nap. It still amazed me how much time cats spent sleeping. I opened the door and he strolled right by me, clearly still miffed about his late start to breakfast. I figured two could play the ignoring game, so I headed back to decorating central with the drinks.

He must have heard Gertie singing because instead of stopping at his food bowl, as he usually would have, he followed me into the living room. I handed Gertie her drink and she took it, then her eyes widened.

"Uh-oh," she said.

I followed her gaze and saw Merlin staring at the Christmas tree as if aliens had just landed. He stood midstep, frozen in place like a statue, his huge green eyes locked on the twinkling tinsel.

CHAPTER FOUR

GERTIE OPENED HER MOUTH TO SAY SOMETHING BUT BEFORE she could get the words out, Merlin sprang from the middle of the living room floor and right into the center of the Christmas tree. He wasn't a huge cat, but he'd carried the momentum of an NFL linebacker. And since he'd hit the tree midway up and the stand was as old as the tree and a little loose, the whole thing started to sway.

As I rushed to grab the tree, Merlin took the movement as a sign that he needed to exit, but he didn't opt for running down, which would have benefited us all. No, in true cat form, he went straight up the wobbling tree, then launched from the top of it onto the stairs. That final kick from his hind legs was all it took to send the tree toppling over.

I attempted to shove Gertie out of the way, but the cord for the lights was wrapped around her leg, so instead, she fell sideways into the tumbling tree. I saw a flash of blinking lights and tinsel before the whole shooting match came crashing down on top of us.

"It's electrocuting me!" Gertie yelled.

I flailed around a bit, sliding on tinsel, and as I crawled out from under the tree, the front door flew open and Ida Belle ran in, guns blazing. She took a couple seconds to make sense of the mess, then dropped her gun in the recliner and came running over to help me lift the tree off of Gertie, who was yelling "ouch" every couple seconds.

The frayed light cord wrapped around her ankle explained everything. I leaped over the tree for the wall and yanked the extension cord from the outlet. Gertie flopped back onto the floor in relief, her leg bent up as she tried to reach her ankle.

"Are they going to have to amputate?" she asked.

"Good Lord, woman," Ida Belle said. "You've got a couple of pink marks. A bite from a fire ant would have done more damage." She grabbed the offending light cord and held it up for Gertie to see. "What were you doing, using damaged lights?"

"I thought I'd fixed it," she said as she sat up.

"You could have burned Fortune's house down," Ida Belle said. "This is exactly why I have a giant plastic Santa in my living room and nothing else. No mess. No risk of fire. And what the heck happened here anyway?"

I told her about Merlin's magnificent tree leap and she shook her head.

"Christmas trees are like taunting cats in their own space," she said. "The medical clinic does the bulk of its December business on Christmas tree injuries. Cats, drunks, and kids. That's the order in which the destruction plays out."

I frowned at Gertie. "That would have been useful information to have before I agreed to put up a tree."

"I thought Merlin would be classier," Gertie argued. "Or at least be afraid you'd shoot him."

"Well, apparently, we've established who's in charge at my house," I said. "And it's not me."

Gertie looked at the destroyed tree and sighed. "I guess I better get started cleaning this up."

"It can wait," Ida Belle said. "Merlin can't knock it over twice, and now that the threat of fire is contained, I have something to tell you."

If Ida Belle the Orderly wanted to delay cleaning up the disaster to talk, then that meant she must have found out something about Fake Santa. I pulled Gertie up from the floor and we headed into our war room, otherwise known as my kitchen.

Ida Belle barely slid into her chair before she started talking. "Do you remember Margaret Holden?" she asked Gertie.

Gertie pursed her lips. "That woman from Mudbug who helped with the food drive last year?"

"That's the one," Ida Belle said. "She called this morning about putting together a coat drive for kids after the holiday. I must have sounded distracted because she asked if everything was all right, and I told her about Rollie and Fake Santa. I left out the part about the poisoning, of course. Well, she said they had a problem with their regular Santa this year as well. Apparently, he won a weekend stay at the casino in New Orleans and totally bailed. She'd no sooner put down the phone from talking with him than she got a call from a Santa service saying they still had some slots available and were happy to do things at a discount."

"A Mudbug resident ditching a Santa gig for a free stay at the casino isn't exactly a smoking gun," Gertie said. "It would be harder to find someone who wouldn't ditch for the free casino stay."

"That's true," Ida Belle said. "Except Margaret said the Santa didn't ask for payment after the event. Said the company would send a bill. She thought it was odd so she called the number but it was no longer in service. So she took to the internet to track down the company and it never existed."

"What in the world?" Gertie asked.

"It gets worse," Ida Belle said. "Margaret said that night after the event, someone broke into the photographer's studio."

"Was anything missing?"

"Everything's digital these days," Ida Belle said. "But someone accessed her computer. She can't tell what was done because they reformatted the hard drive afterward so no one can access the history."

"What does it mean?" Gertie asked. "I'm completely lost."

"I'm afraid I am as well," Ida Belle said. "I could have written off their Santa bailing for the casino but combine that with the fake company and the photography studio break-in, and it's just too much to ignore. Especially given the lengths the imposter went to in order to play Santa here. I can't help but think it was the same guy."

"I agree," I said. "I just wish we knew why it's happening. Hey, do you have Rollie's number?"

"Sure," Ida Belle said. "We have to coordinate with him on the Santa thing. But why? I don't know if he'll talk to us about his attacker. Carter probably already read him the riot act."

"This doesn't have anything to do with his attack," I said. "At least not that Rollie will understand. I want you to ask him if he won a free stay at a casino in New Orleans."

"Oh!" Ida Belle said. "Smart. But I think we ought to do it in person. At least then, if he's hedging, we'll be able to tell."

Gertie nodded. "That way we get our answer whether he tells us or not. And he's more likely to say something he shouldn't with a sympathetic audience in front of him."

"Do we have a valid reason to pay him a visit?" I asked.

"He was injured and we have food," Gertie said. "That's all we need."

"Good, then that's on the list," I said. "Who was the photographer for your event?"

"The same one as the other event," Gertie said. "She's new to Mudbug and has been doing all the holiday events for the surrounding towns."

"Is her studio in Mudbug?" I asked.

"Yes, but it's not a separate building. She turned the garage in the house she's renting into her studio," Gertie said, then gasped. "Oh Lord! I guess she wasn't home when the break-in occurred. What if she had been? That could have turned out really bad given how Rollie was handled."

"Then we'll be thankful she wasn't," Ida Belle said. "But what is he after? The only things on the studio computer are pictures."

"Pictures of kids," Gertie said. "If he wasn't already dead, I'd cut off some delicate parts."

"But it wasn't just pictures of kids, right?" I asked. "It was pictures of the entire event."

"That's right," Ida Belle said. "She took pictures and video of the performances and moved around before and after the different performances taking candid shots of the attendees."

She stopped talking and her mouth formed an O. "He was looking for someone."

"I think so," I said.

"But why all the secrecy?" Gertie asked. "Why not just show up at the events himself and see if the person he was looking for was there?"

"Because maybe the person he was looking for doesn't want to be found," I said. "And if they saw him, they'd take off."

"Like an abused wife or adult kid who ditched a crappy parent," Ida Belle said. "That would make sense. Playing Santa, he could be right in the middle of things but the person he was looking for would never be the wiser."

"That's way too stalker for my taste," Gertie said.

"Which is probably why he's dead," I pointed out.

"Good riddance," Gertie said. "I mean, I know Carter has to figure out what happened because that's his job and all, but do we care?"

Ida Belle frowned. "I'm more than a little irritated that someone's shady behavior caused me to spend half the night in the ER. Not to mention the undue amount of attention I received for it. Given that it's Christmas, I would normally let it go...in the spirit of the season. But what if this isn't over? He was looking for someone. Who? And are they still in danger? Or was he the only person looking for them?"

"So someone in Sinful might still be in danger," I said.

"Or Mudbug," Gertie said. "Or I suppose any of the other towns he might have hit up. We don't know that it was only these two. He might have had more on his list for later on as well."

"But he was killed here," I said. "So that's where the trail ends."

"Oh!" Gertie's eyes widened. "You're right. But if we have no idea who he was looking for, we can't warn them. That's bad."

Ida Belle said. "It's worse than bad. We don't even know the identity of the dead man, which might give us a clue as to who he was looking for."

Gertie clapped. "I love a good puzzle."

"This isn't a puzzle," Ida Belle said. "This is a black hole."

"I have to admit, I wouldn't even know where to start," I said.

"Until we know who he is, we can't figure out who he was looking for," Gertie said. "Not like they're going to up and volunteer that when they're probably the one who killed him. So motive is out but we've still got opportunity."

"That's true," I said. "Of course, it would narrow down things to know how the cyanide was administered, but I suppose we could start with opportunity."

"And by start, you mean with a list of everyone who worked at and attended the Christmas event?" Gertie asked.

"So it's not a short list," I said. "But we can narrow it down."

"You're assuming we could even come up with a comprehensive list of people who were there," Ida Belle said.

"Well, you know all the volunteers," I said. "And we could ask your ladies to help us flesh things out—where everyone was at what time."

"Oh goodie!" Gertie said. "Another case."

I shook my head. "Not another case. We have no client. This is just us poking our nose into police business, and you know how everyone but the three of us feels about that."

"Bunch of stick-in-the-muds," Gertie said. "Fine. So we'll be quiet about it. We can do quiet."

Ida Belle stared. "You just acquired a bird that repeats everything you say. How is that quiet?"

"So we don't talk business at my house," Gertie said. "Not like I'm going to bring Francis over here. Especially with Merlin on a tear."

Ida Belle looked at me. "I noticed a scratch at your hairline."

"I slept through his breakfast," I said.

Ida Belle nodded. "And you two wonder why I have no pets."

"I don't wonder," I said. "And let the record state that I didn't actively seek a pet myself. Merlin moved in and I'm afraid to kick him out."

"Makes sense," Ida Belle said. "So how do we approach this non-case? I suppose we could talk to Rollie first. He probably doesn't know much but maybe Fake Santa said something while he was shoving him in the closet. Maybe he'll be outraged enough to talk, even if Carter told him not to."

"Maybe," I agreed. "So yeah, might as well start there. What do you bring for a drop-in after an assault? Does a casserole work for that too?"

"My casserole works for everything," Gertie said.

"She's right," Ida Belle said. "Gertie is pretty much famous for two things—causing trouble and her casseroles. People probably tolerate the first mostly because of the second. I'd bet she provides the entire town with at least one meal per year."

"Okay, then we grab one of your creations and pull a drop-in on Rollie." I stared out the window for a moment, watching the tide rolling in on the bayou, and suddenly a thought hit me.

"I'm an idiot!" I half yelled, startling Gertie a bit.

Ida Belle raised one eyebrow. "I'm not going to come right out and disagree until I hear what occurred to you, but in general, I'm going with you're not."

"Fake Santa didn't drop in from the sky," I said. "All we need to identify him is his license plate."

"Holy crap!" Gertie said, now yelling herself. "That's genius."

Ida Belle frowned. "Except there weren't any other vehicles in the parking lot when we left the school. And we were the last to leave."

"You're sure?" I asked.

She nodded. "It's a constant habit of mine...looking at cars. I can't help but to notice one. Old cars, new cars, fast cars, slow cars. It's an addiction, really. Trust me, the parking lot was empty."

"Maybe he had an accomplice," Gertie said. "A getaway driver."

"And he got away when Fake Santa died?" Ida Belle said. "Not much of an accomplice if he didn't even call for help."

"Let's back up a bit," I said. "Who let Santa into the cafeteria?"

"Since my group furnished the bulk of the snacks—thanks mostly to Ally and her incredible skills—Celia's group was responsible for organizing that end of things."

"So one or more of her people would have let Santa in and told him where to set up?" I asked. "I wonder why they didn't notice that it wasn't Rollie? Wouldn't they have talked to him?"

"They probably would have tried," Gertie said. "But remember, Rollie wasn't much of a talker with adults. Just kids. I think he found them less judgmental. He's kinda an odd duck."

Ida Belle nodded. "You'll see when we visit him. I don't think he's ever been tested, but I'd guess he's a genius. People with those huge brains sometimes have a problem with social skills."

"But they would have noticed if he had someone with him," Gertie said.

"I don't think he had an accomplice," I said. "It doesn't fit. Fake Santa went to great lengths to get into the event in disguise. We have to assume that's so he couldn't be recognized, which means we also have to assume that someone is on alert."

"The person he's looking for," Ida Belle said.

"Exactly," I said. "So if he had an accomplice, that's a strange person hanging around who no one knew and given

Rollie's hermit tendencies, it would be unlikely he would have acquired a friend."

"Maybe he waited in the car," Gertie said.

"And left when he saw the ambulance?" I asked. "They took Santa out in a body bag. He'd have no way of knowing who was in it unless he asked someone. And if some strange guy was sitting in a car at a children's school, wouldn't someone have mentioned it?"

"Definitely," Ida Belle said. "Sinful residents jump on a new face right away, and a stranger lurking around kids wouldn't have made it five minutes without someone asking them who they were."

I nodded. "So if there wasn't a vehicle in the parking lot, he either parked somewhere else or used a car service."

"The second doesn't seem likely," Ida Belle said. "If you check around, you can get car service out of New Orleans to drive you to Sinful, but it's hard to get them to come out here for a pickup. And if he had someone waiting, they would have come looking for him."

I put my hands in the air. "So there's a vehicle somewhere. We just need to find it. I say we check the streets near the school before we head over to Rollie's. Because if Carter hasn't thought of it already, he will."

Ida Belle jumped up. "And he would have the car towed. We'll clean up that mess in your living room later."

We hurried out and headed for the middle school, doing a quick check of the parking lot there first, but it was empty as Ida Belle had declared. Then we started circling the streets surrounding the school, starting with one block away. We had just turned on a street with houses that backed onto the school playground when we saw Carter parked at the curb, leaning against his truck and staring right at us.

"Crap," I said. "I know that look."

"He beat us," Gertie said, and sighed.

He walked toward the SUV as we approached, and Ida Belle rolled down the window. "Can I help you, Officer?" she asked politely.

"Yeah," he said. "You can go home and wrap gifts or strings lights or watch Christmas movies. Basically, anything but interfere in my investigation."

"You found the vehicle, didn't you?" I asked.

His expression shifted from slightly annoyed to blank, but he didn't say a word.

"He found it," I said. "Won't you at least tell us who the guy is? We're going to find out eventually."

His jaw twitched. "You'll find out when I'm ready to make a public statement concerning the case."

I smiled. "He doesn't know. What happened? The car was stolen?"

He turned around and walked back to his truck, climbed inside, and drove away. Ida Belle pulled over to the curb and parked.

"So what now?" she asked.

"I'd still like to get a look at that vehicle," I said. "At least the license plate would tell us if it was stolen, which at least gives us an area to start looking."

"It will be at the impound," Gertie said. "Even if we could just waltz in there and snap a picture, we wouldn't know which license plate to take a picture of. And they're not going to tell us."

Ida Belle looked at me and smiled. "She's right. They won't tell us anything, but they might tell the property owners."

"I don't understand," I said.

"The impound doesn't own the property," Ida Belle said. "They lease it. The property owner would have the right to go onto the property and in this case, I bet they could convince someone to tell them what vehicles were towed in since last night."

I knew Ida Belle had investments, but I'd always thought they were mostly stock market. "Don't tell me you're the property owner?" I asked.

Ida Belle shook her head. "But the owners are friends of yours. The Heberts own the property."

Gertie perked up. "Oh, that's right!"

I stared at her. "Law enforcement leases their impound lot from the Heberts?"

That was wrong on so many levels I couldn't quite wrap my mind around it. The Heberts had several legitimate businesses that they operated and filed taxes on, but everyone knew that their real income was from the sort of things the IRS never heard about. As far as I knew, they didn't participate in any hard-core criminal activities. No gunrunning or drugs. In fact, they had an issue with both. But they did dabble in loan-sharking and bookmaking and probably a host of other items that kept them in the know among criminals. Of course, I knew those lines of work were necessary for the other role they played—federal informants. But no one else was aware of their duplicity, which is why Carter still believed the worst of them and everyone else in the area steered clear unless they were foolish enough to do business with them.

"How the heck did it happen that the Heberts are leasing to law enforcement?" I asked.

"Now that's an interesting story," Ida Belle said. "Apparently, an accountant for the state had his hand in the till to cover his gambling debts, so he wasn't paying the property taxes. He was also ditching the late notices when they came in. By the time his boss found out about it, the property was up for auction and the Heberts had the winning bid."

"Let me guess," I said. "The Heberts held the accountant's gambling debt."

Ida Belle grinned. "Well, there was no evidence of that at the time, and since the accountant had a heart attack and died right after the auction, no one is ever likely to ever prove it."

"You have to give them props for flair," I said. "So why didn't the cops just move the impound lot?"

"Too much money to rebuild," Ida Belle said. "Concrete isn't cheap, then there's all the fencing and the security required. And since the budget was already stretched and the government was trying to downplay their screwup, they weren't about to ask taxpayers for the dollars to build a new lot when leasing was way less."

"I'll bet the Heberts laugh every month when they get that lease payment," I said.

"Probably. So anyway, that's why I figure you can get the information, because the guys working impound aren't likely to tell the Heberts no. But I guess I'm wondering what good you think it will do. If you don't think Carter got anything out of it, what can we hope to find?"

"I don't know," I said. "But I'd still like to know what he knows."

Ida Belle started up her vehicle and pulled away. "Then I guess we're paying the Heberts a visit."

"Oh goodie!" Gertie bounced up and down in her seat and clapped. "I just love the Heberts."

Ida Belle shook her head. "Said no one in Sinful ever."

I laughed. I kinda loved the Heberts too.

CHAPTER FIVE

I HAVE TO ADMIT, I WAS MORE EXCITED ABOUT VISITING THE Heberts than I probably should have been and far more excited than Carter would have liked. He still had trouble deciding what he should think about them. He was grateful that they'd helped me at a pivotal point in my life, and one could have argued had helped save it. Their right-hand man, Mannie, had actually saved Carter's life. So he was grateful and felt indebted, but since they were technically on the wrong side of the law, he was also conflicted.

Because I was now a free agent, I could cavort with all manner of people without concern about what they were doing when I wasn't around. My life had gotten a lot more interesting since I stopped caring about following the rules. I mean, I hadn't exactly been successful at rule following when I was with the CIA, but I'd cared more about it then. Now I figured my code of ethics was strong enough that the occasional departure from the letter of the law wasn't that big a deal. Especially if it helped me nab bad guys.

Carter, of course, had a much different view, but then he had to. As a deputy, he had to document everything, and winging it the way I did would buy him a one-way ticket to the unemployment line or even worse, get him brought up on charges. Plus, if Sheriff Lee didn't outlive us all, I figured Carter would eventually go for that position. He'd been doing the job for years. He might as well have the pay and the title to go along with it.

The Heberts' office was in an old warehouse about twenty miles up the highway from Sinful. I suppose I could have called first to make sure they were there, but I couldn't recall a time when they weren't. Since the warehouse was huge and I rarely saw people there other than Big and Little Hebert and Mannie, I wondered if they lived there as well. It wouldn't surprise me. Big's nickname was for good reason. He was beyond enormous and I couldn't imagine he moved around much. Plus, the security at the facility was excellent.

Which is exactly why Mannie was standing at the front door when we pulled into the parking lot. The smile he wore when he greeted us was genuine and he thrilled Gertie by giving her a kiss on the cheek. Ida Belle just rolled her eyes. On the way back to Sinful, we were sure to hear about all the things Gertie would do if she were "twenty years younger."

"The Heberts were happy to see you pull in," Mannie said as we headed for the elevator. "It's been a while."

"It has," I agreed. "How are you guys doing?"

"Great," Mannie said. "Business is up and defaults are down, which gives me more free time than I'd like, but what's a hired strongman to do?"

Gertie nodded. "I have the same problem. People talk about all dressed up and nowhere to go. I'm all stocked up and nothing to blow up."

Mannie laughed. "If I ever get in a situation that requires that kind of firepower, I know who to call."

"Please don't encourage her," Ida Belle said. "She's probably packing enough in that purse to significantly expand the Gulf of Mexico."

Mannie knocked on Big's office door before opening it and then waved us in. Big Hebert was in his usual spot, on a park bench behind his massive desk. His son, Little, was standing to the side, ready to shake hands and offer us chairs and drinks. Gertie opted for a shot of whiskey while Ida Belle and I went for a soda.

Before Mannie could make his exit, Big stopped him.

"You might as well stay," he said. "These ladies don't make social calls, so I'm likely to need your services."

Mannie gave him a nod and stood against the wall near the desk where he could see everyone. Little passed out the drinks, then took a seat in a chair next to Big's desk.

"It's good to see you three," Big said. "I've been keeping up with your exploits. You're making quite a name for yourselves as detectives while putting a dent in the criminal element in these parts. And your foray to Florida was especially impressive, managing to get the job done on foreign turf. Highly commendable."

Little nodded. "And we've especially loved the videos of Gertie on YouTube. You're quite the social media sensation. The Christmas show was particularly entertaining."

Mannie grinned. "Far more interesting than the original."

"Thanks." Gertie was beaming like she'd just been crowned Queen of England.

"The Christmas show is kind of why we're here," I said.

Big perked up. "Really? We heard that Santa died, but as there was no explosion, we assumed Ms. Hebert was not part of that particular occurrence. The general buzz was that the unfortunate gentleman had a heart attack."

"That's what we thought," I said, then I explained what had really happened.

When I was done, all smiles were gone and Big, Little, and Mannie were exchanging concerned looks.

"I'm sure I don't have to tell you how troubling I find this," Big said finally. "Especially as it would appear that children could be part of whatever this man had planned." He looked at Ida Belle. "And I'm particularly distressed that you risked exposure to a deadly chemical over such a person, especially as it turned out to be a completely different man than you thought and one with questionable motives."

"What would you like for us to do?" Little asked. "I'm sure we're happy to help in whatever manner possible. If someone in Sinful or their child is at risk, that threat might not have ended with this man's death."

"That's our worry," I said. "So here's what we need." I explained about Fake Santa's car.

"It was smart to look for the vehicle," Little said. "I suppose we can't fault your deputy for coming to the same conclusion."

"I can pay the guys at the impound lot a visit," Mannie said. "I'm sure they'll be happy to give me the information the ladies are looking for."

I held in a smile. I was pretty sure the guys at the impound lot would give Mannie their firstborn if he asked. The man was imposing to say the least. I wouldn't want to tangle with him, unless it was with a sniper rifle and from five hundred yards away. I couldn't imagine what the average human being felt when confronted by the six-four wall of solid muscle.

"Why don't you just give them a call?" Big said. "I'm sure they'll be happy to assist when you explain that I'm the one who requires the information, and that will provide the ladies with what they need sooner rather than later."

Mannie nodded and exited the room.

"May I ask what good this information will do you?" Little inquired.

"Maybe no good," I said. "If I had to guess, it didn't do Carter any good. He was rather cagey when I asked him if they'd figured out the guy's identity once I knew he had the car."

"So then we have to presume he's waiting to see if the ME can ascertain identity?" Little asked.

I nodded. "But there's no chance of us getting the ME report. The car is an angle to work. Even if it doesn't give us identity, it might provide more information about what area he lived or operated in. Assuming we can get information from the plate."

Little looked over at Big, who gave him a slight nod.

"It happens," Little said, "that my father and I might be able to assist you with the er...running of the vehicle."

"That would be great," I said, holding in a smile. I was hoping they'd offer.

Big leaned forward and looked at Gertie. "So tell me more about this bird of yours. How did you come about owning it?"

"Well, first some nuns found him and he lived at a convent for years," Gertie said. "That's how he got the name Francis, after Saint Francis, who talked to animals. When the convent closed, he was sold and somehow drug dealers or gunrunners or something of the like ended up with him. He was seized in a raid and I bought him from a police auction."

Big frowned. "Criminals allowed a talking bird around their operations?"

"Oh yeah," Gertie said. "You should hear the things he says about body dumps and where the money and guns are stashed."

"What a most unfortunate choice of pets for a criminal," Little said.

"Given Gertie's internet dynamite buying habits, it's not the best choice for her either," Ida Belle said.

"I have started making all my important calls in the garage," Gertie said.

Big started to speak again when the door opened and Mannie walked back in. He didn't look happy. I wondered if maybe he hadn't been able to get the information. He leaned over and spoke to Big, his voice so low I couldn't hear him. And since he had his back to me, I couldn't read his lips. Big's expression hardened and when Mannie stood back up, he looked at us and frowned.

"Mannie was able to procure the information you wanted," Big said. "I don't suppose you have a photo of this man?"

"I'm afraid not," I said. "By the time Gertie realized it wasn't the man it was supposed to be, Carter was right there. If I'd taken a picture, he would have deleted it. But I can describe him."

I launched into a description of the man, at least of his face, and as I talked Big glanced up at Mannie, then back at me. When I was finished, he nodded.

"We won't need to run the car," Big said. "And you were right when you assumed it wouldn't do you any good. It's registered to a woman who died years ago. But I know the man who drives it now, and he looks as you described this imposter Santa."

This was it. Big was about to tell us this guy was a human trafficker or worse. And he'd been sitting right there in a Santa suit, pretending he was a decent human being.

"Who was he?" Gertie asked.

"He was a private detective," Big said.

"Oh!" I said, and glanced over at Ida Belle and Gertie, who appeared to be as surprised as I was. "That wasn't what I was expecting."

"It wasn't what I was expecting either," Big said. "His name is Peter Cooke. He's not what people would consider a principled man. I know this because I hired him to do a couple jobs for me and he had no problem in letting his methods fall well below the legal lines to accomplish what I asked. He also had no personal interest in the cases themselves. It was never about the work. Everything was simply dollar signs to him."

"Assaulting someone and leaving them tied up in a closet so you can steal their Santa role is definitely well below the legal lines," I said. "So given this information, I guess we have to assume he was on a job."

Ida Belle frowned. "Which means the threat to someone in Sinful is still viable."

Big nodded. "The question you need to answer is, who hired Cooke and who were they trying to find?"

"I don't suppose he had an assistant or a business partner who would give you that information, did he?" I asked.

"I'm afraid not," Big said. "Mr. Cooke was not the type of individual that inspired one to want to partner with him or be employed by him. And given his unique choices while on the job, I'd say most didn't want to go to jail with him."

"Or the grave, as it turns out," Gertie said.

Little nodded. "And that's the most interesting part about all of this. I think we have to assume that Mr. Cooke arrived at the event in full costume. Which means that someone knew what he was up to without ever seeing his true face."

I stared at Little. "You're right. That *is* interesting. And confusing."

"Yes, very," Little agreed. "Because in order to poison him, someone had to be expecting him. Assuming, of course, that people don't wander around everywhere with cyanide in their pockets."

"Maybe someone warned them?" Ida Belle said.

"It's possible," Little said. "Or there were other events that tipped them off beforehand."

"There was a situation in Mudbug," I said, and explained about the fill-in Santa and the break-in at the photographer's studio.

Ida Belle nodded. "That kind of gossip travels quickly between towns. If whoever Cooke was after heard it, then they'd be checking out Santa closely. Any sign that he wasn't who he was supposed to be could have set them off."

"We need to find out who hired Cooke," I said. "Killing him only delayed the inevitable. The kind of person that would hire Cooke wouldn't hesitate to hire someone else to keep on the trail."

"But how are we supposed to do that?" Ida Belle asked. "Even if Cooke kept records—and given the way he does business that's questionable—they would be in his office or house or whatever."

"We've been known to invite ourselves into locked places," Gertie said.

Big chuckled. Given that his storage facility was one of the locked places we'd invited ourselves into, he was well aware of our stance on trespassing and breaking-and-entering. The only reason he'd given us a pass was because we were trying to spy on the ATF and he'd found that amusing. I was pretty sure the Heberts had tolerated all of our earlier questionable behavior because we entertained them while offering up no threat to their business. Now that they knew exactly who I was, they were even more on board with our shenanigans. One of my "questionable behaviors" during my stint with the CIA had saved a young girl from their village back in Italy. I was officially "in" with the Heberts on a lifetime basis.

"Given that the man was just murdered," I said, "it might not be a good idea to go poking around his house."

"Especially since Carter will probably be there," Ida Belle said. "Or in keeping with our luck, show up when we're there."

"Carter didn't have a problem with us on the last case," Gertie said.

"We had a client facing a murder charge on the last case," I said. "And Carter didn't think he did it, so there was a lot more leeway on that one."

"So things are better between you and the good deputy if you are official, so to speak?" Little asked.

"Seems like it," I said. "Of course, we've only had the one case so far."

"And did an excellent job," Big pointed out. "Little and I don't know Whiskey well, but he's a respected businessman in his line of work. And we're aware of the situation with his father. You did a good thing for a good man."

Little looked at Big and smiled. "Then perhaps we can assist the ladies on the client end of things."

Big nodded. "An excellent idea. Mr. Cooke was a business partner of ours from time to time, so we could argue having legitimate concerns with his untimely death. I would hate for our names to get dragged into whatever unfortunate business Mr. Cooke has taken on simply because of our prior association."

Gertie clapped. "We're official! Carter can't complain about us poking our nose in now."

Ida Belle shook her head. "I have a feeling Carter will be less than impressed with Fortune's choice of clients. No offense to the Heberts, of course. But I'm afraid we're not out of the woods on this one."

Big smiled. "The deputy cares about his lady and prefers she not do business with such nefarious characters as Little and me. One can hardly fault him for his feelings. If I had a lady like Ms. Redding on my arm, I would do the same. But

Little and I would never do anything that put Ms. Redding in a situation she couldn't walk away from. She's too valuable an asset to Sinful and we want her to remain here for the rest of her very long life."

"Absolutely," Little said, and looked at Mannie. "So perhaps we could assist with the perusal of Mr. Cooke's records. I believe some of our staff has complained of underutilization as of late. This assistance probably wouldn't involve the more... spectacular of your abilities, but you might enjoy the change of pace."

Mannie grinned. "You know I would."

"I can't let Mannie do my job," I said. "If you hire me then I'm on the clock and we'll need to do a contract and everything to make it official. I can't document Mannie breaking the law in my records."

Big raised one eyebrow. "How were you planning on documenting *you* breaking the law? Neither the dead man nor the police are likely to invite you into his home or office to look around."

"Busted," Gertie said. "I say we take the stork approach to documentation—the information just dropped out of the sky and into our laps."

"Yeah, because that will work," I said. "Okay. How about Mannie goes with us to Cooke's office or house or whatever and after we assess the situation, we make a decision on how to move forward. But ultimately, it has to be my decision."

Big held his hands up in acquiescence. "I have complete faith in Mannie's ability to work with you to make the correct judgment once you have reviewed everything."

I'd expected pushback but had gotten none, which left me at a bit of a loss for what to do next as I'd been prepping an argument. But since I couldn't find anything wrong with a plan that still left me with a vote and not just sitting on my hands back in Sinful, I supposed there was only one thing left to do.

I rose from my chair and extended my hand across the desk. "It appears you've just hired yourself a PI. I'll bring a contract by later."

"No need to waste your time on such trivial matters," Big said as he shook my hand. "Just email the contract to Little and I'll sign and get the contract and a retainer delivered to you. Can I assume ten thousand will be enough to get started?"

"That is more than enough," I said, and motioned to Ida Belle and Gertie.

"I'll get the information on Cooke's residence and office, if he had one," Mannie said. "Then I'll contact you to set up a time to case it. Give me an hour or so."

"Great," I said. "That gives us time to go talk to Rollie and for me to send that contract."

Little shook everyone's hand. "It's always a pleasure to see you ladies. You might be the only people we do business with that we like."

"Probably true," Big agreed. "I look forward to an update on this situation."

We headed out for Rollie's house, which wasn't too far from Big and Little's office. I should have figured that an intro-vert didn't live in town. Unfortunately, that had made it easier for Cooke to accost Rollie in his home since no one was around to see. We'd grabbed a casserole from Gertie's stash before we'd headed out, as Gertie had claimed Rollie would appreciate receiving it frozen. Then he could choose when to heat it up or cut it into smaller portions before heating since there was only the one of him.

Rollie's house surprise me at first, but I suppose it shouldn't have. I guess when I think single dude living in the woods, I think rustic and not overly concerned about things like landscaping and potted plants. But I'd forgotten to include 'engineer' in my equation. They tended to be more on the precise side, and Rollie's house reflected that. It was white siding with navy blue shutters and front door. The porch spanned the length of the front of the house and had a swing and a rocking chair on it. Pots with flowers hung between the porch posts and huge azalea bushes lined the front of the structure.

"This is pretty," I said.

"Rollie's got a green thumb," Gertie said. "I've been trying to get him to enter some of his roses in flower shows for years, but he won't do it. Too many people."

We knocked on the door and a couple seconds later, it opened.

Five feet ten. Two hundred sixty pounds, most of the extra in his belly. Introvert's habit of glancing at a person, then looking down. Easy to see how Cooke got the advantage. No threat unless armed and actually looking at me before firing.

And his poor face and head.

The bruises had already set in on his jaw and both his eyes. His nose was still swollen and there was a lump at his hairline. Cooke had really done a number on him.

Rollie didn't look overly thrilled at the idea of company but he didn't look irritated either, so that boded well for us. Gertie held up the aluminum pan.

"I brought you a chicken casserole," she said. "We figured you might have a headache and not want to move around. It's frozen, so you can heat it up whenever you're ready."

Rollie perked up when he saw the casserole. Score another point for Gertie's cooking. The entire town must be hooked on it.

"That's so nice of you," he said, and gave me a curious look.

"I'm so sorry," Ida Belle said. "This is our friend, Fortune Redding. She's a new addition to Sinful."

"Oh, right," he said. "The CIA agent. I've heard about you."

"I get that a lot," I said.

"Would you like to come in for tea?" he asked, clearly finding no good reason to avoid social niceties. "I just brewed a batch."

"That would be great," Ida Belle said as we followed him to his kitchen. "We won't keep you long. You need your rest. We just wanted to make sure you were okay after that unpleasant business with that fraud of a Santa."

Rollie shook his head as he served the tea, then took a seat. "It's certainly not the kind of thing you think of happening. I keep asking myself what in the world could he have been up to? Then I hear he died and I figure karma came back on him."

"It wasn't karma," I said. "He was poisoned."

Rollie's eyes widened. "What? Are you serious?"

"Yes," I said. "Cyanide. And as Ida Belle had given him mouth-to-mouth, she got to spend a good portion of her night in the ER making sure she didn't contract any of it from him."

"Good Lord Almighty," Rollie said, his body language and facial expression shifting from reserved to sympathetic and open. "I'm sorry that happened. Here you are, trying to do something good and that's what comes of it."

"Same could be said for you," Gertie said. "You volunteer to be Santa every year. I'm sure you never figured on being attacked for it."

"True," he agreed. "So who poisoned him?"

"No one knows," I said. "Carter is investigating, of course, but he's got to figure out who the guy is first. You didn't recognize him, did you?"

"Not at all," Rollie said. "That whole time I was locked up

71

in the closet, I figured it was one of them home invasion things like I see on the news sometimes. When Carter let me out and told me what had happened, well, you could have knocked me over with a feather. It just didn't make any sense. None of it. And now that I find out someone killed him, it just gets stranger."

"Indeed it does," Ida Belle agreed.

He blew out a breath. "I guess I should feel sorry the man's dead, but I can't work up to it. Given the way he went about things, he couldn't have been up to any good."

"We definitely agree with you there," Ida Belle said. "But we're also worried."

He scrunched his brow. "Why? The man's dead."

"Yes, but if he was after something or someone, a Sinful resident might still be at risk," Ida Belle said. "There could be others besides him. Or he could have backup. I know it sounds dire, but I just don't feel right about all of it. It's *too* odd. Even for Sinful."

He frowned. "I hadn't thought about it that way."

"Did he say anything while he was here?" Ida Belle asked. "Anything that might give you an idea why he was doing this?"

"No," Rollie said. "He didn't say anything when he was knocking me around. Although I have to admit, after a couple of blows to my head, I don't remember anything until I woke up in that closet, all tied up."

Gertie flashed an angry look at me and I shook my head. Rollie was lucky he hadn't sustained serious damage due to the beating. I found myself thinking, once again, that the world might be a better place now that Cooke was gone.

"Oh well," Ida Belle said. "I guess we couldn't really expect that he'd give you a rundown of his plans. But we figured it didn't hurt to ask. It worries us that someone might be in danger."

"Of course," he agreed. "Worries me too now that I know more about it all."

"This whole Christmas show thing has been a doozy," Gertie said. "And after all that trouble my bird created, I bet there's some people wishing I'd taken that free trip to the casino that I was offered."

I looked over at Gertie and held in a smile. Great segue.

"You got one of those too?" Rollie asked. "I figured it was bull. I mean, I wouldn't have gone anyway...not my thing, you know?"

I looked over at Ida Belle, who raised one eyebrow. Bull's-eye. I'd bet anything Cooke had been the 'contract' Santa at the other celebration. His plan had worked on Mudbug's usual fill-in but hadn't worked on the introverted engineer. So Cooke had reverted to plan B. The gap between the two plans was rather disconcerting, even for me. Offer a guy a free trip to a casino or beat a guy unconscious and lock him in a closet. Cooke was either a sociopath who got off on that kind of thing or was really desperate for a paycheck. Or maybe the paycheck was big enough that he didn't care what it took to earn it.

I was hoping for one of the first two options, because the third presented a whole other set of problems. Where there was one Cooke for hire, there would be others. And among some in our society, ethics had an inverse relationship with money offered.

CHAPTER SIX

AFTER FINISHING OUR BUSINESS WITH ROLLIE, WE HEADED back to my house so I could draw up a contract for Big Hebert and get it emailed. While I worked on that, Ida Belle and Gertie attempted to get my living room back in order. The entire process had been made even more difficult by Merlin, who'd apparently held a party while we were gone. Ornaments and tinsel were scattered all over the house. And he still hadn't eaten his breakfast. He was really on a tear. I made a note to sleep with my bedroom door closed that night.

I had just emailed the contract when Mannie called.

"I've got the address," he said. "Sorry it took a bit to track it down. His credit is crap, so he's got some weekly motel rental."

"Are you kidding me?" I said. "You barely took an hour. Given his living situation, I'm surprised you got an address at all."

"I have my ways."

"Hmm. I wonder if Carter has the same ways you do."

"I doubt it."

"Then we might beat him to the scene."

"There's a chance of that, but given the situation, it's going to be considered a crime scene. Are you sure you want to risk taking a look?"

"Are you?"

"Sure. But I'm not sleeping with the deputy."

"Ah. Good point. I suppose we'll just have to make sure he doesn't find out."

"You have a strange way with relationships."

"No. I have priorities. My priority is to my client and I can't talk about work that I've been hired to do."

He chuckled. "Let me know how that one plays out in the long run."

"Let me worry about the long run. Where do you want to meet?"

"I'm on my way to pick you up now. Give me ten. The motel is just outside of New Orleans, so we have a bit of a drive."

"Don't want to ride with Ida Belle?"

"Not in this lifetime."

I could practically feel him smiling as he disconnected. I closed my laptop and headed into the living room to fill Ida Belle and Gertie in on the living quarters situation.

"That's great!" Gertie said. "Since Cooke is such a loser, everything important should be right there in that motel room."

Ida Belle nodded, but I noticed her excitement level wasn't as high as I expected.

"You all right?" I asked her.

"I was just wondering what you plan on telling Carter," she said. "I know you've got the client confidentiality card to play, but you and I both know that Carter's going to have a fit when he finds out who your client is."

"Maybe. Probably." I threw my hands up in the air. "What

do you want me to say? This is my job and this is me. It's not like he didn't know what he was getting into."

"That's true," Ida Belle said. "But what is he going to think when he finds out you withheld big information pertinent to his murder investigation? Confidentiality aside, he's going to feel betrayed. We can assume Carter has identity from the ME because as a PI, Cooke's prints should have been on file. But unless there was something in the car to tip them off to where Cooke has been staying, we probably got that bit of information before he did."

I sighed. "So you think we shouldn't do this?"

"Of course I think we should do it," Ida Belle said. "I'm just making sure you know what kind of aftermath you're in for if Carter finds out you withheld information."

"You and Mannie are like an echo chamber," I said.

"Mannie's worried about your relationship?" Gertie asked. "That's sweet. I think Mannie is a really nice guy."

"Except for the part where he's a stone-cold killer, I would agree," I said. "But all of you need to stop worrying about me and Carter. Let me worry about that."

"So you've got a plan?" Gertie asked.

"Of course," I said. "Don't get caught."

"Isn't that always the plan?" Ida Belle asked.

"This time it's going to work," I said.

"Are we leaving Gertie at home?" Ida Belle asked.

Gertie gave her the finger and I grinned as I heard a honk in the driveway.

"Come on," I said. "Let's go find some clues."

Ida Belle protested a bit about being a passenger but she knew better than to challenge Mannie over driving. There was no way she was winning that match. Plus, Mannie pointed out that the SUV he drove was equipped with bulletproof windows and doors. She grumbled something about needing to talk to Hot Rod as she climbed into the back seat and I shook my head. Before she was done with her SUV, it would be a rocket ship with tanklike protection disguised as a Chevy.

Mannie's driving speed was on par with Ida Belle's, which seemed to mollify her a bit, but I knew as soon as we got back, Hot Rod would be getting an earful since he built the Heberts' vehicles and hadn't offered her the same options. The drive itself was an interesting one. No one seemed to know what to talk about with Mannie in our midst so bouts of silence were broken by Gertie recounting tales of things Francis said and her latest desire for a flamethrower. That one actually got a response from everyone, and it was an overwhelming no. But I had a feeling the fire department would be getting a call to Gertie's house sometime in the future. I just hoped she used it outside.

The motel that Cooke had been living in was off the highway about ten miles outside of New Orleans, which was a plus because at least we didn't have to go into the city and deal with all the traffic that came with it. The downside was that it looked like the kind of place where you needed a car with bulletproof windows and doors.

"Cooke certainly didn't spend his earnings on his living quarters," Gertie said as we drove by on the access road to get a look at the place before approaching. "If it weren't for the people standing around, I'd think this place was abandoned."

"I'm pretty sure it should be," Ida Belle said.

"Then where would all these fine, upstanding citizens stay?" Mannie asked. "Sometimes it's better to have certain types collected in one place."

"But why was Cooke here?" I asked. "He's a PI, not a criminal. I mean, I know he crossed lines to do his job but that's not gunrunning or drug dealing or the like."

"I only met Cooke once," Mannie said, "but my impression

was he would stay in a place like this because this is what he was comfortable with."

"You think he grew up in this sort of situation," Ida Belle said.

Mannie shrugged. "It's just an impression."

"And probably correct," Ida Belle said. "Fortune is able to size people up like that and she's usually right. We pay attention when she gets a feeling about something."

"It's an instinct I believe some people are born with," Mannie said as he turned onto a side street just past the motel. "So how would you like to handle this?"

"I'd like to get into Cooke's room and see if there are any records of who hired him and what he was hired to do," I said. "But all the rooms are in full view of the highway. No chance for cover."

"It's a gamble, for sure," Mannie said. He turned into the parking lot from the rear entry and drove around to the front. "Let me go in the office and get the room number."

"You've already done enough," I said. "I can do it."

"If it's a young guy in there," Gertie said, "Fortune is your best bet for getting information."

Mannie grinned. "I can see where that would be effective, but cash works as well. Besides, no one can see inside this car. In the event that your deputy shows up, he won't see you walking out of the front office."

"He'll see you," Ida Belle said.

"Yes," Mannie agreed. "But as I discussed earlier with Ms. Redding—I'm not sleeping with him. Be right back."

Before I could launch another argument, he hopped out of the SUV and headed into the office. In no time at all, he walked back out, frowning.

"What's wrong?" I asked as he climbed into the vehicle. "You couldn't get the room number?"

"No. I got the room number," he said. "But the clerk mistook me for the deputy he talked to about ten minutes ago, who was asking about Cooke."

"Crap," I said. "That's Carter. I bet there was something in Cooke's car that tipped him off to this place—matchbook, stamp on a room key, something."

Mannie nodded. "So what do you want to do?"

I blew out a breath. "He was probably calling from Sinful, which means he's a good forty-minute drive at least."

"But he called ten minutes ago," Mannie said. "So thirty minutes."

"That's if the clerk got the time right," Ida Belle said. "Do we really want to roll the dice on the memory of a guy working in this place?"

"And that's assuming he was in Sinful," Mannie said. "If he was calling from the impound lot then he was only thirty minutes away."

"Which leaves us with twenty at the most," Ida Belle said.

"How much crap can Cooke possibly have in there?" I asked.

"He's living there, so who knows," Mannie said.

"I have to get in," I said. "It's the only way to get the information we need, because Carter is not going to share."

Mannie nodded and directed the SUV along the front of the motel until he was at the end of the building. "It's the last one on the top floor. Give me a few minutes. If you see your deputy pull up, then hop over in the driver's seat and leave."

I shook my head. "You're not doing this for me. Big hired *me* to do the job."

"I have to agree with her on this," Ida Belle said. "Not just because she was hired to do the job but because she's the best person to do the job. Fortune has perfect recall. Something she sees that might not seem important ends up becoming the thing that triggers her to a solution later on. It's like she collects all the puzzle pieces in her mind and then in the end, they all fall together while the rest of us just see this jumbled mess. She can't put together the picture without seeing all the pieces."

I could tell Mannie didn't like it, but he understood. "Okay," he said. "When we approached from the side street, I noticed a small window on the back of the rooms. Probably over the bathtub or toilet. But it's high, and it's small, and it's a second-floor drop."

"But it opens," I said. "I noticed them as well. And it's small but I would fit through it. A two-story drop isn't a problem."

"If you have to go that route, I'll pick you up behind the building," Mannie said.

"I don't mean to be the pain in the rear here," Gertie said, "but the clock is ticking."

I held my hand back and Gertie slapped latex gloves, a credit card, and a screwdriver into my palm.

Mannie raised one eyebrow but didn't say a word.

I hopped out and headed up the rickety stairs to the room, then made ridiculously quick work of the door. The inside of the room looked as if it had already been tossed and that wouldn't have surprised me given the element lurking around outside, but since there was a bag of snacks on the dresser, I figured Cooke was simply a slob. Those snacks would have been long gone if someone had broken in here looking for stuff to lift.

The drawers in the nightstands and dresser were empty, which wasn't surprising as it appeared everything was stacked on surface tops, the bed, or simply thrown onto the floor. Thank God for latex, I thought as I lifted dirty clothes to look beneath. The bathroom was tiny so it couldn't hold much, and

I didn't find anything among the sparse toiletries that helped me fill in the blanks. I headed back into the bedroom to do a more intense search. I had only two options left. Either Cooke had hidden the important stuff or he'd had it in his car. I was really hoping for the first option.

I started with the bed, searching underneath the mattress, but came up empty. Then I removed the dresser drawers and checked to ensure nothing was taped on the bottom of them or behind them on the dresser. When I pulled out the lowest drawer, I hit pay dirt. A laptop lay on the floor beneath the drawer. I pulled it out and hoped that Cooke hadn't password-protected everything. I didn't know enough about him to guess passwords and didn't have the time to get to know him. And while stealing the laptop would give me all the time in the world, I figured that was a line I couldn't cross. Not if I expected Carter to ever speak to me again. It was one thing for me to have an investigation parallel to his. It was completely another to hinder his ability to do his job.

I let out a breath of relief when it booted right up to the desktop. I did a quick check to see what the latest file he'd accessed was and opened it. It was a folder containing Santa shots. They must be the pictures stolen from the photographer's computer. I scrolled through them, trying to see if something stood out, but they were all your basic kid with Santa. Aside from the level of terror the kids expressed, there wasn't much difference from one picture to the next.

I opened the next folder and found candids from the event. I didn't know any of the people but nothing looked odd. The first twenty or so were taken of a stage production of the Charlie Brown Christmas show. The ones afterward were just a bunch of attendees chatting and eating and seeing to kids.

I pulled up the next file he'd accessed and found a list of dollar amounts and dates. Ten thousand dollars on both occasions. The last one was the day before our Christmas show. Surely he wasn't paid ten large just to get pictures of a bunch of kids with Santa. That didn't make any sense. There had to be something else in those files. Something I'd missed. But as I scrolled through the photos again, I couldn't see a single thing that gave me that aha moment.

I checked other recently accessed files and found pictures of Harleys and naked girls on Harleys, and that was all going back four months. I pulled up a web browser and was happy to see the pass code was still logged in, so I accessed his email. There was the usual spam and oddly enough, a daily email from Bed Bath & Beyond, and then I struck gold. An exchange between Cooke and someone with the email handle cashmoney767.

cashmoney767: Well?

Cooke: Nothing. He wasn't there.

cashmoney767: What the hell, Cooke? You said that was the place.

Cooke: I said it was probably Mudbug or Sinful.

cashmoney767: I didn't pay you 10 grand to give me nothing.

Cooke: I did my job in Mudbug and you got the photos to prove it. I'll do my job in Sinful. Just as soon as you send payment. I'm taking a lot of risks here.

cashmoney767: I'm paying you to take risks. I don't have to tell you what happens if you're not successful, right?

Cooke: I'll find him. I want my bonus.

cashmoney767: You better or that bonus isn't going to be at all what you were hoping for.

Cooke never replied to the last email, so I assumed he knew what would happen and it wasn't going to be pleasant. Of course, he'd ended up dead and things couldn't get much worse, so there was that.

I emailed the photos and the exchange with cashmoney to a fake email account I had set up for this purpose, then deleted that email. I closed the laptop and stuck it back where I'd found it, unable to help being a little disappointed. Overall, this little visit had been somewhat underwhelming.

My phone rang and I pulled it out to answer.

"Carter just pulled into the parking lot," Ida Belle said. "Get out, now!"

CHAPTER SEVEN

CRAP!

I'd really been hoping to avoid a second-floor drop from a tiny window, but I should have figured that was the way things would go. I ran into the bathroom and hopped onto the toilet to open the window. The latch moved fine but the window itself didn't budge when I pushed on it. I gave it a harder shove and still nothing. Then I noticed the paint caked around the edges. Good God. This had probably been painted over ten times, and now it was practically glued shut.

I pulled out my phone and sent a text to Ida Belle.

Window is stuck. Create a diversion.

Her reply was immediate.

Carter on stairs. Hide!

Hide? Carter was on his way into the room to search it. Where the heck was I supposed to hide? I rushed back into the bedroom and could hear footsteps pounding up the stairs. I took a running leap onto the top of the dresser, pushed one of the ceiling tiles to the side and pulled myself onto the top of the wall. I'd barely gotten the tile back in place when I heard the door open.

Where was my diversion?

I heard Carter talking to himself and the gist of the conversation was that he wasn't any more impressed with Cooke's housekeeping than I had been. He started opening drawers and I held my position, praying that the diversion I needed was coming soon because I couldn't hold this position forever. And since the wall shook if I breathed too deeply, I wasn't certain the wall could hold position much longer, either.

Then there was an explosion.

The boom shook the cheap motel and as I pitched off the wall and through the ceiling of the next room, I heard Carter swear. Fortunately, the bed was below the wall where I broke through so I had a soft landing. Unfortunately, it was occupied. By a naked dude.

Midthirties. Six feet tall. One hundred thirty pounds. There was more muscle tone on a ninety-year-old corpse. Only a threat if you looked at his blinding white skin.

We both sprang out of the bed and he stared at me for a second.

"I ordered a redhead," he said. "And I'm not paying for that damage. You were supposed to use the door."

"Gross!" I yanked the comforter off the bed and tossed it over him to cover all the bright white things I never wanted to see that were in plain view. Then I grabbed a hoodie from the dresser and pulled it on. I cracked open the door to peer outside and saw a crowd of people gathering in front of the office, a debris field all over the parking lot in front of it. Carter was running toward the debris, so I hurried out the door and ran for the railing.

Worried that Carter would look back and see me running away, I didn't bother with the stairs. Instead, I hit the rail with my midsection and flipped over it, landing in a bush at the end of the building. I hadn't seen Mannie's vehicle out front, so I sprang up and sprinted for the rear of the motel. His SUV was coming around the corner and I yanked the hood off my head and waved my arms. He floored it as he approached and I did a running leap through the passenger window. He didn't even hesitate before taking off again.

"Hold on," he said. "We can't go out the front entrance."

He directed the SUV at a set of hedges lining the back of the property, launched over the curb, and tore right through the bushes. Gertie hooted so loud I thought my eardrums would burst. We had a couple seconds of disarray when the windshield was completely covered by foliage, but then the branches fell off in time for him to make a hard right into an alley, barely missing the sanitation truck. We could hear sirens approaching so he turned away from the motel and tore down the backstreets, slowly working his way back to the service road.

When we were finally on the highway and doing a somewhat reasonable speed again, I looked over at them and grinned. "Thanks for the diversion," I said. "I suppose that was a Gertie's handbag special?"

"You know it," Gertie said. "But I picked the wrong one. I just wanted enough pop to get Carter out of the room. I wasn't planning on blowing that vending machine to bits."

"You blew half of it through the front office window," Ida Belle said. "You could have killed someone."

"But I didn't," Gertie said. "Instead, a bunch of people got free snacks. At least, the ones where the packaging didn't explode."

"Is that why you have a candy wrapper in your hair?" I asked.

Gertie reached up and pulled the wrapper out, then took a

piece of chocolate out of it and popped it in her mouth. "Oh, Snickers. I love those."

Ida Belle sighed and looked at me. "Why are you wearing that hoodie?"

I remembered I had the icky boy's shirt on and tugged it off and tossed it onto the floorboard. I explained my hiding place and my subsequent visit to the room next door.

"Yuck," Gertie said. "How come when naked men crop up, it's never the good-looking ones?"

"Because that only happens in movies," Ida Belle said.

Gertie gave Mannie the side-eye. "Some men have been known to drive in the nude. They say it increases reaction time."

"Nice try," Mannie said.

Gertie shrugged. "Can't blame a girl. So did you find out anything? Please tell me I used my good dynamite for a reason."

I gave them a rundown of what I'd found. "It's not much," I said. "But it confirms our thinking. Cooke was definitely working a job and the pay was really good."

"And he's looking for a male," Ida Belle said.

"A male child, maybe?" Gertie suggested. "Since he was doing the whole Santa thing."

"Not necessarily," I said. "The Santa costume gave him access to a lot of locals in one place and with the benefit of not being recognized. He could have been looking for an adult. He had all of the photos on his laptop—the kids and the candids."

Gertie sighed. "You're right."

My cell phone rang and I pulled it out of my pocket.

"Crap!" I said. "It's Carter. Everyone be quiet."

I tried for a normal-sounding 'what's up?' when I answered.

"Where are you right now?" he asked.

"I'm, uh...meeting with a client," I said. "Why?"

"I just encountered a random explosion and my train of thought went in the obvious direction. So if I send Deputy Breaux out, he'll find you with this client?"

I'd hoped to put this particular discussion off until tonight, but since I needed a cover for Gertie's overuse of dynamite, it had to come out now.

"If you send him to Big and Little Hebert's office he will," I said.

There were several seconds of complete silence and I wondered if he'd hung up. Finally, I heard an intake of breath.

"You're working for the Heberts?" he asked.

"Looks like."

"I don't suppose you're going to share what you're working on."

"I'm pretty sure that falls under that whole confidentiality thing. Anyway, Gertie is here with me and we haven't blown up my clients. I'm pretty sure that would hinder our working relationship."

"Fine. I'll talk to you later."

He disconnected and I slipped my phone back in my jeans pocket.

"That went well," I said.

"I take it Carter isn't enthused with your new job," Ida Belle said.

"Not even a little," I said. "And he suspects Gertie for the explosion at the motel."

"Why?" Gertie said. "That would mean we'd not only know the identity of Santa, which he hasn't told us, but also where he was staying, and that's not exactly easy information to come by."

"Carter knows we're sticking our noses in," Ida Belle said.

"And given the complete randomness of the explosion, it's not surprising he zeroed in on Gertie. It's practically habit at this point. And for all we know, he might have had a conversation with the guy in the room next door to Cooke's."

"Surely that guy wouldn't talk since he was hiring a prostitute," Gertie said. "That would be the dumbest thing ever."

"Well, he *did* think I had chosen to arrive by falling through the ceiling," I said. "And his biggest concern seemed to be damages charges and the fact that he'd ordered a redhead, so there's that to factor in."

"So not a rocket scientist," Gertie said.

Ida Belle shook her head. "This is getting complicated. And you only have two choices—either you tell Carter the truth and see how the fallout goes or you deny until your deathbed."

"I vote for denial," Gertie said.

"You live in a constant state of denial," Ida Belle said. "But if Fortune is going to maintain a relationship with Carter, this is not the first or last time this situation is going to arise."

"I'll use dynamite with less oomph next time," Gertie said.

Ida Belle threw her hands in the air. "Not the dynamite part. The lying part."

"Oh, yeah," Gertie said. "That."

"Look," I said. "Carter and I discussed this before. I won't talk to him about my clients or cases because I can't, and he knows it. He won't talk to me about his cases because he can't, and I know it. It's not like I lied earlier. Big and Little are my clients and we're here with Mannie, so it's sort of a meeting."

"What about breaking into the motel room?" Ida Belle asked.

"Anything that Carter can't prove is something he doesn't know for sure," I said. "He can suspect all he wants but I'm not going to volunteer my business to him. If he wants to consider that lying, then that's up to him. I consider it doing my job."

Ida Belle nodded. "As long as you're comfortable with it, I'm good."

"What do you plan on telling Walter about this?" Gertie asked.

"Not a darn thing," Ida Belle said. "It's none of his business."

"He might think differently," Gertie said.

"Then he'd be wrong," Ida Belle said.

Mannie, who'd been silent this entire time, shook his head. "When I'm ready to settle down, I'm going to find a nice boring accountant who knits."

"I knit," Gertie said. "Last week, I knitted sleeves for my dynamite."

Mannie glanced in the rearview mirror as he exited the highway, a slightly worried look on his face. Then I realized he was headed for the Heberts' office.

"Are we meeting with Big and Little?" I asked.

"That's what you told Carter," Mannie said. "Do you think he's sending Deputy Breaux to check?"

I sighed. "Probably. But we don't have my vehicle or Ida Belle's. What are we going to do, stand in the parking lot so that he sees us when he drives up?"

"When the good deputy arrives, I'll be happy to have him wait by the front door until you appear for display. As for no vehicles, I showed up at your house and insisted you come with me. If the Heberts had pursued hiring you on their own, that's exactly how things would have played out."

"Fine," I said. "I suppose I can bring them up to date on what we've found while we're there. Which isn't a lot."

"Nonsense," Ida Belle said. "We know we're on the right track. We just have to figure out who Cooke was looking for."

"Yeah. Starting with all the male attendees at the Christmas gala," I said. "Piece of cake."

"Not all," Ida Belle said. "Only those with the opportunity to kill him."

"But if he *was* looking for a child, that would mean the killer could also have been a woman," Gertie said.

"That still reduces our list to those who were in the cafeteria prior to the show," Ida Belle said. "We need to talk to Celia's crew and see who was on cafeteria setup when Santa arrived."

"We'll get as much out of Celia's crew as we did out of dead Santa," Gertie said.

"It won't be easy," Ida Belle agreed. "But I have the goods on a few of them. Let's just hope one of those women was working the setup."

Mannie grinned. "You know, you guys and the Heberts have similar approaches to business."

I shrugged. "Mafia, government employees, same difference really."

He laughed. "Yeah, but the Mafia has way cooler equipment."

"And I bet they don't pay thousands of dollars for toilets," Gertie said. "You know, I could totally equip us as a regime for under 10k. It's something we should probably consider."

"Who are we going to war against?" Ida Belle asked. "Our nemesis is Celia. The only weapon you need to use against her is an IQ over eighty."

Mannie was still chuckling when he pulled into the parking lot, but I noticed he adopted his stone-faced look as he got out of the SUV. When one was stepping in front of the boss, it was game-face time.

I had just finished recounting our efforts to Big and Little and had allowed them a suitable amount of time for laughter and recovery when Mannie informed us that Deputy Breaux had arrived. I checked my watch and realized only eight minutes had passed since our arrival. It hadn't taken him long to get there. It was a good thing Mannie subscribed to the same school of driving as Ida Belle.

Mannie escorted us down to the front door, then opened it and allowed Deputy Breaux to step inside.

"Anything you see in this building, you will not describe outside of these walls," Mannie said to the deputy.

Deputy Breaux looked ready to pee himself but managed a nod. I held in a smile. There was absolutely nothing to see in the entry except what used to be a lobby and elevators, doors, and hallways. But I knew Mannie was reminding the deputy whose turf he was on. Basically, the Heberts were doing him a favor allowing him in, so he had to mind his place. Since I was pretty sure Deputy Breaux would rather be having a root canal than be in the Heberts' office, I wasn't worried about him getting out of line. In fact, I couldn't remember a time when he'd ever been out of line. He certainly wasn't going to start there.

"I'm really sorry about this, sir," Deputy Breaux said to Mannie. "But Carter insisted."

"It's okay," I said. "We know how he is, always thinking we're up to something. But as you can see, we're here meeting with our client. Mannie picked us up in Sinful and will drive us back when we're done."

Deputy Breaux nodded as a blush crept up his neck and onto his face. "That's good, but there's this one other thing…I really don't want, that is, I wish I didn't—"

"Oh, for Christ's sake, spit it out," Ida Belle said. "Carter has ordered you to do something you don't want to do. We get it. Just get on with it so we can all get back to our jobs."

Deputy Breaux pulled a packet out of his pocket and gave

Gertie an apologetic look. "I'm sorry, Ms. Hebert. But he asked me to swab your hands for residue."

I had to laugh. Carter thought he was upping his game but he couldn't have been more wrong. Gertie and Ida Belle seemed as amused as I was.

"Go ahead," Gertie said, and held out her hands. "But I can tell you already that they're going to test positive. I keep the dynamite right there next to my tissues and cough drops. I have my hands all over that stuff about a hundred times a day."

Deputy Breaux's expression looked like he'd eaten a bad burrito. "You've got...in your purse? Right now?"

"Sure," Gertie said as she reached into her handbag and pulled out three sticks of dynamite. "Got these cheap. The man's wife said she was selling them because her husband got out of all that prepping nonsense, but I think she offed him."

Some of the color washed out of Deputy Breaux's face. "Oh God."

I felt a little sorry for him. Carter knew good and well that Gertie's handbag was full of things that the general public and definitely law enforcement didn't want to know about. Heck, Ida Belle and I refused to search it because it was better on the conscience to suspect rather than actually know. But now Deputy Breaux couldn't decide what he was supposed to do. He didn't want to arrest Gertie but he didn't want to make Carter mad. Since I thought Carter had been a little unfair in putting the deputy in the middle of this, I decided to help him out.

"Confiscate the dynamite and report back to Carter," I said. "Trust me, he does not want Gertie sitting in his jail because that's a set of paperwork that none of you want to answer for if it gets seen up the line."

"I'm not giving him my dynamite," Gertie said.

"It's that or he has to arrest you," I said. "And I really don't want to give the deputy a heart attack, so don't make him do that."

"This is some of my best stash," Gertie argued.

"You got it on sale," Ida Belle said. "Just give him the darn sticks."

"I got it on sale, not free," Gertie grumbled, but handed the deputy the dynamite.

Deputy Breaux stared at the sticks in his hand as if they were going to spontaneously ignite. "Are you sure this will work?"

I nodded. "Look, I know you've known him longer, but I know him better, if you get my drift."

He blushed again and looked down at the floor.

"Are you going to test my hands, or what?" Gertie asked.

"There's not much point, ma'am," Deputy Breaux said. "You just handed me dynamite."

"Oh," Gertie said. "I guess you're right. Okay, then. Are we done?"

Poor Deputy Breaux looked as frightened as he was confused and I knew he was dreading the conversation he was about to have with Carter. It was unfortunate but couldn't be helped. If Carter didn't want to scare his employees, he shouldn't send them out to do his dirty work.

"Thanks for stopping by," I said. "Let us know if we can provide you with any other illegal weapons."

He gave me a pained look before heading out the door. Mannie locked it behind him and turned to us with a grin.

"If you're done stirring up law enforcement," he said, "I'm happy to take you back home."

"Oh, I'm pretty sure we haven't even scratched the surface on stirring up law enforcement," I said. "But we do need to get back to Sinful. We have work to do."

"Talk to Celia's people." Gertie sighed. "And I had to give up my dynamite. This day is going downhill fast."

Ida Belle patted her back. "Don't worry. It's nowhere close to dinnertime. There's still plenty of opportunity for you to get into trouble."

"You think?" Gertie perked up.

"Oh yeah," Ida Belle said. "I'm pretty much betting on it."

CHAPTER EIGHT

I WANTED TO TALK TO THE PHOTOGRAPHER FIRST, BUT SHE didn't answer so we decided to move forward with the inquisition on Celia's group. I'm pretty sure none of us was looking forward to it.

"So who do we start with?" I asked. "Beatrice?"

Beatrice Paulson was a member of Celia's group, God's Wives, but she was a double agent, having been turned by Ida Belle years ago. She kept Ida Belle informed of Celia's shenanigans, at least the ones Celia let on about. I sometimes wondered if Celia suspected Beatrice's duplicity and intentionally kept her in the dark on most things.

Ida Belle nodded. "I already sent her a text to say we'd be by. I know for sure she was working the cafeteria, so she's the best one to begin with. At least she can help flesh out a list."

"And we know she didn't do it," Gertie said. "It's good to start with someone who isn't the killer."

"Beatrice could totally kill someone," I said.

"No way," Gertie said. "She removes spiders from her house. Last time she had an ant infestation, she had a conversation with them politely asking them to relocate. There's no one less likely to be a killer."

"Gertie might be right on this one," Ida Belle said. "She stopped traffic downtown for half an hour last week trying to get a lizard out of the road."

"Was she successful?" I asked.

Ida Belle shook her head. "Sheriff Lee got tired of hearing all the horns honking and went outside and shot it."

"How come Carter never tells me these things?" I asked.

"Probably because he was too mad to talk about it," Gertie said. "The shot ricocheted off the pavement and took out one of the tires on his truck. I heard a rumor that Carter's going to slip blanks into Sheriff Lee's gun as soon as the opportunity presents itself."

I nodded. Given that Sheriff Lee was two thousand years old and had the eyesight and hearing to go along with the age, it wasn't the worst idea.

"Okay," I said. "But unless Beatrice cried over the lizard, I'm still keeping her on my list of suspects."

"She cried, buried it, and gave a eulogy," Gertie said. "She even made a casket out of a shoebox and lined it with silk."

I stared. "I don't even know where to go with that."

"Straight to a psychiatrist's office would be a good start," Ida Belle said.

"Then let's go see what crazy has to say," I said.

Beatrice was waiting at the front door when we arrived. In order to prep her for the upcoming questions, Ida Belle had already given her a short version of her trip to the ER and why it was necessary. Beatrice looked like she needed a Xanax as she waved us inside and back to the kitchen.

"I'm having lemonade and whiskey," she said. "I can offer you that or iced tea...Long Island if you prefer."

We all requested lemonade without the addition and Beatrice poured. I noticed her hands shook as she passed the glasses before sitting down.

"I just can't believe this," Beatrice said. "If you'd told me that someday Santa would be murdered right there in front of me, well, I would have called you crazy. Why would someone murder Saint Nick? And at a Christmas event that centers on children? I hope they're not scarred for life."

"I'm pretty sure parents didn't just blurt out that Santa is dead," Ida Belle said. "They have, after all, managed to convince them that he was real in the first place."

Beatrice looked a bit relieved. "You're right. I should have thought about that, but I'm so rattled. And then all this with the poison. Are you sure you're all right?" she asked Ida Belle.

"I'm fine," Ida Belle said. "The doctor cleared me and since Fortune, Gertie, Carter, and Walter were all there to hear it, you know I'm not hedging on anything."

"It's a good thing Carter and Walter were there," Beatrice said. "Because these two would lie through their teeth if you asked them to."

"Often and well."

"You know it."

Gertie and I both responded at once and Beatrice shook her head.

"We're hoping you can help us out," Ida Belle said. "We want to know who was in the cafeteria when Santa arrived."

Beatrice's eyes widened. "You're not thinking about trying to find the killer, are you? Oh, I don't want to be any part of that. If I told you something and then you got hurt, well, I'd never forgive myself."

"The thing is," Ida Belle said. "We suspect that guy attacked Rollie and became the fake Santa because he was looking for someone and didn't want them to know. What if that person is in danger? What if there are more fake Santas coming after them? We saw Rollie this morning and he was in pretty bad shape. Regardless of how he died, that man was a bad person, and I'm guessing if more come after him, they aren't going to be any nicer."

Beatrice's hands flew over her chest. "Oh Lord! Why is this happening? I know we've had some trouble here this year but this town is never going to live down killing Santa, regardless of how shady he was."

"It is rather a unique claim to fame," Gertie said. "I kinda like it."

"You would," Ida Belle said.

"It lets people know we mean business," Gertie said. "If Santa isn't sacred, then all bets are off."

"She has a point," I said. "In a completely illogical, Sinful sort of way."

"So that list of people," Ida Belle said. "I'd really like to put a stop to this before someone offs the Easter Bunny."

Beatrice looked horrified but nodded. "Celia was there at first, of course, but she left before Santa arrived as she was part of the performance in the auditorium. She left Dorothy in charge."

Dorothy Tillard was Celia's cousin and right-hand woman. She was lower-key but just as unlikable as Celia. Beatrice named several more women who were members of Celia's crew, then paused to take another shot of her lemonade whiskey.

"Outside of Celia's crew, Zach Vincent was there," Beatrice continued. "He was doing the heavy lifting for anything we needed repositioned. Megan Prejean was preparing the punch. And of course, the photographer came over from the auditorium and was setting up right before the crowd arrived. Myrna was doing her face painting thing on some of the babies."

"Did you see any of them interact with Santa?" I asked.

"I mean, most everyone spoke," Beatrice said. "The South lost the war, not our manners. But then, everyone thought he was Rollie."

"Did anyone give him something to drink or eat?" I asked.

"I don't know," Beatrice said. "I got a phone call from Celia shortly after Santa arrived, summoning me to the auditorium."

"Crap," Gertie said. "We're going to have to talk to that butthead Dorothy."

"Can't the police tell what he ate?" Beatrice asked. "You know, from the autopsy?"

"Sure," Ida Belle said. "But they're not going to share that with us."

"Oh, right. I forgot." Beatrice shook her head. "I'm sorry I can't help more. Maybe if I hadn't left..."

"There's nothing you could have done to prevent this," Ida Belle said. "So don't even start down that line of thinking. Someone was determined to make sure that man didn't find what he was looking for."

"But it was so brazen," Beatrice said. "Right there in front of everybody."

"Brazen or desperate," Ida Belle said.

I nodded but didn't say what I was thinking—that desperate probably had nothing to do with it. Beatrice was already so stressed she might pop a vein. But in rethinking everything, Little Hebert's words kept running through my head.

Someone had come to the event *prepared* to poison Cooke.

Desperate was rarely that prepared.

———

ANY FURTHER INVESTIGATING HAD TO WAIT BECAUSE THAT night was the annual Christmas sleigh ride, and we all needed to grab some food and shower and change clothes before heading out. I'd inquired about how one actually accomplishes a sleigh ride without snow and found out that it consisted of horses and four-wheelers pulling flatbed trailers stacked with hay down Main Street and around the neighborhood. The combination of horses and four-wheelers didn't sound like a good one but since this was my first Christmas as a resident, I figured I'd observe before passing judgment.

Since some of the people we wanted to interview would be at the sleigh ride tonight, we headed back to my house for a quick wrap-up and to lay out how we were going to approach the next round of questioning. But all hope of a relaxed conversation over cookies and iced tea was dashed when I saw Carter's truck parked at my curb. He was leaned against the fender and I could tell by his expression that it wasn't going to be a pleasant visit. I grabbed the envelope with the Heberts' contract and retainer check and began to mentally prepare for the worst.

Ida Belle pulled into the driveway and as I climbed out, she gave me a wave.

"I'll pick you up at six," she said.

"You're not coming in?" I asked.

"Not on your life," she said.

Even Gertie shook her head.

"Cowards," I said as I closed the door.

I looked over at Carter and forced a smile.

"You coming inside?" I asked. "Or do you want to just shoot me out here and save my heirs the cleanup?"

"Depends," he said as he walked toward me. "Who are your heirs?"

"Some of them just drove off," I said.

"Inside," he said, and headed for the front door. I sighed. I should have known my last case was a fluke. Carter and I hadn't been at odds on that one. I had a feeling that was going to be the exception and not the rule.

I walked inside and went straight for the kitchen. If I was going to have a fight, I was at least doing it with a beer and cookies. I grabbed a beer out of the fridge and waved it at Carter, who shook his head. Still on duty, I thought. I took out a bottled water for him and sat the drinks on the table before flopping into a seat. Carter was watching me but so far, hadn't said a word. I hoped he wasn't playing the quiet game with me. I was former CIA. We could remain silent longer than dead people.

"Are you really working for the Heberts?" he said finally.

"They hired me to investigate something for them, yes."

"And just why would they need your help? The Heberts know more about what goes on in this neck of the woods than Ida Belle. Maybe even Jesus."

"They don't know about the thing they hired me for."

"And just what would that be?"

I sighed. "You know I can't tell you."

"Can't or won't?"

I narrowed my eyes at him. "What's the identity of dead Santa? Oh wait. You can't tell me that, right?"

"It's not the same thing."

"Sure it is. You have the whole 'open investigation' issue. I have the 'client confidentiality' issue. Different titles on our business card, but same restrictions on our work."

"You have a contract with them?"

I opened the envelope I'd tossed on the table and waved the check in front of him.

He took a look at the note and the amount and shook his head. "Ten thousand dollars? Jesus H. Christ. What do they want you to do? Find D.B. Cooper?"

"I was CIA. I already know what happened to D.B. Cooper."

He stared and I could tell he was trying to decide if I was telling the truth or simply trying to distract him. I wasn't about to let on which.

"I know Mannie called the impound lot to get information on the vehicle," he said.

"Oh? That's interesting."

"It was probably interesting hours ago when he gave you the information."

I threw my hands in the air. "What do you want from me? You knew this was how it was going to be. That our work might cross sometimes. It's Sinful, not Chicago. There's not enough things going on for us to stay out of each other's sandbox."

"There is an enormous difference between us crossing paths and you working for the Heberts—known criminals—on a murder investigation."

"Look. You and I are never going to agree on the Heberts, but you can't deny that without their help, I would never have taken down Ahmad. And Mannie saved your life. I get that you don't approve of their family business. Neither do I. But I still like them. And if they need my help on something, then I'm not going to turn them down."

Carter ran one hand through his hair. The Heberts probably represented one of the biggest conflicts in his life. As a lawman, he couldn't condone their business practices, but as *my* man he couldn't deny that they played a huge part in my being able to quit the CIA and stay in Sinful. It was a real love-hate sort of thing. I imagined Mannie was even worse. Carter owed his life to him and while I knew he was grateful, he probably spent a lot of time wondering when that debt might be called and for what reason.

"You know how much I appreciate everything the Heberts and Mannie did for you," he said. "And for me. But this is a particularly callous murder. And if the Heberts are involved, then it bothers me all that much more."

"I understand. But the Heberts aren't involved in any way that's suspect."

"Then why hire you? Why give you a huge retainer?"

"To cover their butts."

He frowned. "I don't get it."

"Here's how it played out. Ida Belle was pissed off about having to spend the night in the ER and wanted answers. I don't blame her. So as you know, we went looking for Santa's car but you beat us to the punch. Ida Belle knew the Heberts owned the impound lot, so we figured we'd ask for a favor."

"And they agreed. Just like that."

I nodded. "I know you think they're the bad guys, but there's lines they don't cross. And they have huge problems with sketchy stuff happening where they live."

"Unless, of course, they're the ones doing the sketchy stuff."

"Naturally. But they aren't murderers and they would never do anything that could damage children. They're big on family. And given what Santa did to Rollie, they'd already made up their minds on the sketchy part."

He sighed. "So how did you get from them doing you a favor to hiring you to investigate a murder? Where does covering their butts come in?"

It was pointless to play dumb. Carter was not going to let this go and the reality was, the Heberts couldn't care less if I told him what they'd hired me to do and the somewhat fake reason why. After all, they'd been doing me a favor. It was only a 'real' job in the legal sense of the word.

"They knew Cooke," I said, "and had used him for some

side work. Mannie recognized the car and had the license plate on file from when they met. They have strict security at their office."

"I'm sure they do. So they hired Cooke for some stuff. Why does that matter?"

"They want to know who they were associating with and what he was into. For reputation management, let's call it."

"Potential damage control. You're telling me they're really worried about what other people might think because they hired some two-bit PI and he turned out to be shady? I'm sure they already knew he was shady or they wouldn't have hired him."

"They hired me."

"You're not exactly by the book."

"But no one's looking to kill me."

"Give it time." He shook his head. "So you want me to believe that you had nothing to do with the explosion at the motel Cooke was staying at?"

"That's exactly what I want you to believe. A motel? Really?"

He nodded.

"What exploded?"

"A vending machine."

"So tell me how I would get the name of the motel Cooke was holed up in from his license plate? If I was reading you correctly earlier, you didn't even get Cooke's name from the license plate."

His jaw flexed and I knew I was right. Which meant that I had no way of knowing where Cooke was based on his license plate alone. And that was all he thought I had.

"Maybe the Heberts knew where he was staying," Carter said.

"Why would they? He wasn't working for them at the time

and hasn't in a while, according to what they told me. So unless he's always lived at that motel, they wouldn't have cause to know about it. Did you find out how long he'd been there?"

"Two weeks."

I put my hands up. "Then I don't know what to tell you. This is Louisiana. Sinful is not the only place where weird things happen and Gertie is definitely not the only person walking around with explosives. There's probably far more people than either of us want to know about with explosives shoved in their purse or tackle box or on their person."

He sighed.

"Besides," I said, "blowing up a vending machine sounds like something kids or someone on drugs and with the munchies would do. If Gertie did it, she would have been in the middle of the mix collecting candy. I saw her trip a woman at church last month when she went for the last bag of M&M's in the leftover Halloween candy jar."

"You won't drop this case with the Heberts?" he asked.

"No. They hired me to look into things and given the circumstances, I think they have legitimate concerns. Quite frankly, so do I. If Cooke was as shady as it appears, then whoever he was looking for might be in a mess of trouble. Because I seriously doubt someone of Cooke's caliber was working for law enforcement. Shady PI. Shady client."

Carter didn't say anything but his silence implied his agreement.

"Let me make it clearer," I said. "Someone is stalking a Sinful resident and they were using Cooke to do it."

"We don't know that it's a stalker situation."

"Why don't we? Cooke was looking for someone and clearly that person did not wish to be found. Killing someone sends a strong message. If he was working for an attorney looking for an heir to a fortune or perhaps a Publishers

Clearing House winner, I don't think the outcome would have been the same."

"So what's your point?"

"That someone in Sinful might be in danger. Cooke was a hired gun. He's easy enough to replace."

"Someone in Sinful is also a murderer."

He said it quietly and I could hear the exhaustion in his voice. It had been a rough year for Carter. Too many violent crimes had come home to roost. He was tired of looking for a killer among the people he'd been raised around.

"If the person Cooke was looking for knew enough to kill him," he said, "then they know enough to clear town so whoever is after them can't find them here."

"But if they disappeared, especially right before Christmas, wouldn't that be the same as painting 'I did it' on Main Street? Might as well just fill out their own arrest warrant."

"So let's just say you figure out who that person is. What do you plan on doing about it?"

"I want to know why. And I want you to arrest them."

"Even if someone paid Cooke to hunt them down like a wild animal?"

"Yes. Cooke might have been shady but we don't know what he was told by his client, either. He might not have known what he was getting in the middle of. Although it sounds like he was the kind of man who would have taken the job even if he'd known."

"Probably true enough."

"So do you know who he was looking for?"

"No."

I nodded. I already knew he was telling the truth because he didn't get more out of Cooke's room than I did. And it would take time for the computer guys to run down anything. Assuming they could to begin with. Most people up to no good were smart enough to create fake email and reroute the IP address in order to remain anonymous online. Even if they identified the real source of origin for those emails, it could end up being a library or a Starbucks or even someone parked in a neighborhood where people who were foolish enough to have unsecured networks lived.

"I don't want this to be a problem with us," I said. "Not now and not in the future. But I don't see any way around the situation and it's bound to come up again. Probably far more often than either of us would like. So is your problem really with me working this case or is it because of my clients?"

"I can't champion the Heberts or your involvement with them, but my bigger problem is that someone was desperate enough to kill a man at a public event. How do you think they'll handle you if they find out you're onto them?"

"More bodies mean more clues, right?"

He frowned.

"Too soon?" I asked.

He shook his head. "You're going to be the death of me."

"Probably. But what a way to go."

CHAPTER NINE

MAIN STREET WAS A MADHOUSE. WE HAD TO PARK ONE block over because the street was blocked off for the sleigh ride and then walk over to the chaos. A line of trailers attached to horses and four-wheelers stretched single file down the center of the street and people milled around, chatting. The kids all clustered around the horses.

We checked in with Marie Chicoron, one of Ida Belle and Gertie's oldest friends and Sinful's current mayor, and she gave them their assignments. Gertie was the storyteller in the second trailer. Ida Belle was driving the four-wheeler pulling the third trailer. She grumbled a little about not being first, but my guess was they had stuffed her in the middle to keep her from taking the kids on a Daytona 500 sleigh ride.

"There's Dorothy," Ida Belle said. "We should try to talk to her now."

"But I don't want to," Gertie said. "Dorothy's a—"

"We already know that," Ida Belle said. "But if we talk to her here then we don't have to go to her house and take her a food offering."

Gertie perked up. "If I don't have to give that witch one of my casseroles, then I'm all for it."

We headed over and Dorothy frowned as she saw us approaching. "What do you three want? I was rather hoping after that Christmas program debacle, you'd all stay at home."

"Technically, I had nothing to do with the debacle," I said. "Neither did Ida Belle."

"You encourage that one," Dorothy said, and pointed to Gertie.

"You'd be surprised to know just how inaccurate that statement is," I said. "But that's another conversation. Right now, we were hoping you could tell us about what happened in the cafeteria before Santa kicked off."

Dorothy drew her head up and looked down her nose at me. "That's hardly appropriate terminology for a man's death."

"You can say 'kicked off,'" Gertie said. "They're not curse words."

"You don't curse?" I asked Dorothy.

"It's illegal to curse in public during the month of December," Gertie said.

"Of course it is," I said. "Anyway, did you talk to Santa?"

"No," Dorothy said. "I was busy with setup and of course, I thought it was Rollie, so speaking wasn't necessary or desired. By him, I mean."

"So who directed him to his area?" Ida Belle asked.

"I think it was Megan Prejean," Dorothy said, then narrowed her eyes. "Why are you asking all these questions? You're not going to stick your nose into police business again, are you? Because I'm not helping you with that."

"I spent most of last night in the ER," Ida Belle said. "All because I gave a man who'd been poisoned mouth-to-mouth. I could have died as well. Let's just say I have a burning desire to know who could have killed me."

Dorothy's eyes widened. "That imposter was poisoned?"

"Yes," Ida Belle said. "Which is why Carter rousted me at an indecent hour and hauled me to the ER."

"I'd heard you went to the ER," Dorothy said, "but no one seemed to know why exactly. I just figured it was old age."

I held in a grin. Even when outraged, Dorothy still had no problem getting in a dig.

"Nope," Ida Belle said. "It was being a good citizen and Christian that sent me there."

At the word 'Christian,' Dorothy drew herself up. "Well, that's just wrong. For goodness' sake, we spend all this time in church hearing about how we've got to help others, then you do it and this happens."

"It *is* wrong," I agreed. "Which is why we're trying to figure out why it happened. We have to assume that man was looking for someone who didn't want to be found, otherwise why hide behind a Santa costume? But what if he's not the only one? What if the next one comes calling and things go south again? I don't want the next good citizen to end up in the morgue instead of the ER."

"Neither do I!" Dorothy said, getting worked up. "This whole thing is simply outrageous."

"So did you see anyone else talk to Santa?" I asked. "Maybe give him something to drink or eat?"

"I see where you're going with this," Dorothy said. "But unfortunately, I can't help. I didn't see anyone speaking to him after Megan pointed out his spot. I think he might have helped himself to some punch but that couldn't have been what poisoned him or we'd have had a mass murder on our hands."

She scrunched her brow. "I *did* overhear him on his phone."

"Did you hear what he was saying?" I asked.

"Yes. He said, 'I think I found him.' Then he said 'You heard me right. Let me make sure and I'll get back with you.'"

"You're sure about that?'" I asked.

"Positive," Dorothy said. "I didn't think anything of it at the time. I mean, that conversation could have been about anything. But then, I also thought it was Rollie."

"You didn't realize the voice was wrong?" I asked.

She frowned. "You know, I guess I didn't. He must have sounded enough like Rollie that I didn't notice. Or maybe I was so busy I wasn't paying enough attention."

"Did you hear anything else?" I asked.

"I'm afraid not," she said. "I was called over to help get the snowflakes hanging right shortly after and that was on the other side of the room. I didn't venture back that direction until all the trouble happened."

"Can you tell us who else was working the cafeteria when Santa was there?" I asked.

She nodded and rattled off the names we had already gotten from Beatrice and added one we didn't have.

"Seth Prejean brought their baby in while we were setting up. Myrna was preparing to do those cute paintings on the kids' cheeks. Both he and Zach Vincent had her do their babies before grabbing something to eat. Probably smart, as Myrna had a long line after the show."

Ida Belle nodded. "The face painting was a big hit. I heard she worked the Mudbug festival as well. We're lucky to have her in Sinful now."

"We certainly are," Dorothy said. "Especially as she's a good Catholic. Now, if that's all, I'd like to get back to my duties and try to wash all this sordid business from my mind."

Without even waiting for an answer, she headed off toward a table set up with armbands to give to the kids to indicate which trailer they would ride on.

"Well, that just muddied the waters even more," Ida Belle said. "It sounds like Cooke found whoever he was looking for. Or at least, thought he did."

"Assuming Dorothy got the conversation right," I said.

"Dorothy's a pain in the butt, but her hearing's just fine," Gertie said.

I shook my head. "I guess we have to assume Cooke was poisoned before he had time to verify and call back. I'm sure Carter will trace the calls on Cooke's phone, but I doubt that will go anywhere."

"Probably a burner," Gertie said.

"We are getting nowhere fast," I said.

"We might get some help soon," Ida Belle said. "I've got a line on getting that email account traced."

"Really?" I perked up. "I figured it would take one of those cyber geniuses in order to figure out anything."

"We have one," Ida Belle said. "The Sorcerer has reappeared."

"That's great!" I said.

The Sorcerer was one of Ida Belle's online gaming buddies. He was maybe ten years old and so smart he scared the daylights out of me. He owned a huge plantation home in Mudbug and lived there with his parents, who I gather were allowed to be there because he still needed help with life things—like laundry and cooking and reaching the top shelf in the pantry. He'd helped us with a previous problem and had disappeared shortly after. Speculation was that the government had nabbed him and given his ability, it wouldn't have surprised me. Quite frankly, what surprised me more was that they gave him back.

If anyone could track down the origin of the emails, it would be the Sorcerer.

"Where has he been?" Gertie asked.

Ida Belle shrugged. "He hasn't said and no one will ask. I think the gamers are afraid to know."

"They're probably thinking they might get a knock at their own door by the Men in Black," Gertie said.

"That's only for aliens," I said. "Which, come to think of it, the Sorcerer might be."

Gertie's eyes widened. "You can verify the Men in Black are alien hunters?"

"She's joking," Ida Belle said. "I'm sure if our government has alien hunters, they're not letting the CIA in on it. You know how law enforcement agencies are—all peeing on their territory."

"God, isn't that the truth," I said.

"Carter give you a hard time?" Ida Belle asked.

"Yeah, but he'll get over it," I said. "I think he's more frustrated by who my clients are than the actual case."

"He really needs to get over this issue he has with the Heberts," Gertie said. "They're not going anywhere and they like you. There's a lot worse positions to be in where they're concerned."

"I don't think he's worried about them setting me up or anything," I said. "More like he doesn't like them hiring me because he's afraid it fulfills my wishes and entertains them."

"Which is exactly what they did," Gertie said.

"Probably," I said. "I mean, that's mostly it, I'm sure. But they do get their back up when things get too out of line in their neck of the woods. And this is the definition of out of line."

"That's true," Ida Belle said. "Hey, there's Myrna and Becca."

"Cool," I said as we headed that direction. "I wanted to ask Becca about the break-in as well."

CHAPTER TEN

Becca was the photographer from Mudbug and according to Ida Belle and Gertie, Myrna—the face painter—was her mother and lived in Sinful. I'd seen Myrna around town before. She was your typical classic Southern grandmother-looking type. Sixtyish. A bit of extra weight. Colored her short hair a slightly unnatural brown and picked it out in that kinda poufy thing that so many women her age seemed to favor. But I didn't know Becca at all, so I gave her a good look as we approached.

Thirtyish. Five foot seven. One hundred thirty pounds. Needed some more muscle mass. Right forearm had been broken in the past year or so. No threat unless she had her camera pointed at me when I was doing something I shouldn't.

Myrna was helping Becca with her equipment and smiled as we approached. "Hello, ladies," she said.

"Hello," Ida Belle said. "Have you met our friend Fortune?"

Myrna extended her hand. "Not officially, but I've heard a lot about her."

"Don't believe everything Celia says," I said.

"I don't believe *most* of what Celia says," Myrna said. "And this is my daughter, Becca. Becca, this is Ida Belle, Gertie, and Fortune. Ida Belle is in charge of things from the Baptist perspective. Celia hates her."

Becca looked up from her equipment bag and gave us all a smile. "Then I'm sure I like you. Nice to meet you all. Please excuse me if I keep working. I was running late and need to get these lenses in order so I can get night shots."

"Go right ahead," Ida Belle said. "We're the ones interrupting."

"It's a beautiful night for the sleigh ride, isn't it?" Myrna asked.

Gertie nodded. "We're hoping it's a little less eventful than the gala."

Myrna shook her head. "What a horrible thing to happen. And in front of children. And then to find out what that awful man did to Rollie. I suppose karma paid him a visit sooner rather than later with that heart attack."

"Actually, he was poisoned," I said.

Myrna's hand flew over her mouth and the color drained from her face. Becca stopped digging in her bag and rose up, her eyes wide.

"For real?" Becca asked.

"I'm afraid so," Ida Belle said, and gave a brief recount of our night in the ER.

"Oh my God," Becca said. "That's horrible. Are you sure you're all right?"

"Oh, I'm fine," Ida Belle assured her. "But I'd be lying if I said it wasn't unnerving."

"I can't believe it," Myrna said. "And of course it was unnerving. Good Lord, I would have been scared to death. Cyanide is, well, it's a frightening substance. I only saw a case of poisoning once but that was enough for me."

She must have noticed our expressions because she hurried

on. "I'm a retired nurse. I worked the ER for several years but it takes a toll. My stress level got too high and my doctor said no more, so I finished up my career tending to newborns. It was a much happier place."

A room full of babies sounded scary as heck to me, but for a normal person it was probably a much better option.

"Oh, that would have been nice," Gertie said. "Seeing all those pretty babies but not having to take them home and raise them."

Myrna smiled. "That was definitely the big plus. I love my daughter but her father was killed when she was only ten. Single parenting is not for the faint of heart. I was glad I only had one."

"I don't know if you've heard," Ida Belle said, "but Fortune is a private investigator. And she's been hired to look into this situation."

"Oh," Myrna said. "But surely the police..."

"Of course," I said. "But my client has strong feelings about certain types of crime, especially around children, and he's not as invested in law enforcement as other people are."

"I see," Myrna said, but it was clear that she didn't really.

"You were setting up for face painting in the cafeteria, right?" I asked. "I wondered if you talked to Santa or saw anyone else talk to him. Perhaps give him something to drink or eat?"

Myrna shook her head. "I was running late, I'm afraid. Got a dressing-down from Dorothy over it. Some idiot blocked part of my driveway and then my neighbor's son, who just started driving, blocked part of the other side so I couldn't pull out. It took me forever to wake him up and get him to move his car. And the other car was still parked there the next day. I had to call Carter to get it towed."

I exchanged a glance with Ida Belle, who nodded. I'd bet

anything it was Cooke's car that had been blocking Myrna's drive.

"So you didn't talk to him at all?" I asked.

"I said hello when I passed by to get some water for my spray bottle, but he only nodded," Myrna said. "Given how shy Rollie was, I didn't think anything of it."

"Did he stay at the Santa setting the entire time?" I asked.

Myrna thought for a moment, then frowned. "I think I saw him at the end of the food tables at one point."

"He was talking on his cell phone," Becca said. "I was getting my tripod set up and had to wave him back over so I could test the frame."

"And what time was that?" I asked.

"Maybe five minutes before people started coming into the cafeteria," Becca said.

"Did you see anyone else talk to him? Did anyone give him something to eat or drink?" I asked.

Myrna shook her head. "I'm sorry. After I saw him near the food table, I moved to the other side of the cafeteria where my painting station was. After painting a couple babies, I'd slipped out to the restroom with Megan Prejean and didn't get back until after all the excitement. She's been having dizzy spells and her husband didn't want her in the restroom alone. She's first trimester and it's not easy going, I'm afraid."

"Really?" Gertie said. "And they just adopted a couple months ago, right?"

Myrna nodded. "It happens all the time with couples. They can't conceive and as soon as they sign up for adoption or get the baby, they get pregnant. Has to do with stress."

"Well, good for them," Gertie said.

"What about you?" I asked Becca. "Did you see anyone talking to Santa? Anyone give him anything?"

She slowly shook her head. "I mean, Dorothy came by

barking orders when the crowd was on its way over but it wasn't a conversation. I didn't see anyone else over there at all. He had a bottled water but we didn't provide those so I figured he brought it with him."

"And were you at your camera station the entire time?" I asked.

"Once I arrived, yeah," Becca said. "But I was taking video at the show, so I only got there minutes before everyone else."

"I heard there was a break-in at your photography studio," I said.

Becca shot a sideways glance at her mother before answering. "Yeah. That was weird. The police think it was kids looking for something to hock. It happens from time to time around there. I guess it was just my turn."

"Myrna!" Celia's voice carried across the street. "There are people who need painting over here."

"Oh heavens," Myrna said, and smiled. "She's caught me conversing with the enemy. I best run or they'll revoke my Catholic card."

She hurried across the street and I looked at Becca. "You want to tell me what you really think about your studio break-in now that your mom's gone?"

"You caught that, huh?" Becca said. "My mom is a professional worrier. Maybe it's her medical training and those years she spent in the ER. She worked overnights and I know she saw a lot of bad things and probably a lot of bad things that happened to women. Or maybe it was being a single parent. Either way, she can be completely overbearing. We had a falling-out earlier this year over that sort of thing and didn't speak for almost eight months. That's why when I left New Orleans, I moved to Mudbug and not Sinful. Close enough for regular visiting but not so close she was in my business every day."

"Out of curiosity, what made you chose a small town like Mudbug?" I asked. "You seem more the urban type."

She smiled. "What made you chose Sinful?"

"Touché," I said. "Let's just say I was tired of the rush and I enjoyed a slower pace far more than I thought I would. And then there's the people. Some of them aren't half bad."

"I'm terrific," Gertie said.

"You're the reason the pace isn't slower here," Ida Belle said.

Becca laughed. "I was getting tired of the rat race in New Orleans. The competition among photographers is legendary and the hours you have to put in to compete are horrible. Then I had a bicycle accident and broke my arm. I had to stop working for a while and even once I started again, my arm couldn't take the hours I'd put in before."

"That would be rough," I agreed. "Especially with it being your dominant arm."

She nodded. "Mom met a lady a couple years back at the hospital who was from Sinful and said it sounded like heaven. When she retired, she told me she was getting the heck out of New Orleans and away from all the stench and crime. So she moved to Sinful a couple months ago. It took me a month of listening to her go on about how great small-town living was before I finally threw in the towel."

"And you set up your own shop," I said.

"I lucked out, really. The local pro had just retired, so I slid right into his contracts with the schools and organizations. And the residents started calling almost immediately for weddings and other events, so plenty of work before I'd even unpacked. It doesn't pay like jobs in New Orleans did, but with a much cheaper cost of living, it's been totally doable."

"Slim pickin's on the sexy men side of things, though," Gertie said.

Becca laughed at her obvious chagrin. "New Orleans cured me of sexy man desires. Those slick lookers are always trouble."

"Had a bad run, did you?" Gertie asked.

"You could say that," Becca said. "Thought I'd found the one but turns out he was already taken. He totally fooled me. Probably still would be if a friend hadn't found out and told me. Another good reason to leave the city. No risk of running into either of them in Mudbug."

Her expression was both angry and sad and I felt sorry for her. I'd never been in a relationship before Carter. Not a real one, anyway, but I had been betrayed by people I'd thought I could trust. It made it hard to trust anyone. Something I'd had to work on when I'd come to Sinful. Something I was still working on, if the truth be known.

Gertie shook her head. "I'm sorry, dear. Men can be awful."

"Those kind can be," Becca agreed. "My next man is going to be a blue-collar guy who likes watching television and fishing."

"Throw a rock then," Gertie said. "You just described every man in Mudbug and Sinful. Fortune got the only sexy single one here, though."

"Really?" Becca asked. "Who's that?"

"Carter LeBlanc," I said.

She raised her eyebrows. "The deputy? Nice."

I felt a blush creep up my neck and was glad it was fairly dim on the street. I wasn't embarrassed about my relationship with Carter but it still felt strange to get accolades for it. Except from Gertie, of course. She wanted to high-five me every time she saw us together.

"So, the break-in?" I asked, getting back to the reason for our talk.

"Right," Becca said. "I've actually had two break-ins, but please don't tell my mom."

"When was the first break-in?" I asked.

"About a week before the second one. My back door was jimmied but nothing was taken. The police think I scared him off when I came home. They also thought it was kids, but then the second break-in happened, so I don't know what to think."

"The second break-in was the night of the Mudbug festival, right?"

"Yes. I dropped off all my equipment and left my camera uploading the photos from the festival. Then I headed down the street to a neighbor's house for a little get-together they'd invited me to."

She frowned. "It's weird. I have several expensive cameras in my studio but they weren't touched. I even had an envelope of cash from a job I'd done the day before in my desk drawer but it was still there. The only thing the intruder did was access my computer and he reformatted it so I can't tell what he took, if anything."

"I understand your studio is a converted garage," I said. "Did he come into your house?"

"I don't think so. I mean, nothing was missing, which makes even less sense, right? It's not like I have diamonds lying around but I have a couple good TVs and some other electronics."

"Sounds more like he was looking for something in particular rather than just things to steal," I said.

She crossed her arms across her chest. "I told the cops the same thing but they didn't appear to want to work any harder at it than they already were."

"Which was to blame it on teens and do the minimal amount of paperwork required," Ida Belle said.

Becca nodded. "Honestly, the whole thing gives me the

creeps. Some guy inside my studio and in my home, but nothing missing. It doesn't make sense."

"I wonder if our fake Santa was the culprit," I said.

Her eyes widened. "You don't think...? No way. How would he even know me? I never saw him before the Sinful gala."

"Actually, I think you did," I said. "Mudbug's usual Santa canceled at the last minute and a contract service just happened to call with availability. But when the organizer tried to contact them for payment instructions, she couldn't find any proof that the company had ever existed."

"Oh wow," Becca said. "But what possible reason could he have for doing that?"

"I think he was looking for someone," I said. "And by playing Santa, he had access to the bulk of the local population at one time but without them knowing who he was."

"Looking for someone? You mean, like stalking?"

"Maybe," I said. "That's why my client would like us to look into things. In case someone is in danger."

She blew out a breath. "That's seriously messed up. Man, that kind of thing is why Mom left New Orleans. If she finds out, she'll insist on living with me until the cops figure out what he was up to. That would be dire."

"I won't say anything to her," I said. "This is just speculation at the moment, but I can't think of anything else that fits. Not given the circumstances."

"Yeah, it makes sense," she agreed. "In a completely screwed-up kind of way. I just can't believe... What if I'd been at home? What if he's not the only one looking?"

Gertie patted her shoulder. "It will be fine, dear. I'm sure he was after your photos. Seeing if he could find a shot of the person he was looking for in case he missed them during the event."

"I guess so," she said. "But it makes me feel—I don't know

—icky. To think that he stole my work to stalk someone. Oh man! Do you think someone's going to try to steal the photos I took last night?"

"Assuming anyone else is looking for this person, I don't think they'd risk that twice," I said. "But it wouldn't hurt to be careful. I assume you don't have a security system."

"I do now. Got it installed the day after the last break-in," she said. "Twice in as many weeks was too much for me."

"Do you have a weapon?" I asked.

"If you're asking me do I have a gun, then yes," she said. "And I know how to use it. I was the last to leave at a lot of late-night events. A smart woman does not go walking around New Orleans after midnight without protection."

"Good," I said. "I honestly don't think you have anything to worry about, but it never hurts to be prepared."

Gertie frowned. "I think I see Celia motioning to you." She reached up to wipe at Becca's cheek. "You have a smudge."

Becca rubbed her cheek and shook her head. "Probably that reindeer mom put on me last night. That paint is *not* as washable as the manufacturers claim. I'm glad I didn't go with the Christmas tree."

"I wish I wouldn't have." A girl's voice cut in and we looked up to see a teen walking by, pointing to the green spots on her cheek.

Becca shook her head. "The whole parish will be walking around with spots on their faces before the holiday is over."

I made a mental note to avoid the face painting part of the holiday offerings. Not that there was much risk of that happening unless I was held at gunpoint, but Gertie had been known to talk me into things I wouldn't otherwise do. And since 'tis the season, I might have been swayed toward something whimsical if it was going to make her happy.

"Becca!" Celia's voice carried over the crowd. "We need you now!"

"Crap," she said. "I've got to run. You're sure you think I'm safe?"

"I do," I said. "But you should talk to Deputy LeBlanc and tell him what happened. He might have a different view of things than law enforcement in Mudbug."

She nodded as she slung her camera strap around her neck. "I'll do that. Thanks for letting me know."

Becca hurried across the street and I looked over at Ida Belle and Gertie. "We're not getting much," I said. "So far, all I've managed tonight is scaring that poor girl to death."

"It won't hurt her to be on edge a little," Ida Belle said. "Better than the alternative. Maybe we'll get an opportunity to talk to some of the others after the sleigh ride. In the meantime, I see Marie waving at us so we better take our places."

"What exactly am I doing?" I asked as we headed over.

CHAPTER ELEVEN

"YOU HAVE SEVERAL CHOICES," IDA BELLE SAID. "YOU CAN wait around here and mingle with the crowd. Or you can ride with Gertie and listen to her tales of Christmas. Or you can hitch a ride with me."

Jeez Louise. I either had to make small talk with a bunch of people, ride in a trailer of hay with kids, or risk my life on the back of a four-wheeler that Ida Belle was commandeering. I'd had better options on CIA missions.

"I guess I'll ride with you," I told Ida Belle. Since she'd be hitched to a trailer full of kids, that should prevent the worst of her daredevil driving habits, and it was the only option that eliminated the need for me to chat. I still hadn't gotten that whole chatting thing down. I was fairly certain I never would.

Ida Belle grinned. "You just don't want to talk to people."

"Says the pot to the kettle," Gertie said.

"Hey, I could opt to go home and leave you to it," I said.

"But then you might miss an opportunity to interview more people after the sleigh ride," Ida Belle said.

I sighed. She had me there, and I was all about efficiency. Catching several people at one event was a lot faster than doing the whole home visit, drink iced tea, have a snack thing. It was a lot easier on the waistline, too. I'd already had to double my daily running distance to counter the additional calories that Sinful provided, because turning them down didn't seem like a good option. The holidays had multiplied that problem times ten.

I followed Ida Belle to her four-wheeler and noticed it had a big rack on the back.

"A body rack," I said. "Cool. Gives me more to hold on to."

She raised one eyebrow. "In Sinful, we call those deer racks."

"Ha! Yeah, I guess the cargo is probably a little different here."

"Most of the time."

I wasn't even going to ask.

I waited until Ida Belle was in place, then climbed on the back. When the trailers were loaded and everyone had taken a seat, Marie rang Christmas bells and the procession started out. I was somewhat surprised to see that the horses didn't react to the four-wheelers, but then they probably heard that sort of thing all the time. It seemed to be the third vehicle of choice in Sinful, after a truck and a bass boat.

And Ida Belle had been right about the pace. It was decidedly slow. So slow that I was getting bored. The caravan headed down Main Street and into the residential area. The route would take us past the park and in a big loop around the neighborhood until it arrived back on Main Street. All vehicles on the route area were required to be parked in driveways to ensure plenty of room. The entire thing was supposed to take an hour but at the rate we were moving, I was wondering if we'd get back before Christmas.

"Your blood pressure must be through the roof," I said to Ida Belle. "Having to drive this slow has got to be stressful."

She laughed. "It's certainly not my norm. But it would be hard to do much fancy driving with a trailer attached. And then there's the kids."

"Yes. Parents might get upset if you went all NASCAR with their babies."

"Ha! I've seen the way most of them drive. NASCAR would be an improvement."

As we entered the neighborhood, I pointed to my front door. "Look at the wreath Gertie made for me."

Ida Belle glanced at the circle of green and narrowed her eyes. "What are those red things on it?"

"Empty shotgun shells. She even put little lights in them so they glow really well."

"Perfect."

"Hey. Where's Carter?" I'd expected to see him downtown, but Deputy Breaux had been lurking at the start of the trailer parade.

"Why are you asking me? He's your man."

"Do you know where Walter is?"

"Probably sitting in his recliner in his underwear and watching bass fishing."

"That was far too much information."

"I'm just kidding anyway. He and Scooter hang out at the General Store in case any of the four-wheelers needs a last-minute tune-up or part. Since Deputy Breaux was minding the start of the ride, I'm guessing Carter is either at the park or on the last leg of the ride. They space out along the route in case of an emergency."

"What constitutes an emergency?"

"Equipment failure or someone needs to vacate a trailer. Sometimes a kid has a meltdown and has to be removed. And we've had a couple heart attacks."

As we approached the turn for the park, I peered around

Ida Belle but didn't see Carter's truck parked on the street. I did, however, spot Sheriff Lee sitting on his horse at the edge of the park.

"There's Sheriff Lee," I said. "If someone has a heart attack, I don't think carrying them on the back of that horse is a good idea."

The horse was as old as Sheriff Lee and probably as deaf. Two pounds more on his back would probably cause his legs to collapse. As the caravan approached the middle of the park where Sheriff Lee was stationed, I saw movement on the other side of the street. It looked like two people ducking behind the hedges on one of the lawns. My senses went on high alert. People who were minding their own business didn't need to hide behind shrubbery.

Seconds later, trouble erupted.

The first bottle rocket went over the caravan and landed in the park. Sheriff Lee's horse was partially deaf, but even one with reduced hearing would have heard the blast when it exploded, and then there were the sparks shooting off of it as well. The horse reared up, higher than I would have thought possible, and Sheriff Lee managed to maintain his seat. Another feat I didn't think could happen. But when the horse's front hooves hit the ground, he dug his back ones in and took off.

The second bottle rocket came shortly after the first and went right in front of the horses pulling the second trailer. I was just about to jump off the four-wheeler and tackle the idiots with the fireworks when the situation went from dangerous to deadly. Between the firecracker and Sheriff Lee's horse bolting across the park, the horses attached to the trailer made the joint decision that their part in this nonsense was officially over. They reared up and the driver tried to regain control.

When it was obvious that the horses were too far gone to listen, the driver turned and yelled, "Everyone jump!"

The frightened passengers ran to the end of the trailer and jumped off into the street. I saw Gertie handing a toddler to a woman over the side. Then the horses reared again and let out a battle cry. A second later, the driver dived off the front and into the street and the horses took off like they'd been shot. Then they made a complete U-turn and all the passengers who'd just fled scrambled to get out of the way as they raced by, headed back toward Main Street.

With Gertie on board.

She dragged herself up from the bottom of the trailer and looked at us as she flashed by. She appeared startled and a little confused and I hoped that being tossed into the bottom of the trailer hadn't broken any bones.

"Disconnect me!" Ida Belle yelled.

I jumped off the four-wheeler and disconnected the trailer, then hopped back on. I'd barely gotten my butt on the seat before Ida Belle took off after the runaway horses. We had a crisis situation at the moment, but I made a mental note to slap that driver silly just as soon as all of this was back under control. Who bails off a trailer and lets horses run wild?

Because of the delay in unhooking the trailer, the horses had a head start, and they were making the most of it. When we got to the end of the street, Ida Belle made a hard turn and threw her body weight in, sliding the four-wheeler around the corner, then took off again as soon as the tires reconnected with the pavement. We flashed by my house and I saw my crazy neighbor, Ronald J. Franklin Jr., standing on his front lawn, obviously there to check out the commotion. I was pretty sure he was dressed like Abraham Lincoln but didn't get a good look. We caught up to the runaway trailer just before it got into town.

"Get ready!" Ida Belle yelled.

We hadn't actually discussed a plan, mostly because we'd been moving at warp speed, but I assumed we were going for one of those Western moves. She pulled her knife out and handed it back to me, which confirmed my thoughts. It was a nonlethal rescue. I had complete faith in my ability to make the jump. Not so much faith in my ability to handle thousands of pounds of scared, running mass, but something had to be done. As we inched up to the racing horses, I crouched on the back of the four-wheeler, holding Ida Belle's shoulders to balance, and prepared to leap.

When we drew beside them, I jumped.

I managed to land on the back of the horse and grasped the mane and the harness to keep from pitching off in between them. That would have been dire. People scrambled out of Main Street as the horses charged by and I could hear the frantic yelling. I tugged on the reins as hard as possible but it didn't slow them at all. In fact, I think they might have picked up speed just a bit. The end of Main Street was completely blocked with tables holding snacks and bottled drinks, all manned by Celia's group. They all raced for the sidewalk when they realized the horses weren't going to stop.

Except Celia.

Either the woman had a death wish or a God complex, because I couldn't think of any other reason to stand in front of charging horses. Then she actually raised her hands in front of her, like she was directing them to stop. I yelled at her to move and when we were only a couple feet away, she finally realized that her wanting the horses to stop wasn't going to make it happen.

Her eyes widened and she dived, but instead of diving straight to the side, she launched at an angle and landed on the top of the dessert table. I saw a cloud of powdered sugar explode as we blew past and looked back to the see the trailer clip the end of the table, spinning it around. I saw Celia fly off into the crowd before I turned around and realized the situation had just gone from bad to way, way worse.

The horses were heading off the road and straight for the bayou.

CHAPTER TWELVE

I PULLED IDA BELLE'S KNIFE FROM MY BRA AND STARTED cutting the harness straps. I got the first horse loose then did a half jump, half drag onto the other horse and started working on those. I could see the bayou in the moonlight and it was approaching far quicker than I wanted. As I cut the last strap, the horses saw the water and made a hard left turn, pitching me off into the marsh grass. I jumped up just in time to see the trailer continue on the original trajectory and launch over the edge of the bank and into the bayou.

I ran to the bank, scanning the water for Gertie. A couple seconds later, she popped up, blowing water everywhere, and then let out a huge woot.

"Get out of there before the alligators come for dinner!" I yelled.

She started for shore but after about two feet, it seemed as if she were swimming in place. "Something's wrapped around my ankle!" she yelled. "Good Lord, I'm bait!"

I heard people running up behind me but I didn't have time to chat. I dived into the water and swam for Gertie. She was still treading water when I reached her and it was a bit of a challenge to grab her leg as she kicked. I finally located the problem. One of the harness straps was wrapped around her ankle. I pulled Ida Belle's knife out again and cut the strap. As soon as the knife pulled through the last of the leather, Gertie managed to kick me right in the face with her free foot.

I broke the surface and heard people yelling from the bank. "It's a gator!" a woman called. "Hurry!"

Both of us started for shore and a couple seconds later, a shower of bullets rang out overhead. Without even thinking, I ducked below the surface, pulling Gertie with me. Then I swam like crazy. When my hands hit mud, I sprang up from the bottom and turned to see Gertie not far behind me. The alligator was nowhere in sight. Which meant he'd either made the educated decision to leave the area or had gone under, refusing to give up the prize.

I reached back and grabbed her shoulder, practically hauling her to her feet. Carter and Ida Belle scrambled down the bank and half carried, half dragged her up as she coughed. I hurried behind them and sank onto the ground next to her.

"Is she dead?" a man asked, staring down at Gertie.

"Her chest is moving, you idiot," a woman said. "How can she be dead?"

All of a sudden, Gertie leaped to her feet and started jumping around, pulling at her shirt.

"It's got me!" she yelled.

I bolted up, having zero idea what was expected of me. Then she reached inside her blouse and pulled out a live fish with something that looked like a small candle locked between its jaws. Still jumping, she flung the fish into the crowd of people and it hit Celia right across the face. Celia screamed like someone had killed her and then realized she was clutching the fish and screamed again as she tossed it into the crowd.

"What the heck is wrong with you?" a man yelled. "That's a perfectly good bass."

"Look." A boy, probably about fifteen years old, bent over and picked up what the fish dropped out of its mouth. "It's a really cool firework."

By the time what he said registered, he'd pulled out a lighter and lit up the end of the stick.

"That's not fireworks!" I yelled, and lunged for the stick.

I tore it from the shocked boy's grasp and threw it in the bayou. A second after it hit the water, a giant boom tore through the air, and wet hay and fish blew out of the water and all over the crowd.

"Get those bass!" a man yelled.

"I guess my cows will be eating grass this week," the owner of the trailer said.

Carter grabbed the teen by the shirt. "Where did you get that?"

"It was on the ground, I swear," the boy said.

"But I think you have one of the troublemakers who shot fireworks at the sleigh ride," I said.

The teen shook his head. "That wasn't me."

"Do you smoke?" I asked.

He looked confused. "No."

"Then why are you carrying a lighter?" I asked. "And why did you automatically assume that stick was fireworks?"

His shoulders slumped and Carter waved at Deputy Breaux, who was hurrying through the crowd. "Stick him in a cell," Carter said.

The boy's eyes widened. "What? Jail? I can't go to jail. They do things to young guys in jail. And I'm a minor. You can't throw me in jail without my parents knowing."

A man stepped forward.

Six foot two. Two hundred thirty pounds. Good muscle tone. No threat to me, but based on his glare, the boy was in serious trouble.

"That's my son," the man said. "Haul him off. Will do him some good to sit behind bars for a while. Maybe you can keep him through New Year's. I'll give his gifts to his brother. He knows how to act right."

"Dad!" The teen gave his father a horrified look.

A woman stepped up beside the man and clutched his arm. "Honey, don't you think—"

The man shook his head. "What I think is that his foolishness could have hurt a lot of people. There were little kids on that trailer the horses were pulling. I'm tired of you making excuses for him. It's over."

The man gave Carter a nod and stalked off, the woman trailing behind him.

"Well," Carter said as he pushed the boy toward Deputy Breaux. "Looks like we're going to be roommates for a while."

"Maybe while he's there, he'll tell you who his accomplice was," I said. "There were two of them. I saw them move into the bushes right before the horses took off."

"I'm sure it won't be hard to figure out," Carter said. "Are you two all right?"

"I'm fine, but my bra is shot," Gertie said. "That fish really did a number on it."

Celia stomped up in front of us, with straw and powdered sugar clinging to her hair and smelling faintly of fish.

"How long are these three women going to be allowed to terrorize this town?" she asked.

"What the heck are you talking about?" a teen girl yelled. "They didn't shoot the fireworks, and Fortune saved Gertie and those horses. She's a hero and you're a royal pain in the—"

A woman, who I suspected was the teen's mother, clamped

her hand over the girl's mouth. The girl pulled her hand away and waved her cell phone.

"I got the whole thing on video," she said. "Posted it to YouTube already, so go see for yourself, you old windbag." She looked up at her mother. "That's the nicest thing I could think of."

Her mother patted her shoulder. "I understand."

"Maybe if you weren't always in the way, these things wouldn't happen to you," Ida Belle said to Celia. "But it seems no matter what is going down, there you are. You saw those runaway horses coming straight at you. Everyone moved but you. Maybe you should have your head checked."

Celia put her hands on her hips and glared. "If you three had nothing to do with this mess, then where did that fish get dynamite?"

"eBay?" Gertie suggested.

Carter shot Gertie a look that said he knew exactly where the fish had gotten the dynamite but since she was unlikely to have another stick in her bra, he couldn't prove it.

"I see you're going to do nothing," Celia said. "Ever since you took up with that Yankee tart, that's become a habit with you."

"You're going to want to watch what you say," Carter said. "I still have one empty cell."

"You have no reason to arrest me," Celia said.

"Public indecency?" Gertie suggested. "No one wants to look at that sourpuss face."

"Go home," Carter said to Celia. "Or to jail. Given your popularity, I could probably make a case for that indecency thing."

Celia's eyes widened and her chest swelled up. "When that idiot sheriff is gone, you won't have any power. Then we'll see how your girlfriend and her friends fare with real law enforcement."

"Looking forward to it," Carter said, then turned around and walked away, what was left of the crowd trailing behind him.

"Sucks to be you," Gertie said as she traipsed off after the crowd.

Celia huffed a few times, then finally stomped off.

"Should we do anything about the trailer?" I asked Ida Belle.

She shook her head. "Too dangerous in the dark. Scooter will pull it out tomorrow with the tow truck."

As we headed back into town, I brushed hay off my shirt. "Please tell me this is the last of the Christmas events. I don't think I can take much more of Sinful's holiday spirit."

"There's caroling tomorrow night."

"Surely nothing much can happen singing."

Ida Belle shrugged. "Gertie will be there."

———

I'D REACHED THE SEVENTH LEVEL OF EXHAUSTION BY THE time I arrived home. Ida Belle had made Walter open the General Store and lend her plastic to line her SUV seats before she'd allow Gertie and me to sit in it. The entire process had added another thirty minutes to a day that already seemed like it would never end, but she said she wasn't about to smell wet hay and fish for the next two weeks. I probably could have walked home in less time, but I figured I'd already had more than enough exercise for one day.

I trudged into my house, planning on heading straight upstairs and into the shower, when I heard noise in my kitchen. It sounded like a radio or television playing, except that I didn't have either in that room. I pulled my nine out and shook it since it still had a little water in it, then crept down the hall. When I reached the end of the hall, I sprang around the door, gun leveled.

Mannie looked up at me and smiled.

He was sitting at my kitchen table, a beer in front of him, and grinning from ear to ear as he stared at his cell phone.

"That's a great move," he said. "You could stunt double in Westerns."

I groaned. "How do you find those things so quickly?"

"I have alerts set for anything referencing Sinful, Louisiana. When I first set it up, I didn't include the state. That was a mistake."

I grimaced, not even wanting to think about what a term like "sinful" might turn up on the internet. I pulled the chair across from him out and slumped down into it.

"You're really going to have to start knocking on the front door like other people," I said. "What if Carter had been with me?"

"Then I would have left and you'd have never known I was here."

"But you were watching the video when I came in. I could hear the noise. Carter would have heard it too."

"Except that Carter is back at the sheriff's department babysitting a juvenile delinquent who is probably aspiring to be Gertie."

I shook my head. "Is there anything you don't know?"

"Maybe."

"I suppose there's video of the dynamite explosion as well?"

He nodded. "And Gertie's fight with the fish in her shirt. I'm going to be honest with you—she's the only person I've ever met who terrifies me just a little."

"Yeah. I get that."

JANA DELEON

"Is she what happened to your Christmas tree? It looks a little rough."

"That was a joint effort between Gertie and my cat."

"That's why I don't have pets."

"Even if I didn't have the cat, I'd still have Gertie."

"*That's* why I don't have friends."

"Touché. So anyway, I assume you're here for a reason and not because you had the overwhelming desire to have a late-night beer with a woman who smells like bass and bayou mud. Not that I don't enjoy your company, but I'm really dying for a shower."

"Of course. After you left the Heberts' office, I decided to run down some associates of Cooke's. See if any of them had a line on what he was working on."

I perked up. If he hadn't found anything, he wouldn't be here. "And?"

"A two-bit PI by the name of Reynolds said he had beers with Cooke a couple weeks ago. He said he was looking for a woman in Reynolds' neighborhood and wanted to see if he had seen her around anywhere."

"A woman? He's sure?"

Mannie nodded. "He showed Reynolds a picture."

"Really?"

"Yeah, but Reynolds didn't remember much about it. Youngish, long brown hair, brown eyes, which describes half the women in Louisiana. He said he'd never seen her before, but Reynolds spends more of his waking hours drunk than sober, so who knows. Anyway, that's not the most interesting part. When Cooke went to the bathroom, he left his case folder on the table with his cell phone. Reynolds managed to spill his beer and picked up the file to keep it from getting soaked and another picture fell out—but this one was the woman holding a baby. A baby wearing a blue hat."

"Crap." All the implications of hiring a PI like Cooke to track down a woman and a baby ran through my mind, and none of them were good.

"I had the same reaction. This whole thing stank to high heaven from the start, but if the male Cooke was looking for is a baby..."

"Exactly. I appreciate you running down that information. It allows us to narrow down Cooke's potential targets, anyway. Do you think this Reynolds would recognize the woman from the photo if I sent him some more to look at?"

Mannie shrugged. "Honestly? No. He's burned up too many brain cells with whiskey."

"Well, at least he's given me more to go on. I'll get with Ida Belle and Gertie tomorrow and narrow things down. Can't have been too many people in that cafeteria who also have babies." I paused. "Double crap."

"What?"

"That's assuming the picture was recent."

Mannie frowned. "I hadn't even thought about it, but you're right. I suppose it could have been an older photo and the child is no longer a baby. You're good at thinking through all the angles. I think you made a wise choice to become a PI."

"Thanks. I suppose options were a bit limited given my skill set. It's nice to know I have talent for something else."

He smiled. "I felt the same way when I went to work for the Heberts."

I raised one eyebrow. "Is the work really that different from what you did before? I mean, there's probably a lot less swimming..."

Mannie had never confirmed that he was a former Navy SEAL, but I would bet money on it.

"You might be surprised by the extent of my duties," he said. "I'm working on my MBA right now."

"Seriously?" That statement went down in the 'things I never expected to hear' category.

He nodded. "They're looking to expand their business and Big and Little can't handle much more than they're already managing now. When you add in the sometimes-questionable business practices with their trust issues, they don't have a lot of options for viable employees."

"Makes sense."

He rose from the table. "I'll let you get to that shower. If there's anything else I can help with, you know where to find me. Or if you need equipment, we can help with that as well. This investigation is a priority for the Heberts, especially now that we suspect a child is involved."

"What kind of equipment?" I asked out of general curiosity.

He grinned. "Maybe a cowboy hat?"

CHAPTER THIRTEEN

I HAD PLANS TO MEET IDA BELLE AND GERTIE AT THE CAFÉ the next morning. We arrived at the same time and were all dragging a little. Gertie was sporting a couple of ugly bruises on her arms due to being tossed around in the trailer and the subsequent launch into the bayou. She informed us that the one on her butt was even more spectacular and the fish bite on her boob was legendary, but Ida Belle and I both declined the opportunity to see those firsthand.

Ally was all smiles as soon as she saw us walk through the door. Our usual table was available and she had coffees on it by the time we took our seats.

"Everyone is talking about the runaway sleigh ride," she said. "I saw the videos on YouTube and they are frightening, awesome, and hilarious. The frightening part being those stampeding horses, which I saw firsthand on Main Street, the awesome part being Fortune's *Gunsmoke* rescue, and the hilarious part being the fish in Gertie's bra, the dynamite explosion, and everything that involved Aunt Celia."

"The fish part was only hilarious if it wasn't your bra," Gertie said. "That thing is not repairable. Do you know how hard it is to find a good bra at my age? Gravity is woman's enemy."

"I'd argue that bras are woman's enemy," I said.

Ida Belle lifted her coffee cup. "Hear, hear."

Ally laughed. "I heard Aunt Celia called an emergency meeting of God's Wives this morning. She's determined to keep Gertie from 'ruining' another Christmas event. I think kidnapping and holding you hostage might be on the table."

"Last night wasn't my fault," Gertie said. "And as soon as I find that sleigh driver, I'm going to kick him in an inappropriate place."

Ida Belle lifted her coffee cup again. "Hear, hear."

"Didn't you hear?" Ally asked. "He broke his arm in two places when he bailed."

"That wasn't where I planned on kicking him," Gertie said.

"Anyway, you know Aunt Celia," Ally said. "It's going to be a whole lot of nothing, I'm sure, but I just figured I'd let you know. For the record, the Christmas showcase was the best I've ever seen. Francis stole the show. I'm usually dozing off."

Gertie beamed. "Maybe I should bring him to Christmas service this Sunday."

"No!" All three of us responded at once.

"Why not?" Gertie asked. "He was raised by nuns part of his life. He knows church stuff."

"First off, that bird is Catholic," Ida Belle said. "Second, he was raised the other half by criminals and you never know which line of talking he's going to take."

Gertie frowned. "Yeah, I suppose that Catholic thing might be a problem. I need to talk to Pastor Don about converting him. Can you baptize a bird or will he need a full-on exorcism?"

"Good God," Ida Belle mumbled.

Ally grinned and gave me an apprehensive glance before

training a big smile on Ida Belle. "If you have some free time this week, I'd love to discuss your wedding cake with you. I have a ton of pictures to help us get started. Maybe we could review them over dinner."

"Why in the world would it take an entire dinner to pick cake?" Ida Belle asked. "It can't possibly be that hard."

"There are a lot of options," Ally said.

"A lot of options that don't mean anything to me," Ida Belle said. "Look, just make up one of those double chocolate layer cakes you do, throw a couple bass-fishing on top of it, and call it done."

Ally stared. "I am not doing a basic chocolate cake for your wedding. Nor am I putting fishermen on it. Maybe for the groom's cake, but not the wedding cake."

"Why does the groom need his own cake?" Ida Belle asked. "I'll share."

Gertie shook her head. "You see what I've been dealing with? If she even gets a whiff of a bridal magazine, she pulls her gun on you. The other day, I removed a white napkin from my kitchen drawer and thought I was a goner. She thought it was swatches."

"You two are exhausting," Ida Belle said. "We haven't even set a date."

"But these things take time," Ally said. "And testing. Your wedding cake has to be perfect."

"When has cake ever been a bad thing?" Ida Belle asked.

"What about that time Old Lady Morrison grabbed her talcum powder instead of flour?" Gertie asked. "It wasn't as bad as when Eve Jenkins accidentally garnished spaghetti with her son's weed, but it was still a jolt to the palate."

"Does every woman in Sinful need new glasses?" I asked.

"Have you seen their husbands?" Ida Belle asked. "They don't want new glasses."

I shook my head. "If you don't start being nicer, I'm going to have to pray for you."

"Fine," Ida Belle said to Ally. "I'll let you know when I'm available for dinner. But if you're going to make me look at girlie cakes, you better have samples."

"I wouldn't dream of not having samples," Ally said.

Gertie leaned in. "I've got some Xanax you can put in them. Might help things."

"Why in the world do you have Xanax?" Ida Belle asked. "You don't worry about anything. Hell, you're the reason the rest of us need Xanax."

"Actually, Dr. Wilkinson prescribed it for you that time you brought me into the ER after that incident with the bread-making machine and that stray cat."

"Then why didn't you give them to me?" Ida Belle asked. "Me and the stray cat could have used them."

"It was kinda like admitting you might be right," Gertie said.

"On that note," I said, "I'll have eggs and blueberry pancakes. And I've been meaning to ask you—did you work the cafeteria at all the night of the showcase?"

Ally nodded. "I was in and out all evening but ducked out to catch some of the show."

"Did you see when Santa arrived?" I asked.

"Kinda. I was headed for the auditorium when he was coming across the parking lot. I waved but he was on his cell phone. I don't think he saw me." She gave us a worried look. "He was poisoned, right? And could have infected—or whatever you call it—Ida Belle. I don't understand."

"Neither do we," I said. "But we're trying to figure it out."

Ally's eyes widened. "Oh, but I thought Carter...I mean, the police..."

"Carter's investigating, but I have a client who'd like to know what is going on," I said. "So I'm also investigating."

"Uh-huh," she said. "How's that working out?"

I knew she meant between me and Carter and not the investigation.

I shrugged. "A little rough around the edges, but it is what it is."

"Please be careful," Ally said. "All of you. I can't imagine why that man hurt Rollie but if someone poisoned him, then I can't help but think they probably had a decent reason. I don't want to hear that you guys have spent another night in the ER."

"We don't want to spend more time there either," I assured her.

"And we're always careful," Gertie said.

Ida Belle shook her head. "One day, lightning is going to just bolt through the ceiling and strike you where you sit."

"You better hope not since you're usually sitting next to me," Gertie said.

Ally laughed and headed off to the kitchen. As soon as she was out of earshot, I filled Ida Belle and Gertie in on my visit from Mannie.

"I wish I'd come home one night and find a sexy man drinking beer in my kitchen," Gertie said.

"If you find a sexy man drinking beer in your kitchen, you probably walked into the wrong house," Ida Belle said.

"Maybe I should start walking into Fortune's house," Gertie said. "That's where all the hot man action is."

"Anyway," Ida Belle said. "So it looks like our stalker theory might hold weight. But I don't like the baby angle."

"I don't either," I said. "But we can't be sure the child is still a baby. The photo might have been an old one. Still, I think it's better to start with the baby angle and work our way up from there."

Ida Belle nodded. "I agree. Well, that definitely narrows things down. There were two couples in the cafeteria that night and both have babies. Megan Prejean and her husband Seth and Amber Vincent and her husband Zach."

Her voice trailed off as she finished the sentence and suddenly, she stiffened. "Both of their babies were adopted."

I felt my stomach roll as the theories rolled through my mind. "You're kidding."

"I'm afraid not," Ida Belle said.

"When did they adopt?" I asked.

"About three months ago," Ida Belle said.

Gertie nodded. "That's right. In fact, I think they both got their babies on the same day. I remember thinking what a great day it was that two families were made."

"I don't suppose you know anything about the adoptions or the birth mothers?" I asked.

They both shook their heads.

"Boys? Girls?" I asked.

"Both boys," Ida Belle said.

Gertie frowned. "I don't like this at all. It was bad enough when we thought it was an adult being stalked but if it was really all about one of those babies, that means one of those couples and their baby could be in trouble."

"It also means one of those four people is probably the killer," Ida Belle said.

I blew out a breath. "Then that's where we start."

———

FORTUNATELY FOR OUR INVESTIGATIVE TEAM, GERTIE HAD been knitting baby beanie hats for donations and had some she'd just finished. They'd make perfect gifts for both sets of new parents and give us an excuse to make an unscheduled visit and work in some questions while we were there. After breakfast, I dropped off my Jeep at home and we made a quick trip to pick up the hats. Gertie managed to rustle up some gift bags and we were set.

"Do you think we should tell Carter about this?" Gertie asked on the way to Amber and Zach's house.

"Sure," Ida Belle said. "I think she should lead with Mannie sitting in her kitchen when she got home last night."

"Maybe not then," Gertie said.

I frowned. That had been the question that had plagued me ever since my conversation with Mannie. In fact, I'd lost quite a few hours of sleep to it.

"Did you see Carter at all last night?" Gertie asked.

"No," I said. "He called and said he would be held up late with the dynamite teen and he was going straight to bed when he left."

"Did he sound mad?" Gertie asked.

I shook my head. "He sounded tired. And somewhat resigned. I almost prefer mad."

"I would too," Ida Belle said. "It's hard to see a man like Carter so frustrated. He really wants this town to be a great place to live. With all the things going on here lately, I'm sure he feels like he's failing the town and the residents, but nothing could be further from the truth."

"This place would fall apart without Carter," Gertie said. "But I can understand how he feels. I feel the same way sometimes."

"We all have the same personality type," I said. "We see something wrong and want to fix it, which in our case, means direct action. It never occurs to us that we won't be successful so we take risks that other people wouldn't."

"Well, I'm too old to rethink my life," Ida Belle said. "So I guess we just have to live with it. How are we going to play out these interviews?"

I'd been thinking about that since breakfast and I still hadn't hit on the perfect way to approach things. If we didn't provide any information, we might never steer the conversation where it needed to go. But if we did provide information, we'd be tipping the killer off that we were closing in on them.

"I think we're going to have to give some information, in order to get a reaction," I said. "But I'm still not sure how much I want to provide. I'll play it by ear. Just follow my lead."

"It *is* rather tricky," Ida Belle said.

"And after we do the interviews, I'm going to tell Carter what Mannie told me," I said. "I don't have to give specifics on how I got the information."

Ida Belle nodded. "Smart. We get what we can out of them before Carter makes his play."

"That's my thinking," I said.

Ida Belle pulled up to the curb in front of a pretty yellow house with white shutters. A For Sale sign was in the front yard. Ida Belle frowned.

"You guys know anything about that?" I asked.

They both shook their heads.

"I don't really know either couple that well," Gertie said. "They're Catholic. That makes them Celia's domain."

"Let's find out about that first thing," I said.

We headed to the house and rang the doorbell. It sounded like complete chaos inside. I could hear banging and the sound of glass breaking, then the baby started crying. It was almost a full minute before a harried-looking young woman I'd seen in town a few times opened the door. She stared at us for a moment, then her face cleared in recognition as she locked on Gertie.

"Ms. Hebert," she said.

"Hello, Amber," Gertie said. "You remember Ida Belle, and this is our friend Fortune. We're out running Christmas errands and wanted to drop off a baby gift."

"Oh." Amber's expression softened. "That's so nice. Please come in. I just put on a fresh pot of coffee."

We stepped inside and followed Amber through a maze of boxes and into the kitchen. Dishes sat stacked on the counter, a pile of newspaper next to them. The remnants of a broken cup were in a trash can sitting next to the refrigerator.

I heard the baby cry off down the hallway.

"Do you need to go get him?" Gertie asked.

She shook her head as she poured us all a cup of coffee. "Zach has him. Diaper change time."

"It's so nice how young fathers pitch in on things," Gertie said.

"Please excuse the mess," Amber said as she moved a box off the kitchen table before she placed the coffee on it. "We're so far behind on packing and now we're having to rush to get it done in time."

"You're moving?" Gertie asked.

She nodded as she slid into a chair. "Zach's company offered him a management position at their office in Abu Dhabi."

"Wow!" Ida Belle said.

"It's his dream job," Amber said. "He's an internet security specialist and brilliant. He's been wanting to head up his own division for years and he's finally getting the opportunity."

"That's a huge change from Sinful," I said.

"I'm nervous as heck," Amber said. "But the pay is incredible and we've been assured that there are plenty of top-notch private schools. And his company is putting us up in an executive condo for a year, so no rent either. I don't know how I'm going to like living in a huge city with so many people, but Zach said if it doesn't suit, we'll move out after the year and he'll commute."

"That sounds like a big new adventure," Ida Belle said. "When do you leave?"

"We fly out on the twenty-seventh," Amber said. "But we have to get anything we want to ship over to his company mail center by the twenty-fourth. Mostly we're just sending our clothes and pictures and things like that. The dishes and furniture are going to a cousin who just graduated from college and is getting set up in her first apartment in New Orleans."

"That's nice," Gertie said. "She really lucked out."

"She's beside herself," Amber said. "But she deserves a break. She's worked full time to put herself through school. This little boost is just what she needs to hit the ground running."

I heard cooing noises and looked over to see Zach coming down the hall with the smiling baby. Amber made introductions and Gertie handed her the bag with the hat.

"Since the Christmas baby is here now," Gertie said, "give this a look."

Amber pulled the tissue out of the bag and removed the bright blue hat with white snowflakes and smiled. "Oh, it's so pretty! Did you make this?"

Gertie nodded. "I like to give all the new Sinful babies a gift their first Christmas. The hats have always been a big hit."

"I can see why," Amber said as she jumped up and slipped the hat on her son.

I hadn't had the opportunity, or had mostly avoided the opportunity, to be around infants. If I was being honest, they sort of terrified me. So little and fragile. But since so many capable adults were present, I took the opportunity to study Nathan for a minute. He arms and legs were puffy with rolls, like the Stay-Puft Marshmallow Man, and his skin was smooth white except for the blush of red on his face and a tiny birthmark on his cheek. The baby rolled his eyes up and his fat little hands reached up to try to grab at the hat but he mostly succeeded in waving his arms up and down.

"It's really nice," Zach said, grinning down at the baby. "Thank you so much."

"Let me get him a bottle," Amber said.

She fixed the bottle and Zach a cup of coffee and settled back down with us at the cozy table. Now that Zach and Amber were both present, I figured that was my cue to launch into questions.

"I don't know if you've heard through the rumor mill," I said, "but I'm a private investigator."

"Former CIA, right?" Zach asked. "That's an interesting résumé for a place like Sinful."

I smiled. "It definitely stands out a bit. Anyway, I'm currently looking into the trouble at the school the other night."

Amber shook her head. "Wasn't it horrible? Here we all thought Rollie had a heart attack—I was crying as bad as the baby does—and then we find out that Rollie had been attacked and stuffed in his closet by this imposter. This morning we heard it wasn't a heart attack at all. That he'd been poisoned. Is that true?"

"Yes," I said. "That's why I'm talking to everyone who was in the cafeteria before the showcase finished."

"You're trying to figure out who poisoned him?" Zach asked. "But why? Who was he?"

"He was a private investigator from New Orleans by the name of Peter Cooke," I said. "Does that name sound familiar to either of you?"

Neither had shown any sign of recognition when I'd given the name and now, they both shook their heads.

"We wouldn't have any cause to know someone like that," Amber said. "In fact, you're the first PI I've actually met in person."

"Did either of you talk to Cooke that night?" I asked.

"I said hello when he came in," Amber said, "but he didn't respond. Just gave me a half wave and headed for the back of the room."

Zach shook his head. "I helped with some of the setup but I think I was over with Myrna when he came in. She was setting up her painting station and wanted to paint a snowflake on Nathan's cheeks. After that, I chatted with Seth Prejean for a bit while Myrna did his baby. Then we gravitated to the dessert table, figuring we'd snag a plate before the crowd descended. We were on the other side of the room when everything happened."

"You said this man was a PI?" Amber asked. "Was he on a job? Is that why he beat up Rollie?"

"We think so," I said. "We think he was looking for someone and disguised as Santa, he had the best opportunity to check out most of the locals without drawing attention to himself."

"Who was he looking for?" Zach asked.

"A young brunette woman with a baby," I said.

Amber's eyes widened. "And you think...you don't think he was looking for me?"

"Why would anyone be looking for my wife?" Zach asked, somewhat defensively.

"I don't know for certain that he was," I said. "We're working with limited information, but I'm talking to everyone who fits the bill. The thing is, Cooke was a hired hand. There might be others."

"Oh!" Amber said. "You think someone could be in trouble. But for what? Goodness, there are several young brunette women with babies in this town, but the thought of someone hiring a detective to track one of us down is laughable. We're not exactly living lives of international intrigue here."

"Actually, I was wondering about Nathan," I said. "Do you know who his biological parents are?"

Zach's face flushed with anger. "You think someone is after my son? We went through a legitimate adoption process. You're way out of line, lady."

I held up my hands. "I'm sure you did, but I was hoping you'd tell me the circumstances surrounding the adoption. I assume it was private. Did you know the mother? Have information on either of the parents?"

"No," Amber said. "Everything was conducted through an attorney. Mr. Abshire said the mother was young and unwed and the father was long gone and not interested."

"Do you know if he signed over rights?" I asked.

Zach rose from the table, clutching the baby in his hands. "I think you need to leave. We're not going to sit here, in our own home, and defend ourselves from your implied accusations."

"But Zach, if we're in danger—" Amber began.

"There is no danger," Zach said. "We had a legal adoption. And that's more of our private business than anyone needs to know."

He motioned toward the door and we rose from the table and headed out. As soon as Gertie stepped out the door, it slammed shut behind her.

CHAPTER FOURTEEN

"That went well," Gertie said as we climbed into the SUV.

"Zach was definitely defensive," Ida Belle said.

"But why?" Gertie asked. "It's not like we were accusing them of stealing a baby."

"Amber said 'Mr. Abshire,'" I said. "That must be the attorney who did their adoption."

"It's worth doing a check on him," Ida Belle said. "You want to detour to that now or see Megan and Seth first?"

"Let's go see Megan and Seth," I said. "The couples might be friends. If they are, Zach might call and warn them not to talk to us."

Ida Belle nodded and speed up. Megan and Seth's house was just outside of town. Gertie said Megan had inherited it from her grandmother. At one time, it was the family farm, but her grandmother had sold most of the land to neighboring farmers when her husband passed and had kept a pretty, shaded one-acre plot that held her house.

The house itself was exactly what I imagined a farmhouse should look like—white with green shutters and pretty landscaped beds out front that probably held an array of flowers in the spring. Giant oak trees surrounded the house, shading a good portion of the lot. A tire swing hung from one of the huge branches. I noticed a truck and a car in the two-car carport on the side of the house, but another car was parked in the drive in front.

"Looks like they have company," I said. "Do you recognize the car?"

They both shook their heads.

"Should we try another time?" Ida Belle asked.

"No," I said. "We're already here and if anyone was looking out the windows, they saw us drive up. It would look odd if we left. We'll just see who it is and play things by ear."

"Maybe they'll leave," Gertie said.

We headed to the front door and knocked. A young man who I assumed was Seth opened the door and smiled at us. "Good morning, ladies. To what do we owe this pleasure?"

A bit of relief washed through me. Either Zach hadn't called Seth to warn him about us or Seth thought it was nonsense. We'd see how he felt once I started asking questions.

Gertie held up the gift bag. "We come bearing a gift for the little one."

"That's nice," he said. "Come on in. We're trying to get some Christmas photos of Caleb, so excuse the momentary chaos. I think we're about to wrap it up. Then we can all collapse and drink sweet tea or strong whiskey. Depends on how your morning is going."

I liked Seth immediately. He seemed happy and had a good sense of humor. We stepped inside and saw the reason for the potential need to drink. Becca, the photographer, was trying to get pictures of Caleb sitting in front of the tree, but the baby wasn't cooperating. Instead, he flapped his arms like a bird, then tried to scoot away. Megan stuck him back in place and the whole thing started all over again. Finally, Gertie whistled when Megan put him in place again, and he stared up at us, his eyes wide. Becca took a series of shots and gave Gertie a high five.

"Got it!" Becca said. "Good call on the whistling."

"I just distracted him," Gertie said. "He doesn't know me so he had to stop all that moving and try to figure it out."

I made a mental note about whistling if I ever needed to get a baby to be still but I was really hoping I never had to use it. Caleb was making a lot of noise now and I gave him a once-over. I decided he looked more or less like Nathan, with the same chubby arms and legs and rosy cheeks. They must have been about the same age.

Megan scooped Caleb up and grinned at us as Ida Belle made introductions. "He's so cute but such a trial for pictures. If Becca wasn't a friend, she'd have told us to find another photographer a long time ago."

Becca smiled. "I'm happy to do it. And trust me, sometimes adults aren't any easier. Then there's pets. Last week, I had a lady who wanted me to get all twelve of her cats in front of the tree."

"Wow," Gertie said. "Did you do it?"

"God no," Becca said. "I finally got individual pictures of the cats and assured her I could photoshop them all into a picture and it would look like I took it. I'm still working on it."

"Twelve cats?" I said. "I only have one and he barely tolerates me living with him. If twelve moved in, I'd have to sell the house."

Everyone laughed and Megan waved toward the kitchen. "I just brewed a batch of sweet tea earlier. And I can put on coffee if anyone's interested. Let's grab a chair and take a break."

I wondered if Becca would pack up and leave, but she put her camera away and followed us back. Since Megan has referred to her as a friend, that made sense and it wasn't a huge problem to talk in front of her as she already knew we were asking questions about Santa. Megan got Caleb situated in his swing and poured us all a round of tea. Gertie gave her the gift and everyone oohed and aahed and she tried it on Caleb, who wasn't as impressed but looked really cute in it.

"I feel another round of photos coming up," Becca said.

"More than just one," Gertie said. "I understand you're going to have another round of this." Gertie pointed to Caleb.

Megan broke into a huge smile. "Can you believe it? All those years Seth and I tried and as soon as we adopt, I get pregnant. I called the doctor a liar when she told me. But we're so excited. We always wanted two."

"That's great," Gertie said. "I'm happy for you and looks like I'll be knitting another hat next year."

"I'm looking forward to it," Megan said, and laughed. "So are you guys just running around delivering baby hats today?"

"We're sort of combining missions actually," I said, and explained my profession and that I wanted to ask some questions about that night in the cafeteria.

The answers were similar to Amber and Zach's and what I'd expected. Neither had spoken to Santa except a basic greeting. Neither had received a response. Neither saw anyone give Santa anything to eat or drink. Neither had noticed him on his cell phone. Neither showed any sign of recognition at Cooke's name. But there was one difference that contradicted something Zach said.

"I think Zach Vincent might have spoken to him," Seth said. "I saw him over there when I was getting some food, but I'm not sure."

Interesting. Zach had claimed he was with Seth the whole

time on the other side of the cafeteria. Had he merely forgotten or had he lied?

"Are you still thinking that Santa...uh, Cooke, was looking for someone in Sinful?" Becca asked.

"Wait," Megan said, starting to look concerned. "What do you mean?"

"Cooke was a PI out of New Orleans," I said. "One of questionable reputation. I'm pretty sure he was attempting to track someone down and playing Santa was a convenient cover that allowed him to check out everyone without people asking questions."

"Have you found out who he was looking for?" Becca asked.

"Sort of," I said. "A young brunette woman with a baby."

Megan's hand flew over her mouth and she looked at Seth, a fearful expression on her face. "You don't think he was looking for Ashley, do you?"

Seth frowned, looking completely unhappy at the suggestion.

"Who's Ashley?" I asked.

"My sister," Megan said. "She can be a somewhat challenging personality."

"That's putting it mildly," Seth said. "Ashley hates authority and living responsibly. She left home when she was sixteen and hasn't been back. I've seen her exactly one time in the eight years I've known Megan, which is sad since she's Caleb's biological mother."

Okay. That one I hadn't seen coming.

"I assume Caleb was one of those not-living-responsibly things?" I asked.

"Oh yeah," Seth said. "She didn't want any part of raising a child. Hell, she couldn't even be bothered to deliver him to us. Some woman who contracts for the attorney did it. We haven't had a single conversation with her through this whole thing. And she's never once called to ask about how Caleb is doing."

"The attorney said Ashley couldn't deliver him, remember?" Megan said. "The babies were always brought to him and he had them checked out by a hospital nurse just to make sure they were healthy before the transfer. Then his assistant delivered them. That way he could ensure the babies made it to their homes without incident."

Seth waved a hand in dismissal. "Whatever. She could still pick up a phone."

"If she never talks to you, how did you even know she was pregnant?" Ida Belle asked. "How did you process the adoption?"

"I helped," Becca said.

Ida Belle, Gertie, and I all stared.

"I was friends, of sorts, with Ashley," Becca said. "We met at one of those highbrow corporate parties about a year and a half ago. I was hired to take pictures and Ashley was working the bar at the hotel where it was held. She was outside smoking when I stepped out for a break and we got to talking...sorta hit it off over mocking some of the things we saw inside. She's got a wicked sense of humor. We exchanged numbers and got together afterward for a meal sometimes."

"And probably drinks," Seth said. "Not like being pregnant would have stopped Ashley from doing what she wanted."

"She stopped smoking once she found out about the baby," Becca said. "At least, I never saw her smoking again. And she did have red wine with dinner sometimes, but I never saw her hit the hard stuff. I think she was trying."

"I'm sure she was," Megan said. "Despite my husband's obvious frustration with the way she's chosen to live, Ashley isn't evil. She's just not cut out for regular life. Giving up Caleb was the best thing for everyone."

Becca nodded. "She knew she wouldn't be a good parent. But she used to talk to her mother sometimes, so she knew Megan was trying to get pregnant and hadn't been able to. It seemed like the perfect solution."

"But she never talked directly to you?" I asked Megan.

"No." Megan looked sad. "I wish she would have. I miss her. I know she has her shortcomings, but Ashley was only a year older than me. She was my best friend for a large part of my life. I'd like to share things with her, especially now. But she's not interested."

"Have you tried to talk to her?" Gertie asked.

"Of course," Megan said. "But she wouldn't take our calls before, and the number we had for her was disconnected. She signed the documents with the attorney, dropped off Caleb, and simply vanished."

I glanced at Ida Belle and Gertie and could tell they were as troubled as I was by this story.

"Do you know anything about Caleb's biological father?" I asked.

"She said she didn't know who he was," Becca said. "She sometimes had one-nighters with guys from the bar. I don't think she even found out last names. Said it was better that way in case wives came around asking questions."

"See what I mean?" Seth said.

Becca frowned. "Look, Ashley had her issues, sure enough, but she wanted what was best for Caleb."

"Then why has she disappeared?" Seth asked.

"Maybe she thought that was best as well," Becca said. "I don't think it was as easy as you think for her to give Caleb up, even though she knew it was the right thing to do. Maybe she keeps her distance for a reason. Maybe she's trying to figure out how to deal with everything and once she does, she'll contact you."

"So Ashley didn't have a relationship with anyone?" I asked.

"She had this off-and-on thing with a guy," Becca said. "I only saw him once and from a distance. He looked...well, rough was the best way to put it. I think he knocked her around. She'd try to hide stuff with makeup, but it's not that easy."

"You're sure that guy's not the father?" I asked.

Becca bit her lower lip. "Ashley said he wasn't. I hope not."

Seth shook his head. "I knew this would come back to bite us in the butt. The whole thing was hinky from the start. What do you want to bet that guy is the father? And if this Cooke was looking for a woman with a baby, that means he knows Ashley gave birth."

The color washed out of Megan's face. "Could he take Caleb from us? Should we call the attorney and ask?"

"No way," Seth said. "I never liked that guy and don't trust him any farther than I can throw him. As far as I'm concerned, this shouldn't go past this room. For Caleb's sake. If that guy had a PI looking for Ashley, he's not going to find her here. Maybe he'll move on."

Tears formed in Megan's eyes and Seth looked angry enough to punch a hole in the wall. I figured that was our cue to leave. I had plenty to process. I looked over at Ida Belle, who gave me a slight nod and rose, Gertie and I following suit.

"I'm sorry to have upset you," I said. "I just thought people who fit the description of whoever Cooke was looking for needed to know what was going on. As much as I know, anyway."

"It's not your fault," Seth said. "And we appreciate you telling us. We'll know to be on the lookout."

We headed out of the house and as we climbed into the SUV, Becca hurried out after us.

"Do you really think Cooke was hired to find Ashley?" she asked.

I shrugged. "If Ashley was a young brunette with a baby, then it's possible."

Becca nodded and I could tell she was worried. "I've tried to find her, but she quit at the bar and her apartment manager said she skipped out on rent."

"Did you check...?" Gertie's voice trailed off.

"The morgue?" Becca asked. "Yeah, I know the score. I checked the morgue and with hospitals. I really like Ashley but I don't harbor any illusions as to the dangerous decisions she sometimes makes. But I didn't come up with anything. Maybe she found out he was looking for her and ditched."

"It's possible," I said. "And in that case, she wouldn't want to be found. The easiest way to track her would be through family, so Sinful is probably the last place she'd show up. What about her parents?"

"Her father is dead and her mother's in a nursing home in north Louisiana," Becca said. "A stroke, I think. And there was some damage."

"So no chance Ashley is staying with her," I said. "Please try not to worry. Ashley sounds like a resourceful woman."

Becca blew out a breath. "You're right. I'm sure she's fine. Probably just lying low somewhere. She always said she was going to go somewhere tropical, like Mexico. Maybe she did."

"What was her last name?" I asked. "And do you mind giving me her address and the name of the bar where she worked?"

"Of course not," Becca said, looking a little relieved. "So you'll see if you can find her?"

"At this point, I don't think I have a choice," I said. "She might be in trouble."

Becca nodded and gave me the information. "Is there anything else I can do to help?"

"You can give me the attorney's name," I said. "He might have a way to contact Ashley."

"And you think he'd give it to you?" Becca asked.

"No," I said. "But he would probably be willing to pass along a message, especially if it concerned her safety."

"That makes sense," Becca said. "The attorney was Raymond Abshire. To be honest, I didn't like him much either. He seemed sorta skeevy, if you know what I mean. But he got everything handled so I figured that was that."

She glanced back at the house. "I guess I better get my stuff and head out. I don't want to be in the middle of whatever they need to discuss, especially with Seth that upset. Please let me know if you find out anything about Ashley."

I told her I would and then climbed into the SUV. As soon as I shut the door, we all stared at one another.

"Raymond Abshire," I said. "What do you want to bet both couples used the same attorney?"

"That both Seth and Becca think was shady," Gertie said.

Ida Belle started the SUV and pulled away. "Something feels really wrong about all of this."

"Oh yeah," I said. "Swing by the sheriff's department. I'll tell Carter what I know about Cooke."

"What about Abshire and Ashley?" Gertie asked.

I shook my head. "Carter's looking for the killer, and that can't be Abshire or Ashley because neither was there. We're looking for the target of Cooke's investigation."

"But won't figuring out the target help identify the killer?" Gertie asked.

"Probably," I said. "But Carter will do his own interviews and will get the same information we did."

"The question is which one of them isn't telling us every-thing," Ida Belle said.

I nodded and stared out the window, pondering that very thing. Both couples had appeared troubled at the information and both husbands had been downright angry. But was one of them the killer? I felt like things were being held back in both instances but that was usually the case. People always had things they'd rather others didn't know, and it definitely didn't always include murder.

But the likelihood that one of them was the killer was high, especially if one of the adoptive parents felt their baby was at risk.

CHAPTER FIFTEEN

MY CONVERSATION WITH CARTER WENT ABOUT AS WELL AS expected. I'm sure he figured I'd gotten my information from the Heberts, which irritated him, especially as he hadn't been able to rustle up that tidbit on Cooke's investigation himself. But he also knew the score. Law enforcement would never be able to get things out of sketchy people that other sketchy people could get. And as 'sketchy' was currently my client, that meant I was privy to the underground data stream. But in addition to his general aggravation, there appeared to be something else going on. Something he wasn't saying.

Ida Belle and Gertie elected to wait for me in the car. I didn't blame them. This wasn't their battle, and their presence would probably only make Carter surlier, as he knew they were totally with me on how I was handling things.

"Well?" Gertie asked when I climbed into the SUV.

"He's not happy that he doesn't have the inside info on this one," I said. "But he also knows that he doesn't have the same options."

Ida Belle studied me for a moment. "And?"

"He was also a bit weird," I said.

"About you?" Gertie asked.

I shook my head. "I don't think it was personal. Not about our relationship, anyway. More like I think he knows something that we don't. He had that look like he wanted to say something, but he was holding back."

"He's probably narrowed down something and wishes he could tell you to warn you off," Ida Belle said. "He's got the car and the ME report and we don't have any of that."

"You think he's figured out who the killer is?" Gertie asked.

"Maybe," Ida Belle said. "He won't make an arrest until he's built a case for the DA, though. But if he is pretty sure he knows who did it, he might be struggling with not telling Fortune."

"Why?" Gertie asked. "He can't tell her. She knows that."

"Because if I know who the killer is, then there's no need for us to continue investigating," I said.

"Ah," Gertie said. "That makes sense. I wish we knew what he does."

"We always wish we knew what he does," Ida Belle said. "But our options for getting that information have all but disappeared due to our past success. He guards his computer password like it's the key to Fort Knox. He doesn't keep anything printed or written anymore. And I understand the ME's office has a new camera system that the sheriff's department has also requested."

Gertie huffed. "He's really cramping our style."

I laughed. "Yeah, he sorta is."

Then a thought occurred to me. "You know what? I wonder if he already knows who Cooke was looking for."

"Why do you say that?" Ida Belle asked.

"Cooke showed that other PI a photo," I said. "So he had one printed but I didn't find anything like that in his motel room. No hard files at all. So assuming he still had it, that means it was probably in his car."

Ida Belle blew out a breath. "Well, hell. I bet you're right. Here we are doing all this running around and Carter probably has the photo and is ten steps ahead of us."

"But if he had the photo, then why hasn't he been to question Megan or Amber?" Gertie asked.

"Because he wouldn't want to alert them that he's onto them," Ida Belle said. "He'd dig into things and I wouldn't put it past him to do some surveillance."

"Then all we have to do is follow Carter and we'd know who was in the photo," Gertie said.

"I don't think tailing Carter would be as easy as you think," I said. "The job he did for the Marine Corps was one of those that requires eyes in the back and on the sides of your head. He'd see us coming a mile away."

"And he'd be expecting it, so he'd be looking for us," Ida Belle said. "So how do you want to approach this?"

"I think we need to do our thing without regard to his thing," I said. "I gave him information, so we're not guilty of withholding on an active investigation. I think the first thing we need to do is talk to this attorney, Abshire. Then see what we can run down on Ashley Breaux."

Gertie clapped. "Road trip!"

Ida Belle checked her watch. "We have caroling at six. That gives us roughly four hours if we leave time to get ready. Take out an hour and a half for commute and we've got two and a half for detecting."

"Let's go with two hours for commute," I said. Racing toward death would probably limit our ability to investigate.

Ida Belle waved a hand in dismissal. "Fine. Two hours."

"Does that leave us enough time?" Gertie asked.

"It does to get started anyway," I said. "If we run out, then we'll head back tomorrow. Not like the attorney, the bar, or the apartment complex is going anywhere."

"Then let's take ten minutes to grab a sandwich from Francine and head out," Ida Belle said.

Despite a bit of grumbling from her passengers, Ida Belle made the drive to New Orleans in about forty-five minutes. I was pretty sure she was getting negative three miles to the gallon. But despite the crazy speed, she managed to weave in and out of traffic, one-handed, while eating her own sandwich. The woman definitely had skills. They often scared the heck out of me, but I couldn't complain about her efficiency.

I'd looked up Abshire's office on the way and directed Ida Belle to an area just on the edge of the French Quarter. The building was a bit run-down and the area looked a little questionable, but that all seemed to fit with everyone's feelings about the attorney. We headed inside and located his office on the second floor. I tried the door but it was locked. I knocked and we waited.

No one came.

I knocked again, this time harder, but didn't hear anyone stirring inside.

The door to the office across the hall opened and a woman stepped out. She drew up short when she saw us. "Can I help you?" she asked.

"We were looking for Raymond Abshire," I said. "Does he still have an office here?"

"Well, yes, but he's not in," she said. "I'm not sure when he will be again."

It was clear from the tone of her voice that something was wrong.

"Did something happen to Mr. Abshire?" I asked.

She nodded. "He was assaulted. About two weeks ago, a man broke into his house and tied him up and beat him."

"That's awful," I said. "Is he going to be all right?"

"I think so," she said. "But the cops said he was in pretty bad shape. I think he's going to be in the hospital a while."

"He's still in the hospital?" I asked, thinking the beating had been epic if they were still holding him two weeks later.

"There was a complication of some kind," she said. "A staph infection, I think. You keep hearing about that sort of thing, which just scares the daylights out of me. You go in for one thing and then you acquire something else in the place where you're supposed to get better."

"That's very unfortunate," I agreed. "I assume he was attacked as part of a robbery?"

"Seems that way," she said. "The guy who attacked him stole money and electronics. Someone broke into Mr. Abshire's office that same night. It's put everyone in the building a little on edge."

"No security cameras in the building?" I asked.

She gave me a disgusted look. "The landlord can barely be bothered to keep the roof from leaking and the plumbing working. No way he's springing for security."

"Do you have any idea why Mr. Abshire might have been targeted?" I asked.

"No," she said. "The police told us the robber only asked where he kept money. I got the impression that Mr. Abshire didn't have much on hand, though. It doesn't make a lot of sense...beating a man that way for what amounts to very little financial gain in the big scheme of things."

"Probably on drugs," Gertie said.

"That's certainly possible," she said. "I don't work past dark anymore. This area is okay in the daylight but I don't want to be around afterward. And I'm sorry, but I need to get on with my errands or I won't make sundown tonight."

"Thank you for the information," I said.

She nodded and walked away.

"Does anyone think someone broke into Abshire's house, tied him up, beat him, and also broke into his office because they were looking for random cash?" I asked.

"Not even," Ida Belle said. "You think it was Cooke?"

"I do," I said.

"I don't suppose there's any chance that Abshire would give us a description or tell us what Cooke really wanted," Gertie said.

"I'd say ice cube's chance in hell," I said. "He didn't tell the police."

"I wonder why not," Ida Belle said.

"If I had to guess, I'd say because his adoptions aren't always on the up-and-up," I said. "Ashley Breaux might have told him she didn't know who the father of her baby was but did he bother to research that? I get the feeling that his practice operates just this side of the law, which is why he lied to the police about what the man wanted and probably about the cash and electronics being taken."

"That would also explain why Zach Vincent kicked us out when we started asking about the adoption," Gertie said. "I bet he knows Abshire isn't on the level."

"Given that he's a security expert, I can't imagine getting information on Abshire would have been that difficult for him," I said.

Ida Belle nodded. "Cooke must not have gotten anything out of Abshire if he went for the office records. How much do you think was contained in them?"

"Likely, it was the other way around," I said. "I'll bet Cooke broke into the office first and didn't find what he was looking for, then headed to Abshire's house. If Abshire was smart, he didn't keep a bunch of paper around detailing his indiscretions.

Probably stored digitally and with the absolute minimum required to pass through the courts."

"And Cooke couldn't get much from Abshire, because he probably makes a point to not remember the details," Gertie said. "But he must have gotten enough information to know where to start looking."

"Delivery locations," Ida Belle said. "Abshire might not have committed the adoptive parents' or the mothers' names to memory, but I bet he remembered where babies in the time frame given were delivered, especially since two were somewhat local."

"This isn't about the mother," Gertie said.

"No, it's not," I agreed. "Someone is looking for his baby."

CHAPTER SIXTEEN

THE BAR THAT ASHLEY HAD WORKED AT WAS IN ONE OF THE ritzy hotels in the French Quarter, the kind that businessmen preferred when traveling and companies liked for events. It was quiet when we arrived, but we were well ahead of the after-work crowd. Two senior gentlemen sat at a corner table when we walked in. They stopped talking long enough to check us out but must have decided we looked too difficult because they went back to their conversation.

A young woman, probably twenty-five or so, was wiping down the bar and greeted us as we approached. "What can I get you ladies? Wine is half price until five."

"Oh!" Gertie said. "I'll have a pinot grigio."

I heard Ida Belle sigh, but she must have figured we'd get more out of the bartender if we had a drink, so she slid onto a stool. "I'm driving," she said. "Just a Coke for me."

"I'll have beer," I said. "Whatever you have on tap."

She gave me a couple options and I chose one, then she set about pouring the drinks.

"I don't think I've seen you ladies in here before," she said as she served. "Are you vacationing?"

I shook my head. "Actually, we're here on business." I showed her my identification.

Her eyes widened. "Private investigator? What do you want with me?"

"It's not about you specifically," I said, trying to keep her calm. "You just happen to be working. I'm trying to locate Ashley Breaux. Her sister hasn't heard from her in a while and she's concerned."

"Oh," she said, and frowned. "I thought she just quit. You know, walked off?"

"Why would you think that?" I asked.

She shrugged. "She hadn't been the same since she got pregnant. I knew she was giving him up for adoption and she said that was the best thing to do. But it didn't look like she meant it. She seemed really sad...depressed, you know?"

"So she was still working here after she gave the baby up?" I asked.

"Not exactly. She was still out on maternity leave the last time I saw her. She'd stopped in to collect a bonus pay we got for the previous month. Said she'd dropped the baby off at the attorney and it was all taken care of. But when she was due to come back to work, she never showed."

"She didn't give notice?" I asked.

"No way. The boss was hella mad when she didn't show that first night she was scheduled to return. There were two events going on and we were slammed. He had to rustle up some contract help and that cuts into profits, which cuts into his bonus."

"I assume he tried to call her?"

She nodded. "Said her phone was disconnected, and when he tried to send a couple of her personal items she'd left here to her apartment, they came back as no longer at this address."

"She never said anything about leaving? I mean, even before the baby? Future plans? Dreams?"

"Sure. We've all got those. You spend most nights with suits slapping your butt and you have plenty of dreams, but I don't know that she was actively working on anything."

"What about the baby's father?" I asked. "Did she ever mention anything about him?"

"Told me she didn't know who he was. She used to pick up guys sometimes at closing. Or let them pick her up. Whatever. We're not supposed to but that doesn't stop some of the bartenders from working a side angle."

"She was taking money from the men?" I asked.

"She never said so, but that's my guess. I mean, the guys she left out of here with weren't even in her league, you know? Ashley lived kinda rough but she was hot."

"What about a boyfriend?" I asked.

"There was this one guy. He came in several times but I never got his name. Every time I saw him, he was hitting her up for money. She didn't look all that enamored with him. Honestly, if anything, she looked a little scared. I think he tuned her up some. A couple times she had a black eye. Hard to hide that, especially on a long shift when makeup starts to fade."

"Can you give me a description?"

"Maybe. I never paid close attention really. He was probably thirty-five or so. Clean-cut and usually wearing a suit. Looked like good quality, so I never got why he needed her money, but then plenty of people put everything they make up their nose, so... Anyway, sorry I can't give you more but all the suits start to look alike after a while."

I frowned. Clean-cut and wearing a suit was not what I expected and didn't match Becca's description of someone who was 'rough.' Maybe this was a guy Becca didn't know about.

"Have you seen that guy in here since Ashley took off?" I asked.

"Not that I can remember."

"Do you think he was the baby's father?"

She shrugged. "Honestly? I have no idea. Ashley was cool enough and a really good bartender, but she was also odd. She'd tell us things about her one-nighters with guys or about a cool drug trip but didn't talk about the rest of her private life. I didn't even know she had a sister until you said so."

"Has anyone else been in here asking for Ashley?"

"Yeah, there was one guy. Came in maybe a week or two ago. Older, rude. He asked everyone working if they knew where to find her. None of us do but I wouldn't have told him if I did. I got a bad vibe from him. I mean, maybe he was just here trying to collect or something. That happens, but still. You don't go telling a strange man where he can find a single woman, you know?"

I turned my phone toward her and showed her a picture of Cooke. "Was this the guy?"

She studied it for a couple seconds and frowned. "Maybe. Looks cleaner in that photo, though. He looked like he'd been living on the streets a while when he came in here."

I pulled out my card and handed it to her. "If you hear from Ashley, please give me a call. Or if you see that guy in the suit. I'd love to talk to him."

She took the card and slipped it into her jeans pocket. "Sure. Hey, you don't think anything bad happened to her, do you? She had her issues but overall, Ashley was a decent person. Never backstabbed, always pulled her weight and usually more, never stole tips from the other bartenders, always positive and funny...that's really rare in this line of work."

"I hope not," I said. "I'm definitely going to try to find out."

She nodded and wrote a name and number on a cocktail napkin. "If you get anything, would you mind letting me know? I've been wondering but now I'm kinda worried."

I folded the napkin and tucked it in my pocket. "I will, and thanks for talking to us."

"No problem," she said, and headed to the other side of the bar to wait on a group of men in suits who had just walked in.

"You want to check out the apartment now?" Ida Belle asked.

Gertie checked her watch. "It's getting late. Unless you want Ida Belle driving at warp speed, we should probably head back soon."

"When people with guns are chasing us, you don't have a problem with warp speed," Ida Belle pointed out.

"I was sorta hoping to avoid any gun chasing with this investigation," I said.

"I was sorta hoping to avoid warp speed," Gertie said. "I rolled my hair this morning and don't want it going flat before the caroling."

"The apartment building is on our way out of the city," I said, "so let's go ahead and make that stop. I don't figure it's going to take long to hear 'I don't know anything,' which is probably all we'll get from the manager."

Ida Belle started up the SUV and we headed out.

The apartment building had seen its better days, probably fifty years ago when it was built. Or maybe not even then. The brick showed the signs of enduring decades of bad weather and neglect. The patches of lawn were mowed, but the grass that was probably planted there after construction was long gone and had been replaced by weeds and bare dirt. A faded sign at the entrance indicated where to find the office and we parked in front of a small one-story offshoot in the middle of the complex and headed inside. The man working there didn't even bother to get out of his chair when we walked in.

Midfifties. Six foot even. Two hundred fifty pounds. No threat at all as he probably only got out of the chair twice a day.

We must not have looked like his usual renters because he narrowed his eyes at us and barked out, "What do you want?"

This was already going well.

"I'm a private investigator," I said, not bothering to give my name. "I'm looking for Ashley Breaux."

He snorted. "You're not the only one. But I'm surprised someone paid a PI to find her. Must have stiffed them for more than a month's rent."

"I can't really disclose client information, but let's just say my client has a vested interested in locating her."

"'Fraid I can't help you," he said. "I went around knocking when she was two days late on the rent. Got no answer and no one had seen her in a while. Hadn't no one complained about a bad smell, but I figured I best check anyway. Her clothes and bathroom stuff was gone. All that was left was a bit of kitchen stuff and some furniture that was falling apart."

"Did she have a car?" I asked.

"She never registered one," he said. "And I never saw her in one. Saw her catch a bus to the Quarter most days. Assumed that's how she got to work."

"Did she have an emergency contact?" I asked.

"Her mother," he said. "But she said she hadn't seen or heard from her in weeks."

"You think she was telling the truth?"

He shrugged. "Don't see any reason for her to lie. Not like

she'd be on the hook for the rent. And she got all upset with me...insisted I call the cops and report her as missing."

"And did you?"

"Why would I? It was clear she left on her own accord or all her stuff would have still been in the apartment. The cops don't care about someone skipping rent. All they would have done is told me to take it up in civil court."

I nodded. I knew he was right. Despite the fact that no one could account for Ashley's whereabouts, that didn't mean she'd been the victim of a crime. And since her personal belongings were gone, that indicated she'd left of her own volition. Or someone who wanted to harm her had been very careful. I really hoped it was the first option and not the second.

"Do you mind telling me which unit was hers?" I asked. "I'd like to see if any of her neighbors know anything."

"Room 165," he said. "But they ain't likely to tell you anything, even if they know. People who live around here don't like questions, and they figure if someone wants to be found then they'd let people know where they were."

"Thanks," I said, and headed out. I knew he was right. Even though I wasn't a cop, a lot of people saw PIs as something along those lines.

We knocked on the doors of a few of the apartments near Ashley's, but no one answered. Since I heard noise inside all of them, I figured no one was interested in talking to strangers. We didn't look like cops but they didn't know us, either, so that automatically made us suspect.

"Looks like no one wants to talk to us," Gertie said as we headed out.

"Couple of old gray-hairs and one young woman," Ida Belle said. "They probably think we're pushing Jesus."

"Who are you calling old?" Gertie asked.

"There is no time for this discussion again," Ida Belle said, and looked over at me. "So what do you make of all this?"

"Nothing good," I said. "Could be the suit was Ashley's off-and-on love interest and maybe the father of her baby. I figure Abshire skirted the line on things to make a buck and the suit, or whoever the father is, found out and is looking for his child. Ashley knew the whole deal was shady and dropped the baby, then hightailed it out of town."

"Then Cooke roughed up Abshire to get information about the adoptions," Ida Belle said. "It's definitely not good but you're right, it does fit."

Gertie shook her head. "So what do we do now?"

"That's a good question," I said. "We've narrowed down our pool of suspects at least."

"Yes," Ida Belle said. "But I don't want any of them to be the killer. Megan and Seth are good people and they don't deserve problems. And with Megan pregnant now...this is a mess."

"Don't forget Becca," I said. "She had opportunity and she was friends with Ashley. And I'm guessing she knows more about the entire situation than she's saying."

"Do you really think so?" Gertie asked. "She seemed scared when you told them about Cooke. If she already knew someone was looking for Ashley's baby, would she have looked that surprised?"

"Maybe she looked scared because she did it," Ida Belle said.

Gertie huffed. "I hate this. All these people just trying to protect a baby from an abusive man and one of them is probably going to end up in prison over it."

"Unfortunately, that's not our call," Ida Belle said.

"What about Zach and Amber?" Gertie asked. "Are we striking them off the list?"

I shook my head. "Not yet. I still think it's possible their adoption wasn't on the up-and-up, and I think Zach knows it. Probably Amber does as well. They're just not admitting it because they got what they wanted."

"The question is what lengths would they go to in order to protect themselves?" Ida Belle said. "And a surprising number of otherwise-average people have taken extreme measures when it came to their children."

"So we're back around to what do we do now?" Gertie asked.

"I honestly don't know," I said. "I don't think we're going to get any more than we already have out of the couples and Becca. We could continue talking to the other people who were working the cafeteria. Maybe someone saw one of our five suspects hand Santa food or drink."

I looked over at Ida Belle. "Did you send the files to the Sorcerer?"

"Yes. He said he had to finish up a project, then he'd take a look at it and let me know. I was hoping to hear something today."

"Good," I said. "I'd like to identify the man behind all of this. Nothing about him sounded nice, and hiring Cooke doesn't help his case any. If we can dig up dirt on him, it might help make an argument against him getting custody."

"And might help build sympathy for the defense," Ida Belle said. "Not that I'm excusing murder, but there are mitigating circumstances here."

"If it turns out Cooke was the one who beat up Abshire, that might help the defense as well," Gertie said.

"I hate this!" Ida Belle said, and I stared at her, somewhat surprised at the amount of emotion in her voice.

"The killer is supposed to be a bad guy," she continued. "And we're supposed to be racing toward him like we're trying to capture the devil. Instead, we've got a bunch of otherwise good people in the middle of a nightmare. And the biggest victims from the legal end of things are the shady attorney and the equally shady PI."

I nodded. "I think this is why cops are always saying, 'We don't get to pick the vic.'"

"A good reminder of a crappy reality," Ida Belle said.

CHAPTER SEVENTEEN

GIVEN THE WAY THE HOLIDAY EVENTS OF THE WEEK HAD gone so far, I had no idea what to expect from caroling. I'd seen it on those Hallmark Christmas movies Gertie had forced me to watch—groups of people walking through the snow from house to house and singing at the front door. I suspected the Sinful rendition wouldn't sound like the professionals they used on television, but it was the spirit of the thing that counted.

That spirit, according to Ida Belle, was why Gertie got to participate.

As I'd heard Gertie sing many times in church, I was well aware of why she wasn't in the choir and probably never should be. Yes, there was all that joyful noise nonsense and all, but I had my doubts that even the most pious among us would find Gertie's singing joyful. I usually lip-synched, so never had to worry about that form of judgment, but then I didn't enjoy singing the way Gertie did.

When we parked on Main Street, I spotted a four-wheeler with a trailer attached at the end of the street and frowned.

Surely we weren't going to revisit the whole sleigh farce again. Not after last time.

"That's not what we're going caroling in, is it?" I asked.

Ida Belle nodded. "Usually we do the whole horse-drawn thing. It's better for pictures. But after last night, everyone felt the four-wheeler was the better option."

"You're not driving, are you?" I asked, because if Ida Belle was at the wheel, our chances were probably better with the horses.

"No," she said. "I'm the unofficial song director so I have to be in the trailer."

"Do I have to be in the trailer?" I asked. "I mean, I've had more Christmas joy packed into this week than all of my previous life. I could probably sit this one out and wouldn't feel like I was missing anything."

"Nonsense," Gertie said. "Caroling is awesome. Besides, most of the residents bring us baked goods, and some have eggnog...the whiskey-laced kind."

"Hmm." I considered the new facts introduced. I didn't exactly have a shortage of baked goods at my house, but the lure of sampling random baked goods and chasing them with whiskey-laced eggnog might be just enough to keep me from jogging back home.

"Fortune!" Emmaline's voice sounded behind me and I turned just in time for her to gather me into a hug and kiss my cheeks. Carter's mother was a lovely woman whom everyone in Sinful adored, including me. Fortunately, she seemed to like me too, which made me extremely happy and made living in Sinful and dating Carter a lot easier than if she'd taken an immediate disliking to me.

"With all this holiday flurry, I haven't seen you in forever," she said. "I didn't figure you for the caroling type, but I'm glad to see you here."

"Gertie and Ida Belle made me come," I explained.

"The potential for baked goods and whiskey eggnog are keeping her here," Gertie said.

Emmaline laughed. "Don't let on you know about the whiskey part or none of us Baptists will be able to drink the eggnog. We've been pretending ignorance for decades."

"My lips are sealed," I said. "Until I lift a cup of eggnog to them."

"Smart lady," Emmaline said. "I knew there was a reason I liked you. In addition, of course, to capturing my son's attention. I was worried that he'd follow in Walter's footsteps."

"Can't say that anymore," I said. "Not with the upcoming nuptials."

She leaned in close to me and whispered, "I'll believe it when I see them walk down the aisle."

I nodded. I didn't think Ida Belle would toy with Walter that way. She wasn't cruel and she was definitely a woman who knew her own mind. But her getting married still seemed a bit surreal. And like Emmaline, I wanted to see it happen before I was ready to invest in it a hundred percent. Right now, it still seemed like a script for a Hollywood movie.

Emmaline sighed. "Here comes everyone's favorite person."

I looked over and saw Celia marching toward us like a military general and the expression on her face just as pleasant.

"I should have known you three wouldn't have the decency to sit this out," she said.

"Why would we?" Gertie asked. "We haven't done anything wrong. If we had, Carter would have invited us to sit it out in jail."

"Please," Celia said. "As long as he's involved with this hussy, that will never happen."

"That's hardly a Christian attitude at a religious celebration," Emmaline said. "I expect better of Sinful residents. Even you."

Celia's eyes widened and I heard some chuckling around us. I didn't even bother to hold in my grin. Neither did Ida Belle and Gertie. Celia glared at all of us, then stomped off. I could hear her mumbling as she went.

"*Someone's* getting coal in her stocking," I said.

"The stocking will be happier with coal in it than Celia's leg," Gertie said.

Ida Belle grinned. "Let's load up and I'll get ready with the song list. I think we'll start with 'Grandma Got Run Over by a Reindeer.' Celia hates that one. Argues to have it removed from the list every year. In fact, we might sing it at every darned house."

"That's the Christmas spirit," Emmaline said, and smiled.

As people started loading onto the trailer, Carter pulled up behind us in his truck, Deputy Breaux in the passenger seat. I strolled over and he rolled down his window.

"You spying on me?" I asked.

"That's actually not far from the truth," he said. "Deputy Breaux and I are damage control. Just in case there's another holiday mishap."

"Well, we already killed Santa," I said. "Is deer hunting season still open? Could be a bad omen for Rudolph."

"Ha," Carter said. "We're worried more about the citizens than the deer."

Deputy Breaux held up a first aid kit and a fire extinguisher.

I nodded. "In any other place, I might accuse you of being over-the-top, but in Sinful it makes sense."

Carter studied me for a moment. "So you really plan on singing? Because I know you lip-synch in church."

I shrugged. "I'm just here due to promises of home-baked goodies and whiskey-laced eggnog."

"Completely valid," Carter said. "Maybe while you're there, you can keep Gertie out of trouble."

"You're asking me for a Christmas miracle?" I asked.

Deputy Breaux snorted.

Ida Belle yelled for me as they were about to leave and I gave Carter a grin and hurried to jump on the trailer. I grabbed a seat on a hay bale in between Gertie and Emmaline and we were off.

"How do they know which houses to stop at?" I asked as we made our way into the neighborhood.

"There's a sign-up sheet at the General Store," Emmaline said.

"That's cool," I said. "So anyone can just sign up and get some singing but it's not forced on anyone."

Emmaline laughed. "Only you would consider Christmas caroling forced if it wasn't asked for. You were really in the city too long."

"The people who don't sign up just don't want to bake anything to give to the carolers," Gertie said. "Which is stupid, because you *can* improvise."

Emmaline nodded. "The year Ida Belle had a broken foot and couldn't come with us, she handed out ammunition. Deer season was still open, so it was highly appreciated."

"I'll keep that in mind if I'm ever injured at Christmas and craving a cartload of people, including Celia, to stop at my house and sing."

Emmaline patted my arm. "I have a feeling you'd do just fine with a beer and the television."

We stopped at our first house and I went through the motions of singing with the group. Celia frowned the entire time we were singing the Grandma killed by a reindeer song, which almost made the entire thing worth it. Then the homeowner, a nice elderly lady, handed us all small bags with cookies in them that smelled like heaven. No whiskey eggnog at this house. She was Baptist. Couldn't be caught handing out banned materials.

The next house was a Catholic couple and the eggnog had apparently been in full swing for a while before we got there. The couple were swaying back and forth as we sang, but since they weren't in time with the music, I had a feeling it wasn't voluntary. The husband presented everyone with cups of eggnog when we were done. The whiskey was so strong I probably could have taken rust off a car bumper with it. But I noticed it didn't stop everyone from downing it, the Baptists all pretending it wasn't laced. The wife handed out tiny loaves of banana nut bread to everyone, except Celia, whom she gave a blueberry pie.

"One of Celia's crew," Gertie whispered. "She doesn't participate as much. Claims it's her arthritis but everyone knows she's on the eggnog on a regular basis...without the eggnog."

"If you have to be friendly with Celia to rank a pie, I'll stick to banana nut bread," I said.

"You're not settling," Gertie said. "All the drinking hasn't affected her baking in the least."

"I have a feeling that statement applies to more than one Sinful resident," I said. "So who's up next? I'm really enjoying this goodie collection. It's like trick-or-treating for adults, but better—no costumes."

"I have this sexy elf costume—" Gertie began.

"No." Ida Belle cut her off. "There's not enough laced eggnog in Sinful for you to wear that outfit in public."

The trailer slowed and I glanced up and realized we were close to my house. Too close. In fact, we were stopping in front of my next-door neighbor's house—the undoubtedly insane Ronald Franklin Jr.

"Are you kidding me?" I grumbled. "He's more likely to give us all poison than a treat. He hates people."

"He hates you," Gertie said. "He tolerates most everyone else."

"He doesn't even go to church," I argued. "He doesn't have a single Christmas decoration anywhere. I'm pretty sure he worships at the altar of crazy."

"Oh, you're not wrong about that one," Emmaline said. "Ronald is an evolutionist. He believes we all came from fish. So he signs up every year so he can try to persuade us to his side."

I sighed. "Of course he does."

The door to his house opened and Ronald came out. At least, I was pretty sure it was Ronald. He was wearing a fish costume, complete with a long tail. I said a quick thanks that this outfit covered everything important and didn't include high heels. Ronald was a natural disaster when breathing, but when wearing heels, he took things up several notches.

"How come he gets to wear a costume?" Gertie asked.

"Because he's an idiot," Ida Belle said as she motioned for everyone to get off the trailer.

"I didn't realize intelligence was a factor in suitable dress," Gertie said.

"Apparently it is for caroling," I said, and hopped down.

We stood in rows in front of Ronald, and Ida Belle prompted us to start singing. As soon as we broke into song, Ronald started shouting, telling us all about the 'real' creation of humans starting with us swimming in the sea. His voice grated like ten women whining in sync and to make matters worse, he insisted on swiveling his hips as he talked in order to make the fish tail flick around like he was swimming.

I didn't even bother with the lip-synching routine for this one. Ronald was probably handing out fish at the end of all this and I didn't think it was a good pairing with my banana nut bread. I glanced over at Carter and Deputy Breaux to see what they thought about it all. Apparently, they'd been expecting something stupid because Carter was reading a magazine and Deputy Breaux appeared to be making a fishing lure. Maybe he could hook Ronald and throw him in the clink.

I looked back toward Ronald and caught movement behind him on the stretch of lawn between his house and mine. The lighting between the houses was practically nil and whatever it was wasn't much taller than the grass, meaning I couldn't figure out what it was. I had locked Merlin inside before leaving so it wasn't him. I hoped he didn't have a friend lurking around because if another cat moved in, I'd have to put the house up for sale.

Then the thing I saw started coming directly toward us, and fast, but stayed in the shaded area between the two houses. It was maybe thirty feet away from Ronald when it moved into a lighted area and I got my first good look at exactly what had zeroed in on my crazy neighbor. I pulled my pistol from my waistband and shoved my way through the front line of carolers.

"Gator!" I yelled, and leveled my pistol for a shot. But before I could take aim, the gator ran directly behind Ronald and I lost line of sight. I yelled at Ronald to shut up and run for the trailer, but no way was he taking orders from me. The other carolers either believed me or had caught sight of the beast because I heard scrambling behind me as they fled. Truck doors slammed and Carter yelled at Deputy Breaux as I moved to the side, hoping to get in a shot.

I didn't make it.

The gator grabbed the end of Ronald's wiggling fish tail

and flung him onto the ground. Ronald screamed and started thrashing around, which only made him look like a flopping fish in distress. The gator still had Ronald's tail in his mouth, shaking it around like a dishrag and preventing me from shooting since I wasn't sure where the suit ended and Ronald's feet began. If I shot off his leg, no way we could continue to live next door to each other. Carter and Deputy Breaux moved up beside me, both with guns drawn, and that's when I heard running behind me.

Gertie ran right past us and toward the raging gator.

"Don't shoot!" she yelled. "It's Godzilla!"

CHAPTER EIGHTEEN

I HEARD CARTER CURSE AND HE SHOUTED FOR GERTIE TO get out of the way. I knew there was no way Gertie was going to allow anyone to get off a shot at that gator, even if it meant flinging herself over him to defend him from the bullet. The only way to solve this was with food. I sprinted for the trailer and jumped over the side, sliding in the hay before stopping in front of Celia. I reached down and grabbed the blueberry pie but before I could make off with it, Celia grasped the other side.

"You're not taking my pie!" she shouted. "Thief! Thief!"

"Either you give that pie to the gator or he eats Ronald," I said. "I am personally up for the second option, but it's probably not the right thing to do. Especially at Christmas."

Ida Belle took the more direct approach and reached over to whack Celia on the wrists, causing her to let go of the pie. I whirled around and sprinted for the gator. Gertie was standing behind him, yelling for him to stop. I yanked the pie out of the box and tossed it to her. She moved close enough for Godzilla to catch sight of the baked goody. It must have looked enough like one of Gertie's casseroles to fool the gator, because he stopped shaking Ronald. For a couple seconds, he appeared to be considering his options—a treat from the person who used to feed him awesome things versus a giant fish.

I understood his dilemma. Ronald would be good eating for weeks. The baked goods, while better tasting, wouldn't last nearly as long. But ultimately, Gertie's cooking must have won out because the gator let go of Ronald's fish tail and headed off after Gertie, who hurried toward the bayou. Carter and I started off behind her, ready to shoot if Godzilla got too close and showed any signs of attacking. I knew Gertie trusted the prehistoric monster, but I only expected wild animals to be themselves.

Gertie was practically sprinting for bayou and when she got close, she flung the pie to the edge of the water. Godzilla ran past and tilted his head to the side, as if to say thanks, then snagged the pie and disappeared into the water. Carter and I put our guns away and we all headed back for the street.

And that's when the yelling began.

The glow of light coming from the trailer was too large to be the battery-operated candles we were supposed to be holding when we sang. And the streetlights barely produced any light at all.

The trailer was on fire.

We took off running and got there in time to see Deputy Breaux dash to the trailer with the fire extinguisher. Everyone was bailing off the sides as he took aim and let the foam fly.

Just as Celia was climbing over the side.

The foam hit her right in the face and she screamed, then whirled around, clutching her eyes. With all the whirling, the lack of ability to see, and her crap balance, she hit the curb and pitched forward right into Deputy Breaux, sending them both tumbling. As he fell, Deputy Breaux still had his hand on the trigger and the foam went straight up in the air and then rained down on everyone within a ten-foot radius.

I heard screaming from the ground but wasn't sure if it was Celia or Deputy Breaux, who had Celia's chest planted firmly across his face. Deputy Breaux's situation was unfortunate but not the biggest emergency, so Carter grabbed the fire extinguisher from him and attacked the rest of the fire. I didn't want to touch Celia, but my sympathy for Deputy Breaux outweighed my discomfort.

I grabbed her around the waist and hauled her off the deputy, then dropped her on the ground next to him. Celia flopped around to get onto her back, then sat up and glared.

"You did that on purpose," she said.

"You're not exactly a lightweight," I said. "I'm not throwing out my back to lift you all the way up."

"How did that fire start?" Carter asked, holding the empty fire extinguisher. "Was someone smoking?"

"Celia was using a real candle," Emmaline said.

"You've got to be kidding me!" Carter exploded. He whirled around to glare at Celia. "And you think Gertie is a problem? Who is stupid enough to have a lit flame in a trailer full of hay? You are officially the dumbest person in the state. I ought to arrest you for attempted murder just to make people happy and your life as miserable as you make everyone else's."

"You can't talk to me that way," Celia said.

"Yes, he can." Sheriff Lee's voice sounded behind us and I turned to see him on his horse, trotting across the lawn. "In fact, since I have insomnia, I'm going to go ahead and take Carter's recommendation. Deputy Breaux, arrest that woman for disturbing the peace. We'll both spend the night in jail. Of course, I'll be playing video poker and drinking beer in a nice office chair, but it seems only fair since I didn't ruin Christmas caroling."

Deputy Breaux hopped up and looked from Sheriff Lee to Carter.

"You heard the boss," Carter said, and I could tell he was struggling not to laugh. "Handcuff her and take her in for the sheriff. Then come back to pick me up. It's going to take a bit to sort out this trailer mess."

"Help! I can't get up. My arms are going to sleep."

I shook my head. We'd completely forgotten Ronald, who was still laid out, facedown on the lawn.

Carter looked over at him in disgust. "I think this is the part of your story where you sprout legs and walk into your house."

"Evolution takes time!" Ronald shouted. "I can't just evolve because it's convenient."

"I know," Carter said. "The whole town has been waiting for you to evolve into a normal person for decades now."

Ida Belle pulled out her knife, which was about the length of Ronald's leg, and headed his way. He took one look at the gleaming metal and started thrashing about again.

"She's going to fillet me!" he yelled.

"Darn right I am," Ida Belle said, and grabbed the tail of his costume. She stuck her giant knife in and slit the suit all the way up to his neck until it was completely open.

Exposing every square inch of his bare butt.

"If he stands up and that suit falls off, I'm pressing charges," Gertie said.

Carter stomped over and yanked Ronald up from the ground, making sure he was facing his house. "Get to walking, and if I see so much as a backward glance, I swear I'll shoot you."

"Sinful should pass a law that requires you to wear under-garments when you leave your house," I said.

"It already has," Gertie said. "If you have company, you're even supposed to wear them when you shower. In case an emergency exit is required."

"What do you know?" I said. "Ole Ronald is breaking the law. Maybe he should sit in a cell next to Celia."

Deputy Breaux, who had managed to get Celia in cuffs, paled.

"Please, I'm begging you," he said.

Ronald heard my suggestion and picked up the pace, now half running, half skipping, clutching the remnants of his fish costume as he went. His white butt almost glowed in the porch light as he scuttled up the stairs and into his house.

I looked at the smoking remnants of soggy hay and shook my head. "I hope there's a big store of feed in this town for livestock, because Christmas has been hell on the cows' dinner."

"Forget the cows," Gertie said. "What about caroling?"

"I was rather hoping you'd call it a night," Carter said.

"No can do," Ida Belle said, and slipped her phone into her jeans. "Walter is on his way. Everyone who wants to continue caroling can pile in the bed of his truck. It won't be comfortable, but at least we won't disappoint the people who signed up."

Carter sighed. "You're all wearing fire extinguisher foam."

"So it looks like we were standing in a snowstorm," Ida Belle said. "It wouldn't work for Halloween but it's perfect for Christmas."

"I give up," Carter said. "But you're on your own. I've got to get to the sheriff's department and help Deputy Breaux, and the extinguisher is empty."

"We've got firepower and baked goods," Gertie said. "What else do we need?"

I looked at Carter, feeling about as optimistic as he looked. "Maybe we could borrow that first aid kit?"

———

COMPARED TO THE GODZILLA AND RONALD FIASCO, THE rest of the caroling was uneventful. Thank goodness. What made me even happier was that this had been the last official event of the year. I didn't have to worry about hungry gators, runaway horses, flaming hay, or naked butts again until New Year's. I took the longest shower in recorded history, then headed downstairs to fix myself a bite to eat. I'd just pulled the ham out of the refrigerator when I heard a knock at my front door and Carter call out as he let himself in. I smiled, knowing that the dual warning of knocking and yelling was so that I didn't shoot him thinking he was an intruder. It was nice when your boyfriend acknowledged your lethal side.

"You look to be in good spirits for a man who just finished damage control on yet another Christmas fiasco," I said as he walked into the kitchen.

"At least this one isn't trending on social media."

"Sure it is. Godzilla is a big hit. Ronald's bare butt, not so much."

He sighed. "I'm going to start arresting people for posting that stuff. It makes the town look bad."

I grinned. "Well, you're going to have to start with your mother then."

He gave me a pained look.

"I'm having a ham sandwich and homemade blackberry pie," I said. "You interested?"

"You couldn't get me out of here, even at gunpoint."

"I don't know. I might be able to."

He considered it as he grabbed a beer out of the refrigerator and sat. "Gertie's purse would probably clear me out faster."

I fixed up the sandwiches and slid them on the table.

He took a big bite and smiled. "If the pie is half as good as the ham, I'll be the happiest man in the world."

"What are you in such a good mood for?" I asked as I plopped down in my chair. "Did Celia list her house for sale?"

"I wish. You know that will never happen. She's going to stay right here, aggravating the general population, until she dies."

"I wouldn't count on it."

"On her staying?"

"No. On her dying."

He laughed. "Yeah. You might be right."

I studied him as I ate. He really was far more relaxed than the last time I'd seen him. His jaw wasn't clenched, and his shoulders were loose, not hunched up like they were when he was tense. His forehead was relaxed and even his posture was less rigid than before.

"So what gives?" I asked. "Something cheered you up and I don't think it was locking Celia up, although I'm sure there is some level of satisfaction to it. I would say it was because you were coming to see me, but I'm not that vain."

"I love seeing you. Most of the time."

"Ha. Not lately."

"Lately has been...rough. I agree."

"So spill. To what do I owe the pleasure of this new and improved Carter LeBlanc?"

"I shouldn't be telling you this, but I knew I was going to as soon as everything was confirmed. I've been waiting all evening for official word."

I perked up. "Something about the case? Did you catch the killer?"

"Even better."

"The killer turned themselves in and it's Celia? Or Ronald?"

"Not that much better. But I know how Cooke ingested the poison and it wasn't someone from Sinful that gave it to him."

"Seriously! That's huge. How can you be sure?"

I felt my hopes leap over the moon. If the killer wasn't a Sinful resident, then that changed everything. I mean, Cooke was still dead, but as long as it didn't have anything to do with our town, that made all the difference in the world.

"There was an unopened bottled water in his car," Carter said. "It had cyanide in it. There was a tiny injection hole near the lid."

I frowned. "But if it was unopened..."

"Forensics collected all the trash from the cafeteria. There was the same brand water bottle with traces of cyanide in it and Cooke's DNA on the mouth."

"Wow!" My excitement built until a huge grin broke through that I thought might be permanent. "That's incredible. Talk about Christmas come early."

"I know. I mean, the guy was still murdered, but given this new evidence, the New Orleans police have decided it's their problem."

"Given his reputation, they've got their work cut out for them."

"I'm pretty sure they'll be starting with Abshire."

"I guess you made it around to him during your inquiries."

He nodded. "I followed the woman-with-a-baby trail, same as you."

"I can't say I'm sorry he's on police radar, but why? The

man's in the hospital and based on what I heard, it didn't sound like he was leaving anytime soon."

"Men like Abshire have all kinds of people on the down-low payroll. There's rumblings that a task force was already looking at him for the adoption thing."

"But Abshire told the police he didn't know who attacked him."

"Yep. That's what he said, but I don't think anyone is buying his robbery story."

"I didn't. So the cops think Abshire recognized Cooke and passed his name to one of his shady connections?"

"They didn't come right out and say it, but it was implied. My buddy in New Orleans said they've had Cooke on their radar for a while as well. Apparently, he's a suspect in two homicides but they couldn't get enough to pin the murders on him. They weren't exactly sad to hear he was dead."

"You think Cooke was a hired gun masquerading as a PI?"

Carter shrugged. "Who knows? Maybe he started out legit but couldn't make enough money and diversified."

"That's a heck of a diversification."

"For some people, it's not that big of a stretch."

"True." I held up my beer can. "A toast. To no one in Sinful killing Santa."

Carter clinked his can against mine.

"I guess this means we're both off the case," he said.

"I suppose you're right," I said.

But I didn't think that at all.

Carter was only tasked with finding the killer, and now that the task had shifted hands, he could close his file and happily move on. But part of my investigation was figuring out who Cooke was after. Just because Cooke was dead didn't mean it was over for me. If the baby's father had hired a man like Cooke to find his son, then he wouldn't stop at finding another

Cooke to take the dead man's place. That meant Caleb was still at risk. Or Nathan. But my money was on Caleb.

Unfortunately, I wasn't sure what I could do about that situation other than identify the man who'd hired Cooke. Unless the police could conjure up evidence that he'd directed Cooke to assault people, he'd just play the innocent father looking for the son who was stolen from him by the biological mother. With no criminal activity to put on him, there was a strong chance he'd get custody.

And a family would be broken apart.

"You all right?" Carter asked.

"Me? Sure. Just mulling it all over. This was a twist I didn't see coming. Don't get me wrong, I'm really happy about it. I'm just trying to put it all in perspective."

He frowned. "You're worried about the babies."

"And the families. Whoever hired Cooke will just send someone else. If Abshire was crooked, then the fallout could be devastating."

"Yeah. That's crossed my mind more than once, but unfortunately, there's nothing we can do about it. That will all have to play out in court."

"I know you're right but I still hate it. They're all nice people."

"Maybe Cooke didn't find his target here," Carter said. "He might have had other towns lined up to check or it could be that he was off base entirely."

"I hope so," I said. But I didn't believe it for a minute. Not given what Dorothy had overheard Cooke say on his phone. But as far as I knew, Carter hadn't gotten around to questioning all of the workers in the cafeteria, so he probably didn't know about that conversation at all. And now that he knew Cooke had brought the poison with him, he would never conduct those interviews.

"So anyway," Carter said. "I stopped by my house and took care of Tiny before I came over...in case you're interested in making this an overnight celebration."

I smiled, pushing all thoughts of Cooke and the babies out of my mind. There was nothing I could do about it tonight. And I had a hot man I loved sitting in my kitchen.

"Best. Idea. Ever."

CHAPTER NINETEEN

As soon as Carter headed out the next morning, I sent a text to Ida Belle and Gertie telling them I had info from Carter and they needed to get to my house pronto. Ten minutes later, they arrived. Despite the fact that it was only 7:00 a.m. Ida Belle looked like she'd been up and running for hours. Gertie looked like she'd thrown back the covers, put rollers in, and walked through a war zone.

She marched straight through my front door and into the kitchen without saying a single word. She grabbed a handful of coffee grounds and licked them like salt before a tequila shot, then lifted the coffeepot and poured a stream of the steaming liquid directly into her mouth.

"What the heck do you do while you sleep?" Ida Belle asked.

Gertie carried the entire pot of coffee to the table and flopped into a chair. "What sleep?"

I poured Ida Belle and me a cup before Gertie drank it all, then put the rest into a thermos for Gertie before starting another pot.

"Francis?" I asked as I sat.

She nodded and took a gulp out of the thermos.

"I thought you were going to cover him at night," Ida Belle said.

"I did," Gertie said. "But he was on a roll so it didn't make a difference. Started quoting Revelations. Gave me nightmares. Every time I'd doze off, he'd start talking about the apocalypse and I'd bolt out of sleep thinking I needed to either grab my gun or pray. I was so confused one time I shot a hole in my dressmaker's mannequin. And I was working on a new dress for Christmas. Can't wear it now. Not unless belly button holes become the new rage at church."

"I wouldn't count on it," Ida Belle said, and looked at me. "So what's up? You look all perky this morning."

"That's because she had a non-slumber party with Carter," Gertie said. "Although if I had a hot man in my house all night, I'd look exhausted, not refreshed."

"If you had a hot man in your house all night, you'd be arrested for kidnapping," Ida Belle said.

"Sounds like she had the four horsemen in her bedroom," I said.

"Nice." Ida Belle gave me an approving nod.

"But yes, I do have exciting news," I said, and filled them in on what Carter had told me the night before.

"That's great!" Gertie said, perking up more from the news than the coffee. "That means nobody we like is the killer. Heck, that was worth coming over here in my pajamas. That might have been worth coming over here naked."

"But we're all glad you didn't opt for that," Ida Belle said, and I could tell she was pleased. "I have to admit, I didn't sleep all that well last night with this on my mind. That news is really a load off."

I nodded. "I feel the same way. But..."

Ida Belle blew out a breath. "One of those babies is still at risk."

Gertie frowned. "Surely a judge wouldn't give a baby to a man who hired someone like Cooke. Especially if all Cooke's misdeeds are exposed."

"The client isn't responsible for what the PI does unless they specifically directed them to do it or participated," Ida Belle said. "If the father kept his nose clean then there's a better than good chance that he could get custody."

"What if Ashley comes back and takes the baby?" Gertie asked. "Assuming that Caleb is the target."

"Being the biological mother would weigh in her favor," Ida Belle said. "But if she put the baby up for adoption without notifying the biological father, that's going to outweigh anything else."

"That stinks," Gertie said. "Caleb has a great home with parents who love him. He doesn't belong with some abuser who hires hit men to track people down."

"I agree," I said. "Which is why I figured we should concentrate our efforts on figuring out who the father is and then getting all the dirt we can on him."

"Oh, I like that plan!" Gertie said.

"So do I," Ida Belle said. "And it just so happens, I can help in that arena. I heard from the Sorcerer early this morning. He traced the email back to an investment firm in New Orleans. He can't get it narrowed down any more than that, though."

"That's amazing," I said. "I figured that email would be routed all over the world."

"It was," Ida Belle said. "But the Sorcerer said he found it amusing that people thought they could hide."

"Not from him," I said. "I'm pretty sure ghosts can't hide from him."

Ida Belle nodded. "To be honest, I'm kinda surprised he's

out among us regular people. I figured the government would lock him up somewhere and force him to do their bidding."

"You've been watching too many movies," Gertie said.

"As a former government employee," I said, "I'm going to have to go with Ida Belle on this one. Maybe he figured out a way to turn the tables—get enough on them that they had to let him go."

"That sounds like something he'd do," Ida Belle agreed.

I grabbed my laptop off the kitchen counter and opened it. "What was the name of the investment firm?"

"Bayou South Investments," Ida Belle said as she and Gertie pulled their chairs over next to mine.

I did a search and found a website for the company. So far, so good. I pulled it up and was pleased to see it contained a page for staff. Assuming our guy held a position important enough to be listed, he might be on there. I scrolled down the page and we examined the faces and bios.

"Five guys total," I said. "Two of them are silver, so I'm going to eliminate them."

Ida Belle nodded. "That leaves three, and all fit the vague description the bartender gave us."

"Search social media," Gertie said. "Find out if any are married."

"What difference does that make?" Ida Belle asked.

Gertie sighed. "Never mind."

"She brings up a good point though," I said. "The logical default for a married man would be wanting to hide a child with his mistress," I said. "I mean, they don't usually show up at home and present their wives with another woman's baby, do they?"

"Not usually, or my guess is the murder rate would be a lot higher," Ida Belle said. "Okay, then search on marital status and we can put them in order based on that criteria."

I located all three on social media. One was clearly married and had two kids. He went to the bottom of the list. The second listed his status as single and I didn't find any reference to a girlfriend. The third had a private profile so we couldn't see anything on him. I did a couple more searches and didn't come up with any more information.

"Drew McEntire and Cory Guillory are tied for the top spot," I said.

"So what now?" Gertie asked. "We go to New Orleans and follow them around?"

"We can't follow both of them," I said. "Not at the same time."

"And he's hiring a PI to do his dirty work anyway," Ida Belle said. "So we probably wouldn't discover much by following him."

I downloaded two of the pictures and sent a text to the bartender, asking her if either looked familiar. She texted back a couple seconds later indicating that it could be either one but she'd remembered that the last time the guy had been in the bar, he'd been limping on his right leg.

"That was months ago though," Ida Belle said. "If he wasn't limping every time, it was probably an injury and he's recovered by now."

I accessed Drew McEntire's social media again and scanned the posts and pictures back to that time frame. "No mention of an injury."

"Then he's probably not our guy," Gertie said. "When men are injured, they tell everyone who will listen and most people who won't."

"That's true," Ida Belle said. "Walter had an ingrown toenail removed last year and sales at the General Store dropped for two weeks. Everyone got tired of hearing about it and went up the highway to the big grocery store."

"I think we need to make another trip to New Orleans," I said.

"To spy on Cory Guillory?" Gertie asked.

"That, and I'd like to talk to the attorney, Abshire," I said. "Assuming we can get in. And assuming he'll talk to us."

"Oh, we can get in," Gertie said. "One way or another. It's just a hospital, not a police station or prison."

"We can get arrested in New Orleans," Ida Belle reminded her.

"We can get arrested in Sinful," Gertie said.

"Yeah, but in New Orleans, Francine isn't going to bring us dinner and our cellmates won't be as pleasant as the Swamp Bar drunks," Ida Belle said.

"Celia's in jail right now," I reminded them.

"I forgot about that," Ida Belle said. "Another good reason to avoid jail."

"I'm not suggesting we burst into the hospital with bazookas," Gertie said. "Besides, I only have one. I was thinking about doing an undercover thing."

I winced a bit at the bazooka comment but didn't have the nerve to pursue that line of questioning, not this early in the morning. Apparently, Ida Belle didn't either, but she subconsciously shifted her body away from her friend, giving her the side-eye.

"What kind of undercover thing?" I asked, figuring talking was a promise of action.

"Scrubs," Gertie said. "We get scrubs and some fake badges and we stroll right in like we work there."

"But we don't know what they wear," I said, not completely hating the idea. "If they're all color-coded then we'll stand out worse in the wrong color scrubs."

"I happen to know that the employees are allowed to choose their own scrubs," Gertie said.

Ida Belle narrowed her eyes. "How do you know that?"

"Remember when you went on that three-day offshore fishing trip last year?" Gertie asked. "Well, I might have made a side trip to the casino."

"And you spent the night at a slot machine next to a hospital employee?" I asked.

"Not exactly," Gertie said.

Ida Belle snorted.

"So how, exactly, did you get that information?" I asked.

"You know those huge slot machines with the giant arm?" Gertie asked. "They have one at the entrance. It's a gimmick thing but the top prize was a new bass boat so I put in five bucks and pulled the arm. I didn't realize it was that heavy or that it would drop that fast."

Ida Belle sighed. "Or that maybe you should stand to the side as it was coming down?"

"Maybe that too," Gertie said. "Anyway, it bopped me right on top of the head and knocked me out cold. So I got a trip to the ER and they made me stay a couple hours. It was so quiet that night that everyone was bored, so I spent the night playing poker with a nice nurse. She told me all about how things run there. You don't want to eat the mashed potatoes."

I was afraid to ask. "So where can we pick up some scrubs?"

"I've got scrubs," Gertie said.

"Why?" Ida Belle asked.

"Part of my costume collection," Gertie said.

"I'm not wearing sexy anything," Ida Belle said.

"They're normal," Gertie said. "Unless you think Hello Kitty is sexy."

"There's a place that sells scrubs right off the highway on the way into New Orleans," Ida Belle said. "We'll just make a quick stop."

"We don't all need scrubs," I said. "It will be difficult enough for one of us to sneak past hospital staff and into the ER."

"So what were you thinking?" Ida Belle asked.

"I want you two to create a diversion," I said. "Something that gets staff away from the desk so that I can slip through the door."

"I'm not having a heart attack again," Gertie said. "I'm always having a heart attack. One of these days, I'm going to have a real one from all this pretending. It's a karma thing."

Ida Belle waved a hand in dismissal. "You don't believe in that crap and don't tell me for a minute you have a problem pretending. Besides, you're a better actor than me. I can't even fake being pleasant, much less injured."

"That's true," Gertie said, seeming mollified. "Then I guess I'm having another heart attack."

"Let's just wait until we get there," Ida Belle said. "Then we can see what we have to work with and make a decision."

Gertie perked up. "Improv. I like it."

"Most comedians do," I said.

"I'm not a comedian," Gertie said.

"Tell that to your YouTube following," I said.

"We're burning daylight," Ida Belle said. "Let's print you up a fake badge and get Gertie dressed and head out."

"I don't need to change clothes to have a fake medical emergency," Gertie said.

"You do if you're with me," Ida Belle said. "You go in public that way, and you might have a real one."

"Dressed is better," I said. "If anyone takes a closer look at things, it might be odd that you drove all the way from Sinful in your pajamas to fall out in the ER in New Orleans."

"It's only illegal to go in public in your pajamas if the temperature is above eighty," Gertie said.

"Why in the world would the temperature make a difference?" I asked.

"Because when speckled trout were running at dawn, the race to get to the hottest spots first led to some less-than-desirable fishing attire," Ida Belle said. "Everyone's okay with winter pajamas, but what some wear in the summer isn't fit for public consumption. Quite frankly, they probably scared the fish."

I grimaced. "Did those who sleep in the nude get dressed at least?"

"Unfortunately, no," Ida Belle said. "There was also the year *someone* was sleeping in Saran Wrap because she thought she'd lose weight."

"I dropped two pounds," Gertie said.

"That's because you weren't wearing clothes," Ida Belle said.

"So about that badge," I said.

It was going to be a long drive into New Orleans.

CHAPTER TWENTY

I CHOSE A SOLID-COLORED NAVY SCRUB AT THE MEDICAL supply store. Gertie thought it was boring so I knew I'd chosen well. Standing out wasn't exactly what I was going for. When we arrived at the hospital, I parked in the lot in front of the ER entrance and we studied it for a minute.

"Circular drive with drop-off," Ida Belle said. "Standard sliding glass doors to the inside. Looks like two nurses at the front desk and another behind them in the files."

"If you can draw those nurses just outside the entry, I can sneak past," I said.

"You don't think doing something farther in the parking lot would allow you more room to operate?" Gertie asked.

"It would, but I don't think the nurses will go that far from their station," I said. "But if something happened just outside the door..."

Ida Belle nodded. "They'd call for help but they'd also move to assist as it's right in front of them."

"I'm not sure about a heart attack fake, though," I said, frowning. "I'm afraid if Gertie claims heart trouble, they'll haul her in for tests and won't release her."

"We've spent too many useless hours in the ER already this week," Ida Belle said.

Gertie nodded. "And I'm not interested in a stress test. That last time almost killed me. The darn test is designed to give you a heart attack. I think it's all a ploy to increase cardiac patients."

"Most people don't set the treadmill on fire during the test," Ida Belle pointed out. "It's probably a lot less stressful without the fear of burning to death."

Gertie looked back at the front of the hospital and smiled. "The sprinkler system is running."

"So they've got nice landscaping," Ida Belle said. "Who cares?"

"If one of those sprinkler heads was broken and I slipped into that landscaping," Gertie said, "you yelling about a lawsuit would probably get the nurses moving."

Ida Belle stared. "That's genius."

"I know," Gertie said. "Just part of my everyday thinking."

"Don't push it," Ida Belle said.

I grinned. "Let's do this then. You two go summon up an attorney threat while I go summon up the actual attorney."

We headed to the entry, Ida Belle and Gertie walking ahead of me. I moved over as we approached the entrance and stood off to the side of the doors, pretending to talk on my cell phone. Ida Belle walked by the nearest sprinkler head and gave it a solid kick, breaking it in two. Water started bubbling out onto the walkway and Ida Belle motioned for Gertie to do her thing.

Which Gertie never did halfway.

She took two steps into the running water, then let out a high-pitched scream and fell directly into the flowers. The nurses all jumped up, staring outside, and Ida Belle waved frantically at them. I stepped over a little to the side and the doors opened.

"Help!" Ida Belle yelled. "My mother fell because of your broken sprinkler system. If she's injured, I'll own this hospital before it's over."

"Your mother?" Gertie shot Ida Belle a look that could have melted metal. "There might be a real injury coming."

The nurses rushed from behind the desk and ran outside. As soon as they cleared the entrance, I slipped inside and hurried through the door to the ER. I had no idea which room Abshire was in, so I had to peek into every room, hoping a doctor wasn't in residence. I'd seen a photo of Abshire on his business website, so I would know him when I saw him. I hit the jackpot behind Door Number 3. He was awake when I walked into the room and glared at me as I walked toward him.

Late fifties. Six foot even. One hundred seventy-five pounds. The number of bandages and bruises indicated that he'd been put through the wringer. No threat at all to me but had probably committed an unknown number of assaults on families through his practices.

"You just took my temperature and blood pressure," he said. "How the hell is a person supposed to get better if you never let them rest?"

"I'm not here to do any of that," I said.

"Don't tell me they've scheduled another test. I'm done with tests. I just want you to fix this infection and let me go home. You people have caused more problems than you've solved."

"I'm not a hospital employee," I said. "I just dressed like one to get in to see you."

"I'm not talking to reporters."

"I'm not a reporter. I'm a private investigator and I'm

looking for a former client of yours that's missing. I was hoping you might be able to help me with some information."

He gave me a suspicious look. "What kind of information?"

"A way to contact her, perhaps," I said. "Her cell phone is disconnected and her family is worried. I was hoping you might have another way to get in touch."

"Even if I did, I couldn't give it to you."

"But you could use it to pass a message on from her family."

"Not from here, I couldn't. And I don't see that any of this is my problem."

"It's not. I'm asking you to help alleviate some stress on a family right before Christmas."

He narrowed his eyes at the Christmas reference and I knew my attempt to guilt him into helping hadn't worked in the least. I had a feeling Abshire was only interested in helping himself. But curiosity got the better of him.

"Who is the missing woman?" he asked.

"Ashley Breaux."

"Ashley Breaux?" The name didn't register recognition and I wondered for a moment whether his injuries had affected his memory or he simply cared so little about anything but the money that he'd already forgotten her name. I suspected it was the latter.

"Her sister, who lives in Sinful, adopted her son," I said, hoping the additional information might prompt his memory.

I saw a flicker of recognition at the word 'Sinful.'

"Yes, I remember now," he said. "Very straightforward. Always easier when it's a family member."

"What about the father?" I asked.

"What about him?" he said.

"Was he notified that his son was being adopted?" I asked. "Did he give his consent?"

226

He frowned. "I haven't committed the details of all the adoptions I handle to memory. But when the father is present, then of course, he has to give consent."

"And when he's not present?" I asked. "Do you make an attempt to find him?"

"Look, my clients are not necessarily the models of society. Sometimes they don't know who the father is. How am I supposed to identify the father when my client can't? Surely you're not suggesting I take out ads in the paper, asking everyone who's had sex with a certain woman to contact my office for DNA testing."

"So you don't make any attempt to identify the father."

He put his hands up in the air. "My guess is, even if I took out that ad, I wouldn't have any takers. Most likely, the fathers are married men who don't want their wives to know about their indiscretions or men who aren't interested in being financially strapped for two decades over a fling."

"Got it. So do you have a way to get in touch with Ashley besides her cell phone or address?"

"Why would I?" he asked. "My paperwork would contain her contact information from the time of the transaction, which I assume is what her family has. I don't create or maintain personal relationships with my clients."

I stiffened at his use of the word 'transaction' but then I supposed that's all the babies were to Abshire.

"I'm sure you don't get involved personally," I said. "If you knew too much about their lives, you might not be able to adopt out their babies."

Anger flashed across his face. "I'm done answering your questions. I have no idea how to find Ashley and I don't know who the father of her baby is."

"Is that what you told the guy who beat you up?" I asked. "I'm guessing lack of answers is how you ended up in here."

"That man robbed me," he said.

"I'm sure that's what you told the police, but I'm guessing that the man who robbed you was the same man who showed up in Sinful disguised as Santa...most likely looking for Ashley. I figure he wouldn't have known where to start looking unless he got that information from you."

"I don't have any idea what you're talking about. You are the only person who's asked me about Ashley Breaux."

I nodded. "I suppose you should stick with that story, especially since that man ended up murdered. Might not look good for you if the police knew he was the same man who put you in the hospital a couple weeks before."

"Get out! Or I'm calling security."

I held my hands up in defeat. "I'm gone. But I'm guessing I won't be the only person to visit you and ask these questions. The next set will probably have badges. Can't threaten them with hospital security so you might want to come up with a better story than what you gave me."

If Abshire wasn't injured, I'm pretty sure he would have launched out of the bed and throttled me right there. Or he would have tried. It wouldn't have worked out at all as he'd thought, but the desire was certainly there. If there had been a shred of doubt before, it was all gone now. Raymond Abshire was definitely not a good man.

I trailed out of the ER and headed for the parking lot. I didn't bother to hurry as I knew Abshire wasn't going to make good on his security threat. He was too afraid I'd summon the police. Gertie and Ida Belle were still in the lobby. An orderly and two of the nurses from earlier were trying to convince Gertie to get on a gurney so they could check her out, but she was refusing. As soon as she caught sight of me, she lifted her handbag and whacked the orderly across the shoulder. I had no idea what she was carting around in that bag, and didn't want to know, but whatever it was had enough weight to shift him a couple inches and cause him to clutch his arm.

"That does it," he said, and stomped off.

"I'm so sorry," Ida Belle said. "Mother has these spells sometimes, and she's not fond of men."

I could barely keep from laughing as I walked outside.

I headed out to the SUV and climbed inside. A couple minutes later, Ida Belle and Gertie joined me, Gertie still grousing about the whole mother thing.

"It was the best call," Ida Belle said. "It doesn't sound nearly as threatening for me to say my friend is pushing up your daisies and I'm going to sue. 'Mother' holds a lot more power."

"She's right about that one," I said. "This whole Southern mother thing is a serious business."

"I do not look old enough to be your mother," Gertie grumbled, but she couldn't argue the Southern mother angle of things.

"So did you get anything?" Ida Belle asked.

I filled them in on my conversation with Abshire and they both looked as impressed as I was with the shady attorney.

"He knows that adoption wasn't on the up-and-up," Gertie said.

"He suspects, at least," Ida Belle said. "I imagine he makes sure he doesn't know anything for sure. That's his legal out."

"Maybe this beating from Cooke will teach him a lesson, and he'll change the way he does business," Gertie said.

"I wouldn't count on it," Ida Belle said. "His kind gravitate to that sort of thing because it's who they are to begin with. I don't think Abshire is capable of living a moral life. The lure of the easy money is too great."

"You're right," Gertie said. "But I wish you weren't."

Ida Belle glanced over at me. "You're awfully quiet. Is something wrong?"

"No," I said. "I mean, yes, the whole thing is wrong. But there's something that bothers me about the conversation, more than the obvious. I just can't put my finger on what it is."

"You think he knows how to find Ashley?" Gertie asked.

I shook my head. "Like Ida Belle said—the less he knows the better. But when I first asked him about her, the name didn't register. Not even a twitch. It wasn't until I mentioned Sinful and her sister adopting that he showed any sign of recognition."

"He'd probably already forgotten," Gertie said. "After all, it was months ago and it's not like she mattered."

"Yes, but if that beating he took was from Cooke, that was only a couple weeks ago," I said. "Surely her name would have stuck after that."

Ida Belle frowned. "That *is* strange. You think he has a head injury?"

"Quite possible," I said. "He had the lingering spots from bruises on his face, and his head was still bandaged. His short-term memory could be sketchy."

"But you don't think that's it?" Ida Belle asked.

"I just don't know."

"You'll figure it out," Ida Belle said. "You always do."

I nodded. That was true enough. I just hoped this time I figured it out before guns were blazing.

IDA BELLE PARKED AT THE CURB ACROSS THE STREET FROM Bayou South Investments and we all stared at the entrance, not sure what to do next.

"We don't even know if those guys are at work," Gertie said. "A lot of people take off right before the holidays."

"Even if they are, what are the options?" Ida Belle said.

I sighed. "Yeah. I've been thinking about that and we have a bit of a quandary. I know we talked about trying to get some dirt on the father, but shadowing someone that way is a 24-7 job. And we don't even know who the father is."

"Maybe you should just go talk to them," Ida Belle said. "You could still do it under the guise of looking for Ashley because the family is worried. Since Cooke was murdered, the father isn't likely to admit he even knows her, much less mention the baby. But you would be able to tell if he's the one."

I nodded. "That could work. And it's definitely a more efficient option than following them around and hoping they do something in public that indicates they're the one."

Gertie pulled lip gloss and tissue out of her purse. "Put this on. Men respond better to a pretty woman. Just try not to appear so capable."

I frowned but put on the lip gloss, then blotted with the tissue and handed it all back to Gertie, who sighed.

"The tissue was for your chest. You're not wearing a push-up bra and that T-shirt isn't doing anything to emphasize your assets."

"It's an investment firm," Ida Belle said. "That's not the kind of assets they're interested in."

"All men are interested in those assets," Gertie said.

CHAPTER TWENTY-ONE

THEY WERE STILL ARGUING WHEN I HOPPED OUT OF THE SUV and headed into the building. A perky young woman with a big fake smile greeted me as I walked in.

"I'd like to speak to Cory Guillory and Drew McEntire," I said.

"Mr. McEntire has already left for the holidays," she said. "But Mr. Guillory is in. Do you have an appointment?"

I pulled out my PI license. "No. But I'm hoping I don't need one. It will only take a minute."

This was clearly not one of the things she'd been trained to handle. She stared at me for a moment, bit her lower lip, then picked up the phone.

"Mr. Guillory, there's a lady in the lobby that would like to speak to you. She doesn't have an appointment but she's—"

I heard a curt voice cut her off, telling her to send me back. As she started to reply, he hung up.

"Second door on the left," she said, her voice as apprehensive as her expression. She was probably already calculating the number of ways she was going to be in trouble once Cory found out I wasn't a potential client.

I tapped on the partially open door and poked my head in. The man behind the desk stood up and smiled, motioning for me to enter.

Six foot even. One hundred eighty-five pounds. Nice muscle tone. Typical pretty boy in a suit. Probably hits the gym five nights a week but couldn't win a fight with a ten-year-old. No threat unless I give him my money to invest.

He extended his hand and I shook it before taking a seat.

"How can I help you Ms....?" he asked. "Are you looking to make some investments?"

"Not at this time," I said, and handed him my business card. "I'm a private investigator. I was hoping you might be able to help me."

He looked at the card and scowled. "PI? What could I possibly help you with?"

This was going about as well as I expected. "I'm looking for a missing woman and I have reason to believe you are acquainted. Her name is Ashley Breaux."

He stared at me, unblinking. "I've never heard of that person."

"She was a bartender at one of the hotels where your company holds events," I said, and named the hotel. "Thirty years old, long brown hair, pretty."

"Do I look like the sort of person who associates with barmaids?"

"All sorts of men associate with a pretty woman. Their profession isn't often relevant."

"Maybe not to some, but it is to me. I married Annabelle Leighton three months ago."

He stared at me like that statement had weight.

"Sorry," I said. "I just moved to Louisiana. I'm not familiar with Annabelle."

"The daughter of state Senator John Leighton. You see,

Ms. Redding, I believe family should benefit one's status and future. They're just another form of partnership, after all. A pretty face with nothing to offer is of no interest to me."

Holy crap, this guy was cold. I wondered if his wife was aware of her role in the relationship or if he adopted a different personality when it was all about getting what he wanted.

"You have political aspirations then?" I asked.

"Of course. I have the best track record at this firm and I'm involved in my community. I'll be an asset to the people."

"I'm sure," I said, struggling to keep the sarcasm out of my voice. "Well, one of the families in your future constituency would really like to find Ashley for the holidays. She recently had a baby, and they're anxious to do the whole first-Christmas thing."

He frowned. "Are they afraid something happened to her?"

"No. It appears that she left on her own accord, but they'd like to at least confirm she's all right."

He shook his head. "Sounds like an irresponsible person. Bartender. Apparently, unmarried but with a baby, skipping out on her family. I can't imagine why they'd want her to be part of their lives. Seems like she'd be an embarrassment."

"Well, none of them are running for office, so they're in the clear."

He smirked.

"It could be that I have the wrong guy," I said. "There is another employee here that I wanted to speak to, but I understand he's already left for the holidays. Drew McEntire?"

"That would make more sense. Drew shuffles women like a deck of cards and he has zero discrimination."

"So I take it you guys aren't friends."

The smirk disappeared from Cory's face. "We're coworkers."

"So not friends. Got it. Then I don't suppose you'd know where I could find him."

"Not even a guess. But you could ask the receptionist. He spends a lot of time regaling her with tales of his party life. She thinks he's cool."

The disgusted look was back in place and he reached for his phone, clearly signaling my dismissal. "If you don't mind," he said, "I have some calls to make before I close down for the holidays."

I rose from my chair. "Thank you for your time."

He didn't even bother to look up as I left.

I walked back up front and stopped at the receptionist's desk. She gave me a wary look.

"Is he always that pleasant?" I asked, hoping to win her over with our mutual dislike for Cory Guillory.

"Sometimes he's worse," she said. "Was he awful to you? I wouldn't take it personally. He's that way to everybody unless they have money or connections."

"Yes. I got that loud and clear. I feel sorry for his wife, unless she's as horrible as him. Then I don't."

The receptionist frowned. "Feeling sorry is the right call. Annabelle is actually nice. Painfully shy and sorta plain-looking. It's obvious to everyone why Cory married her. And that stinks, especially after everything she's been through."

"Oh? What's that?"

"Cancer. The female kind. But she was a trouper. Still showed up to her daddy's reelection events although sometimes it looked like she was going to pass out. The senator used her to make a big push over women's issues so he had to put her on display. I have a feeling being married to Cory isn't going to be any different than being Senator Leighton's daughter. She's useful when they need to put on a show."

She looked disgusted when she said it and I didn't blame

her. Life for Annabelle Leighton didn't sound all that awesome. I hoped one day she gained the strength to break free of all the men using her to gain a political seat.

"That's really crappy," I said. "Fortunately, it turns out Cory probably isn't the person I needed to speak to. I think Drew McEntire might be the one who can help me out with my case. I don't suppose you know where I can find him?"

She gave me a pensive look. "Oh, I don't think he'd want me to tell people where he is on his personal time."

"I'm sure he wouldn't, but this is sort of an emergency. I'm looking for a missing woman that I think Drew knew at one time. I'm talking to anyone who might be able to give me an idea where to find her. The family is really upset, especially with the holidays coming up."

"That's awful. Well, I guess he wouldn't mind. I mean, since it's important and all. He left for his camp. It's this huge place on the bayou. They have these wild parties down there—at least, that's what I hear. I've never been invited."

Her disappointment was apparent.

"Do you know where the camp is?" I asked.

"Off the highway going toward Sinful is all I know," she said. "Maybe you could look up the address online."

"Probably so. Thank you for your help."

She nodded. "I hope you find the lady you're looking for. And Merry Christmas."

I headed out to the SUV and recounted my chat with Cory Guillory.

"Sounds like a real a—"

"We get it," Ida Belle said, cutting Gertie off. "But it doesn't sound like he's our guy."

"There wasn't even a twitch when I said Ashley's name," I said. "When I told him she was a bartender, he looked offended that I was even asking him about her."

"Well, that figures," Ida Belle said. "A future politician in the making is just the sort of person who would consort with a man like Cooke."

"Totally," I said. "I think Cory Guillory would stop at absolutely nothing to get what he wants and apparently money and power are on the agenda."

"So I guess it's good news that he's not the father," Gertie said. "He sounds like a sociopath."

"A narcissist at least," I said, and relayed my conversation with the receptionist.

"So Drew is one of *those* McEntires," Ida Belle said. "Phillip McEntire built that camp, but he's probably seventy if he's a day."

"So maybe a grandfather or great-uncle?" Gertie said.

"You know the family?" I asked.

"By reputation only," Ida Belle said. "Old money. The girls are all about the social scene in New Orleans. The boys are all playboys, if the rumors are to be believed."

"Sounds like party boy Drew is following family tradition," I said.

Ida Belle frowned. "But why would a guy like that want to be saddled with a baby? He sounds like the definition of the kind that would claim it wasn't his."

I shook my head. "Maybe we're on the wrong track altogether."

"But the email came from that company server," Gertie said. "I don't think the Sorcerer made a mistake."

"Neither do I," I said. "But a family member or friend of an employee could have accessed the computers here. Heck, for all we know, it could be someone on the cleaning crew."

Ida Belle pulled away. "Let's track down Drew McEntire and see."

The camp was a good bit off the highway and after a single

glance, I decided it was more than pretentious to call it a 'camp' in the first place. I'd been to plenty of camps during my time in Sinful. None of them looked like this. At least ten thousand square feet of distressed wood and glass, overlooking the bayou. A hot tub was visible from the parking area, as were several bikini-clad women climbing into it. There were at least ten other cars parked in the drive and from the sound of the booming music, the party was in full swing.

"This must be the place," Ida Belle said.

"I'm glad you remembered where it was," I said.

"Not many mansions on the bayou," Ida Belle said. "Hard to forget. You want to handle this one on your own?"

"I don't see the point," I said. "Let's all head inside and spread out...try to locate Drew."

It didn't take long.

As soon as we stepped in the front door, we had a clear view of the huge back patio, which is where most of the activity was located. Drew was standing on a table, funneling beer, with a crowd of people standing around him, cheering him on.

Gertie snapped a picture. "In case he's the father."

I couldn't wrap my mind around the guy on the table hiring a PI to track down a baby he fathered out of wedlock, but I'd learned that Louisiana held all kinds. For all I knew, Drew was just itching to trade in hot babes and hot tubs for binkies and diapers.

We headed outside and waited for the funnel to empty. When he was done, Drew sprayed a huge stream of beer in the air and all the people cheered, despite the fact that they were being showered with spit and beer that had swished around in another man's mouth. Then he jumped off the table, grabbed the nearest bikini-clad woman, and planted a kiss on her

239

mouth. When he let her go, he grabbed the next one and repeated the process.

I looked over at Gertie, who was filming, and shook my head. I had a feeling this was going to be a waste of time. Drew McEntire didn't fit the profile of the man we were looking for on any level.

When he'd made it through two more women, he caught sight of us standing at the edge of the living room and squinted, probably trying to figure out if he knew us or not. I waved at him, hoping that would draw him over. I didn't want to make introductions in front of his fan club. He ambled our way, grinning, and gave me the up-and-down when he stopped in front of us.

"I should remember a woman as hot as you," he said. "But for the life of me, I'm drawing a blank."

"That's because we've never met," I said.

"Thank God!" He did an exaggerated brow wipe. "I thought I was losing my touch."

"You don't appear to be," I said. "My name is Fortune Redding. I'm a private investigator. I was hoping you could answer some questions for me."

He frowned. "PI? What do you want with me?"

"Maybe nothing," I said. "I'm looking for a missing woman and I think you might have known her. I'm talking to anyone who did in an effort to track her down. Her family is worried."

"Missing? You think something bad happened?" he asked.

"There is no reason to suspect foul play at this time," I said, easing his mind. "It's more likely she simply took off, but her family would like to know for sure."

He nodded. "Sure. Christmas and all. Need to know whether or not to hang the stocking, right? So what's her name?"

"Ashley Breaux."

Drew's eyes widened and I forced myself to remain calm. "Ashley? Seriously?" he asked. "She took off?"

"Looks like," I said. "Skipped out on rent. Did a dip on her job."

He shook his head. "I had no idea. Of course, I haven't been by the bar in forever. Can't even remember the last time."

"So you and Ashley were involved?" I asked.

"'Involved' is a serious word, and there was nothing serious about me and Ashley," he said. "Sometimes we hooked up. Ashley was a good time, but that was as far as it went."

"For her too?" I asked.

"Sure," he said. "She was a party girl. Made me look like an amateur if the truth be told."

I glanced around. "Seems like a pretty fancy place you've got here. How come you used to go to the bar to hit up Ashley for money?"

He gave me an indignant look. "Says who?"

"The other bartenders. They've seen her giving you money."

He nodded. "And they probably have. Let's just say Ashley had a penchant for certain items that I had access to."

"Drugs?"

"I'm not saying. But you can bet that any exchange of money between Ashley and me was purely business."

"I'm curious," I said. "How come you speak of her in past tense?"

"Because once she got pregnant, the fun was over."

"So you knew about the baby?" I asked.

"It would have been kinda hard to hide after a certain point, right? But the truth is she told me right after she found out. Said she had to get off the party train."

"Are you the father?"

He laughed. "Do you think I'd be foolish enough to get a

woman pregnant? Especially a woman like Ashley? My parents would disown me and that would be dire."

"Do you know who the father is?" I asked.

"Never asked. Never cared. Like I said, Ashley and I just had some fun together."

"You didn't even ask if the baby was yours?"

He smiled. "I didn't have to. Given the money I've got coming someday, I knew the gold diggers would be out in full force. I had a vasectomy when I was twenty. Get tested twice a year to make sure it's good. No woman is going to make me a permanent paycheck."

"I hope your future wife feels the same way about your choice."

"There are other ways to get a baby. Ways that don't ruin a woman's body. My ego isn't tied up in having my own DNA walking and talking."

"I don't know why not. There's plenty of that ego to go around."

I could tell he was aggravated by my statement but I didn't care. Everything about Drew McEntire rubbed me the wrong way and if irritating him was the most I could do to him, then I was darn well going to do it well.

"Look," he said, "everyone gets to decide their own life. I'm not into kids. I leave that to the churchgoers and the people with political aspirations. All that image stuff."

"Like your coworker, Cory. He didn't seem to think much of you when I spoke with him earlier."

He shrugged. "Nobody at the firm likes me. My parents own the place. They all know that no matter what they do, they'll never to get to sit in the big chair. It's all coming to me."

"Didn't sound like jealousy," I said. "More like disdain."

Drew's jaw tightened and I saw his expression shift. The

previously cocky look vanished as if a steel door had closed on top of it, and it was replaced with anger.

"Cory should watch what he says about other people. He's not the angel he makes himself out to be. Now, if you ladies are done with your worrying-about-Ashley routine, I've got people waiting on me. I don't know where Ashley is, nor do I care. She wasn't anyone to me but a bit of fun. Don't try to make it more."

He stood up and walked away.

"You think he's telling the truth?" Ida Belle asked.

"Unfortunately, yes," I said. "I think he's too in love with himself to lie."

"That's a shame," Gertie said. "Because I really wanted to shoot him."

"Me too," I agreed.

"Let's get out of here before one of us changes our mind," Ida Belle said.

"None of this makes sense," Gertie said as we headed back to the SUV. "The emails to Cooke came from Bayou South Investments and Drew admitted to partying with Ashley. If he's not the father, then who is? Is it possible that two different men from the same company were sleeping with her? And if so, who's the other one? Drew and Cory were the only two that fit the profile and it doesn't appear to be either of them."

"She's right," Ida Belle said. "We followed the logical trail and found all the pieces but they appear to belong to two different puzzles."

"Maybe Drew *is* the father and his parents found out and hired Cooke," Gertie said. "I know he says they'd disinherit him but it would be their grandchild. Some people get crazy over their bloodline."

"That's a better theory than what I've come up with," I said.

"What did you come up with?" Gertie asked.

I sighed. "Nothing."

"Gertie's got me beat on this one too, I'm afraid," Ida Belle said, and looked over at me. "You didn't get a sense of something off or wrong or anything from either of them?"

"I've gotten a sense that something wasn't completely right with everyone we've interviewed," I said. "None of them were lying but I doubt any of them were giving the full story, either."

"Of course not," Gertie said. "People rarely offer up personal business when it's embarrassing, much less illegal."

"And I'm sure they all have things they'd rather not become public knowledge," Ida Belle said. "Everyone does."

"Not me," Gertie said. "My life is an open book."

"Your life is a YouTube video," Ida Belle said. "But you still don't want anyone looking in your purse."

"True," Gertie said. "So what now? We start looking in handbags? Metaphorically speaking?"

I shook my head. "I think we head back to Sinful, wrap gifts, and see if we can make a dent in baked goods."

"You're giving up?" Gertie asked.

"No," I said. "I'm giving myself time to sort everything out and decide on a next course of action. And I need to check in with our clients. They might be ready to call it quits since it appears Cooke wasn't killed by a Sinful resident."

"But we've still got a baby in danger," Gertie said. "And Ashley missing."

"I know," I said. "I'm not saying we won't keep poking around. I'm just saying I probably shouldn't be charging the Heberts for it."

Ida Belle nodded. "We've had a lot to process in a short

while. I think a break to get it all in order is a good idea. Sometimes when I'm stuck on how to proceed, I wash my vehicle or pressure-wash the driveway...things that require motion but not a lot of thinking. It seems to loosen up my mind."

"Or shooting things," Gertie said. "I always think better when I'm shooting."

"Well, thank God for that," Ida Belle said. "It's hardly the time to let your mind wander. But she does have a point. We could load up some ammo and guns and head out in the boat for a shooting session. Might get rid of some frustration, anyway."

"Can we put a picture of Celia on an old pier post and let 'em rip?" Gertie said.

"It's a requirement," Ida Belle said.

I smiled. "Then I suppose we have an activity planned. At least there won't be any loose livestock, and we can't catch anything on fire."

Gertie shook her head. "Never underestimate me."

CHAPTER TWENTY-TWO

WE RELAXED OVER A SNACK AND THEN MADE SEVERAL TRIPS from my supersecret closet to the boat to load up weapons and rounds. There were a couple of guns that I had inherited with the house that I hadn't tried yet, and I was looking forward to giving them a whirl. We headed back inside to fill up the cooler and grab our phones, and that's when we realized we all had text messages, and voice mail, and a million missed calls.

All from Walter.

"What the heck is that man up to?" Ida Belle asked. "He better not think marrying me means he gets to keep tabs. I'll rescind my 'yes' if that's the case."

I figured this was all Ida Belle's business and Gertie must have as well, because neither of us made a move to return the call. Ida Belle didn't even hesitate. She poked in his number, put it on speaker, then started in as soon as he answered.

"Why are you blowing up our phones?" she asked. "Is Celia dead? Did Christ return? This better be good."

"If you'd shut up a minute, I'll tell you," he said. "Myrna got a call from the Mudbug police. Becca's alarm was going off but she's not answering her phone. She called here asking if I'd seen her. I'd no more than hung up with her when a man I'd never seen before walked into the store, asking how to find FM 614."

Ida Belle sucked in a breath. "That's where the Prejeans live."

"Myrna said Becca was supposed to take more pictures there sometime today," Walter said. "Said they got a puppy and wanted some with the baby. But no one's answering at the Prejeans' either. Now, maybe they're all busy with the picture taking."

"What did the man look like?" I asked.

"City slicker. Expensive suit. Bad attitude."

My back stiffened. "Call Carter and send him to the Prejeans' house."

"Already did," Walter said. "But he's on a call at the Swamp Bar and can't get away and I've got a store full of people. That's why I'm calling you."

"How long ago did the man leave?" I asked.

"Fifteen minutes."

"We've got to hurry," I said, and started for the front door.

"Wait!" Ida Belle yelled. "There's a bayou that dips down just off the back of the house. We'll get there faster in the boat."

"And the weapons are already loaded," Gertie said.

We all ran out the back door and I could still hear Walter yelling on the phone as I shoved the boat off the bank and jumped inside. Ida Belle passed me her phone and I told Walter we were on it before disconnecting. Ida Belle fired the boat up and we took off at warp speed. I clutched the arms of my chair and squinted into the blasting air, wishing I'd grabbed sunglasses before I left. I looked down at the stack of weapons in the bottom of the boat and said a quick prayer that we wouldn't need them.

But I had a feeling things had gone seriously south. And my chat with Cory Guillory had set it all into motion. How had I missed this? I would have sworn that Cory was telling the truth when he said he didn't know Ashley but apparently, he was the best actor ever. And by handing him a business card with my address and telling him I represented her sister, I'd sent him right to her front door.

I wondered why Cooke hadn't made the familial connection, but then remembered what the bartender had said—that she hadn't even known Ashley had a sister until I'd mentioned it. No one was looking for a sister and since Megan was married and didn't share the same name, there was nothing to connect them. Until my visit.

Given what Cory got from me, a PI could have tracked Megan down in a matter of minutes with simple record searches—birth, marriage, property deeds. Still, it seemed a gross oversight that Cooke didn't bother to trace Ashley's family more thoroughly. But maybe he preferred roughing people up for information rather than cruising computer files.

The part that really confused me was why Cooke hadn't gotten that information out of Abshire. Was the attorney really that strong? He'd seemed to remember Ashley's baby had been adopted by her sister when I talked to him. Had Cooke literally knocked the information clean out of his mind and he was only now able to recall it? But then I remembered the payments—ten grand per town. Maybe Cooke had deliberately kept the information on Megan from Cory so that he could collect the payment for Mudbug as well as Sinful.

I shook my head. Too many things still didn't make sense.

I glanced over at Ida Belle and took in the grim look on her face. I knew her well enough to guess what was going through her mind, and it was the same thing that was going through mine. I'd already labeled Cory a narcissist and now we knew he'd hired Cooke. That made him an unknown quantity when it came to violence. Certainly, he wasn't above paying someone else for it. The question was, had his desperation reached a level where he'd get his own hands dirty?

Either way, this was a confrontation that we'd been hoping to avoid. If Cory insisted on making a play for his son, then I'd hoped he'd hire an attorney and file the proper paperwork... make his case through the legal system. Confronting the Prejeans, who didn't appear to be part of a conspiracy to keep the biological father from his child, wasn't the way to go. It was reckless and it had the potential to be dangerous given how high emotions were running.

Ida Belle made a hard right when we reached the lake and skirted the edge for a bit before making another hard right into a narrow bayou. The boat flew across the top of the water, the sides brushing the grass on the banks at time due to the limited width. I could see Gertie clenching the edges of her custom-made seat cushion and knew she was feeling the pressure as badly as I was. The fact that she wasn't hooting at the top of her lungs was also an indication of just how worried she was about what we were going to find at the Prejeans' house.

It was probably only a couple minutes that Ida Belle navigated the tiny channel, but it seemed like forever before she cut the throttle and pulled up against the bank.

"The house is through that tree line," she said and pointed to a grouping of trees about fifty yards away.

I jumped off my chair and Gertie hefted the duffle bag of weaponry onto the bench. I already had my nine-millimeter on me but I pulled out a scope and a sniper rifle. Ida Belle gave me a hard look.

"Just in case," I said.

She gave me a single nod and grabbed another rifle. Neither of us wanted things to go down that way, but if it was a choice between Cory and one of the others, then my allegiance was definitely with the others. I already knew what kind of person Cory was. I just hoped he elected to cause a scene by mouthing off and didn't take things to the level Cooke had.

We ran to the tree line then paused at the edge to assess our approach to the house. Becca's car was in the driveway and a BMW was parked behind it. That had to be Cory. A later model Accord was parked next to Becca's car, and I wondered if it belonged to Myrna or even Ashley. Either way, that meant we had at least four adults and one child inside...and Cory Guillory.

A storage building stood in the backyard and, if we angled in behind it, blocked the view from any of the house's windows. I pointed to the shed and took off, Ida Belle and Gertie trailing behind me. When we got to the shed, I peeked around the corner with my scope. The window to the kitchen was open and I could see inside, but no one occupied the kitchen or breakfast nook. They must all be in the living room, which was at the front of the house.

"The kitchen is clear," I said. "I'm going to sneak in the back door. Gertie, you cover me on the rear. Ida Belle, you take the front so we can flank him."

They both nodded and I hurried across the lawn to the back of the house and pressed myself against the side, under the kitchen window. Gertie was only seconds behind me, which surprised me a bit, but then she wasn't carrying her handbag which probably weighed her down significantly.

"I'm going to enter through the back door," I whispered. "Hang back at the door until I motion for you to enter."

The point of that setup was that if Cory, by some miracle of extreme luck, happened to take me out, Gertie had cover and time to take aim and shoot. But mostly, I wanted her out of the potential line of fire. Ida Belle was a sharpshooter and had taken a rifle with her for that reason. I knew she'd hang back rather than charging in, which was why I'd sent her around front. I crept onto the porch and tried the back door, happy to find it was unlocked. I eased the doorknob around and inched the door open, praying the hinges didn't squeak. Then I slipped inside.

I could hear the angry voices in the living room as soon as I entered, and when I peered around the corner into the living room, the worst possible scenario was splayed out in front of me.

Cory Guillory stood near the front door, Caleb clutched in one arm and a pistol in his other hand. Megan, Seth, Becca, and Myrna were across from him, all of them wearing horrified expressions. Megan was staring at Caleb, crying, as the baby wailed and stretched his arms out in her direction. A puppy whined in a crate next to the Christmas tree.

I could have shot Cory, but not without risking injury to Caleb. And besides, if I fired a shot right then, one of the others might have a heart attack. They were already perched on the thin edge of sanity. Add to that, I had no reason to suspect that Cory was going to harm the baby, just take him, and that left me with a thin defense for killing the man. Especially as he was trying to leave with his own child.

I saw no other option but to force Cory into relinquishing the baby. If he knew he wasn't going to get away, then maybe he'd come to his senses and no one would get hurt. I leaned my rifle against the wall and pulled out my pistol, then stepped around the corner, gun leveled at Cory's head.

"This isn't going to work out the way you think it is," I said.

Cory looked at me and sneered. "You think I'm scared of some broad with a gun?"

"You should be," I said. "I'm a former CIA operative. My job title was classified. You know what that's code for?"

I shook my pistol and he smiled.

"You're just another lying whore," he said.

"The only reason you're not already dead is because you're holding that baby," I said. "I understand you're angry. Ashley went through with an adoption without telling you. But this is not the way to exercise your parental rights. You need to let the courts work it out."

I hoped appealing to his rational side would get him to turn over the baby, but when he looked at me, with those cold, dead snake eyes, I knew he was too far gone to care anymore. Why, I had no idea. He'd claimed Ashley was beneath him. He'd married the well-connected woman he thought he needed to get him ahead. It still didn't make sense.

"I told you I didn't dally with cheap women," he said. "This has nothing to do with Ashley and everything to do with that whore right there."

He pointed the gun at Becca and Myrna gasped.

Becca's eyes filled with tears and her entire body started shaking.

"You thought you could take my son from me and give him to these peasants?" Cory ranted. "Raised in this hick town in squalor? That's no life for anyone with my blood. My son is going to have the best of everything available to him. He's going to carry on my name and my legacy."

I looked between Becca and Cory, so confused, and then with Becca's next words, all of Cooke's perceived inconsistencies in his investigation made sense.

"Our baby died!" Becca yelled, choking as she spoke.

CHAPTER TWENTY-THREE

EVERYONE STARED AT BECCA IN DISBELIEF.

"You're lying," he said. "That's all women know how to do."

Becca burst into tears. "Do you think I like saying that? That our baby died? Reliving the most horrible moment of my life? I showed you the death certificate. It's on file with the state. That is not your son!"

"If he's not my son, then why did you run?" Cory asked. "You gave up my son and disappeared, hoping I wouldn't find you. But you weren't as smart as you thought. And now, it's all over. I'm taking my son and you're going to prison for this. And there's nothing you can do about it."

Myrna wrapped one arm around her clearly distraught daughter and grabbed a baby brush from a nearby table. She tossed it on the chair next to Cory.

"This has gone far enough," Myrna said. "Get that hair tested. While *you're* sitting in prison, you can do so without plotting your next act of violence against these people."

Cory glanced down at the brush and I saw a tiny flicker of doubt cross his face. I thought that would be it. That he'd give Megan the baby and have the tests run. That everything could be settled by judges and with no guns. But then his expression hardened again and I saw his jaw flex.

"You've already wasted too much of my time," he said. "Time my wife and I could have been bonding with our son. Time we could have spent presenting him to the press. You won't take another minute from me and what's mine."

The front door was open behind Cory with the screen door closed. I saw a shadow cross the threshold, then Ida Belle stepped into the frame, motioning to Caleb. I gave her a nod and she lifted the rifle and slammed the hilt into the back of Cory's skull. At the same time, I dropped my pistol and leaped forward, snatching Caleb with one arm and Cory's pistol with my other hand.

Cory screamed in pain but was still conscious, so for good measure, as I spun around to hand Seth the baby, I backhanded Cory with his pistol, sending him crashing in a heap on the living room floor. Becca collapsed and dragged Myrna down with her as Ida Belle and Gertie rushed into the room. I bent down and checked Cory's pulse. He was unconscious but still breathing. Even though that was a good thing, I couldn't help feeling a tiny bit disappointed.

Gertie handed me a pair of handcuffs and I snapped them on him.

"Guess he won't become president," Ida Belle said, looking down at Cory. "What with that prison record that he's going to have."

"I'm thinking his wife might have a problem with all this as well," Gertie said.

"I suppose we're going to have to be satisfied with that, since we didn't kill him," Ida Belle said.

"I almost wish you would have," Seth said as he walked up and kicked Cory right in the rib cage. Quite frankly, had a man been holding a pistol on my family and trying to kidnap my baby, I would have done a lot worse.

"Nobody saw that," Gertie said. "If you'd like to do it again."

He shook his head. "No sense any of us getting into trouble over this piece of—"

"Language," Megan said as she ran over to hug each of us, still crying. She was clutching Caleb in her arms, probably squeezing him a little too hard, but the baby had a death grip on her shirt and hair, so clearly he felt the same as she did.

When she broke off the hug, we all stood there staring at one another, not sure exactly what to say. I think everyone was still a little dumbstruck.

"Can someone help me get her up?" Myrna asked.

Crap. We'd completely forgotten about Becca!

Seth helped Myrna lift Becca onto the couch while Ida Belle hurried into the kitchen, then came back with a glass of water. Myrna stuck her fingers in the water and rubbed it onto Becca's face.

"Is she all right?" Gertie asked.

Myrna started tapping the side of her face. "She just passed out. I'm sure it was the stress."

"Yeah, that admission was totally unexpected," Seth said. "Did you know Becca had given birth?"

Myrna shook her head. "We had a falling-out earlier this year. At the time, I thought Becca had gotten in a snit over nothing and she'd get over it, but now I know why she kept me distant for so long."

"But keeping you in the dark doesn't make sense," Seth said. "She couldn't have hidden the baby forever."

"Maybe she was going to give the baby up like Ashley did," Gertie said. "Maybe she figured out that Cory was a horrible person and didn't want her mother to know that she'd made such a huge mistake. Shame is a powerful motivator."

Myrna looked over at Gertie, her expression bleak. "You might be right. But I wish she would have come to me. I could have helped."

I heard a car engine roaring up and looked out to see Carter running inside. He stopped short, his relief apparent, then looked around, taking in everything but clearly confused. I moved forward and attempted to give him the condensed version of who everyone was and what had happened.

"I'll get statements from everyone later," he said as he motioned for Seth to help him cart Cory out. "But I've got enough to book him for now."

He gave me a quick nod as he left and I could tell that he'd been afraid of what he might find. I was certain Walter had called him in a panic, insisting he drop whatever nonsense he was seeing to at the Swamp Bar in order to get to the Prejeans' immediately. He'd probably been imagining a million different horrible things on his way.

Becca stirred a bit, then bolted upright in a panic. Myrna put her hands on her shoulders to prevent her from standing.

"Calm down," Myrna said. "Everyone is safe. Carter just took that awful man away from here."

Becca started softly weeping and wrapped her arms around Myrna. "I'm so sorry I didn't tell you. I should have. But I'd messed up so bad and didn't want you to know. And Cory was so horrible. I was scared of him. Scared of what he might do to me and to you if you were involved."

Myrna stroked her daughter's hair and held her close. "None of that matters now. All that matters is that you're safe and so is everyone we care about. Cory isn't going to bother you again. Carter will make sure of that."

"I'll fix us all something to drink," Megan said. "Spiked.

Except for Caleb, of course. We all need it. Will you ladies please stay with us for a while? I have a feeling we're all going to want to talk things out. I'm thrilled that you're here but also confused about everything."

"You're not the only one," I said. "And we'd be happy to stay."

"Even happier for a drink," Gertie said. "I'll help you with those."

A bit later, we were all sitting in the living room, clutching a stiff drink. Caleb and the puppy were down for a much-needed nap. After the initial flurry of passing glasses around, we all went silent. I think everyone was afraid to be the first to start talking, especially given that the questions we had weren't going to be easy to answer. And Becca needed to answer most of them.

She looked better than she had a few minutes earlier. The color had returned to her face but tears still pooled in her eyes from time to time. Her hand shook a bit as she lifted her glass and I'm sure she felt self-conscious under our scrutiny. Megan was the first to break the silence.

"I have to ask," she said quietly. "Is Caleb Ashley's son?"

It had to be the biggest question on everyone's mind. Myrna had practically taunted Cory to have Caleb's DNA tested. What if he was Cory's son? Would his family make a play for the baby? His wife? Could he acquire rights even as a convicted felon?

"No," Becca said. "Ashley's baby died a couple weeks after he was born. It was a crib death. There was nothing wrong with the baby or with anything she did." Becca looked directly at Seth. "I know that for certain because she was staying with me. Our babies were born only days apart. We thought it would be easier if we shared duties, at least in the beginning.

Plus, my place was closer to the doctors if we needed them and I had a car."

Megan nodded, getting misty, and Seth put his arm around his wife and pulled her close. This was their worst nightmare.

"I swore I'd never tell anyone what happened, but you deserve to know," Becca said. "But to explain it all properly, I have to go back a ways, so please bear with me."

"Take all the time you need," Myrna said.

"I met Cory at one of his company's events at the hotel where Ashley worked," Becca said. "We hit it off and he asked for my number. I was flattered by the attention. He was good-looking and educated and rich. It was stupid to think he would be interested in someone like me. But he was a good actor when he needed to be."

"The worst ones always are," Ida Belle said.

Becca nodded. "I met Ashley that same night on break—outside, like I told you guys before. And we became friends. Ashley used to hook up with another guy who worked at the company, Drew McEntire. A party boy whose parents owned the company. Neither of them was serious."

"Was he the father of her baby?" Megan asked.

"She said no," Becca said. "Ashley always claimed she didn't know who the father was and I believed her. She didn't lie to me because she didn't have to. I didn't have any expectations when it came to her. I knew the way she lived wasn't my way but she was a good friend, and when she got pregnant, she *did* change her life."

"Ashley was telling the truth," I said. "We talked to Drew. He had a vasectomy when he was twenty. Didn't want to be trapped by a woman looking for a permanent paycheck—his words."

"That sounds about right," Becca said. "I should have known better than to get involved with Cory, but I was stupid and lonely. He was charming and sophisticated. He said all the right things and did all the right things, and I thought we were in a relationship. When I got pregnant, I was terrified. I figured he'd be furious but instead, he was happy."

She shook her head. "I should have seen the signs. I'd never met his family or friends. At first, I was happy about that—I had him all to myself. You know, the big romance. At least, that's what I convinced myself of. But keeping me separate from his real life was how he kept me from finding out the truth."

She took a deep breath and slowly blew it out.

"He was just using me to get a baby," Becca said. "And I'm pretty sure I wasn't the only one. Just the first to get pregnant. The entire time I dated him, he was engaged to another woman—one with the political connections he wanted so badly. But something was wrong, and she couldn't have children. Cory wanted a baby desperately. It was important for his image, and nothing but his own blood would do. He thought his DNA was special. His son would be special. Like him."

I shook my head. I'd seen some pretty big God complexes, but this guy was in love with himself like no other.

"But how could he know you'd get pregnant?" Gertie asked. "He was running a risk, having an affair with you while being engaged. And if there were other women as well…"

"We always used protection," Becca said. "I can't take birth control pills and told him that. My guess is he poked holes in the condoms."

"Bastard," Gertie said.

"But he couldn't just take the baby from you," Megan said.

"He didn't think he'd have to," Becca said. "I'd told him that I didn't want kids. I saw how hard it was for my mother after my dad died. I never wanted to risk that for myself or my child. So he thought if he offered me money, I'd jump at the opportunity."

"He offered you money?" Megan asked, clearly outraged.

"A hundred grand," Becca said. "I was so angry. I loved him, and he had used me as a brood mare. Then he assumed I cared so little about the baby I was carrying that I'd sell it and just go on like it had never happened. There's no way I could do that."

"Is that when he broke your arm?" I asked.

She stared at me, a bit surprised.

"It's not really the type of break you get from a bicycle accident," I said. "It's the kind you get from a struggle with another person."

Becca dropped her gaze down to her lap and nodded. "I knew then just how bad things were. I'd thought worst case we'd share custody, but that was before I knew how cruel Cory was and just how far he'd go to get what he wanted. After that, I told him he couldn't come to my apartment. That if he did, I'd press charges and get a restraining order."

Myrna grabbed her daughter's hand and squeezed it. "My poor baby."

"It gets worse," Becca said. "Ashley heard Drew on his phone in the hotel hallway one night. She was going for supplies when she heard him say my name, so she hid behind a plant and listened. It was right after I'd refused to take Cory's money. Drew was giving Cory the name of a shady doctor who would be willing to have me declared mentally incompetent."

Becca swiped tears from her cheek and I could see all the anger and hurt come back on her full force.

"Cory was planning on putting me in some mental institution and getting full custody of the baby. Drew told him if that didn't work, there were other ways of eliminating me as a problem. Permanent ways."

Megan's hands flew over her mouth and Myrna gasped. Ida Belle called Cory a few choice names and Seth contributed to her list. I just shook my head. The evil people could do rarely surprised me but the callousness of all of this was overwhelming.

"So what did you do?" Ida Belle asked.

Becca shook her head. "What could I do? I didn't have the money to disappear and Cory had money and the connections to find me even if I tried. He believed my threat about the police and never came to my apartment again, but during the rest of my pregnancy, he'd drop by the photography studio where I worked. He pretended concern for me but I'm sure he was just making certain I wasn't harming his precious DNA. Every time he left, he'd throw money at me. It made me feel so cheap, which is what he wanted. He was trying to break me down. Get me to give in to his plan."

"I wish I would have kicked him harder and far more," Seth said.

"And in a different place," Gertie said. "That man needs to be sterilized."

Becca nodded. "If I hadn't passed out, I might have shot him. Guess it's a good thing I did."

"What happened after the baby was born?" I asked.

"Cory turned up the heat," Becca said. "He still wasn't allowed in my apartment. Ashley was there by then and no way was I putting all of us at risk. But one night, about five days after the birth, he banged on the door and I called the cops. They told him he had to go through the courts to solve his problems and they didn't want to see him there again. I figured he'd gone by the studio and when he couldn't find me, he knew I'd had the baby."

"You should have filed charges then," Megan said. "Had him thrown in jail."

"It never would have stuck," Becca said. "He'd just married a state senator's daughter. They had connections with local law enforcement and judges. So he upped the ante and offered me twice what he had before. When I refused, he shifted gears and threatened me with attorneys. Said if I had a wellness exam for myself and the baby that he wouldn't make trouble, but he just wanted to make sure both of us were all right. Then he started pushing me to see that doctor that Drew had recommended. By that point, I'm sure my health wasn't all that great. I was terrified and not sleeping, and I was certain that if I went in front of a judge, they would take one look at me and decide I wasn't fit. I couldn't see any way out of the situation that didn't end with me in a mental institution or a grave."

Tears welled up in her eyes again and several spilled over onto her cheek. "That's when Ashley's baby died. When we took him to the hospital, she told me to tell them he was mine. That way, I'd have a death certificate to show Cory. Ashley knew how much you wanted a baby and said she could get you to adopt my son. That way, he'd be safe. Another bartender she knew had used Abshire to adopt out her baby and she knew he didn't ask questions. Then, just in case Cory ever found out about Ashley and me being friends, she was going to disappear."

"Cory didn't know you and Ashley were friends?" I asked.

"No," Becca said. "He'd never shown any interest in my personal life and I'd never mentioned her. I figured he wouldn't approve of my being friends with her given his straitlaced stance on everything. Turned out to be a good thing, although I guess he found out about Ashley eventually or he never would have tracked things here."

I knew Cooke had connected Becca to Ashley because he'd gone by the bar looking for her, but since she was nowhere to be found and people didn't seem to know about their friendship, I supposed he'd made a note to the file and let it go as a dead end. But after I talked to Cory, something must have clicked in his mind, possibly from notes Cooke had sent him on the investigation. Combine that with the mention of a baby and Sinful and that was all it took to set Cory off in the Prejeans' direction.

"What a horrible decision to have to make," Megan said.

"It was," Becca agreed. "But it was still an answer to my prayers. My son would have a great home and you would have the child you always wanted. Ashley said it was the positive thing that could come out of her baby's death."

"So Caleb *is* your son," Megan said. "Cory will have tests run. Even if he's in prison, his family has money, right? Or his wife's family. They can make things happen."

"No. They can't," Becca said. "Because Caleb isn't mine."

Everyone looked completely confused. "Then whose baby is he?" Megan asked. "Will someone else come looking for him?"

Becca shook her head. "No. I went with Ashley to the attorney to drop off my baby. She carried him in, of course, but when it came time to put him in the nursery room, she handed him to me. The lawyer just thought she was too emotional to do it and directed me to the room where he kept the babies until they were checked out by the nurse before transport to their homes. But I knew Ashley was giving me a chance to say one final goodbye. When I went into the nursery, there was another baby boy there. He was about the same age as my son. So I switched them."

CHAPTER TWENTY-FOUR

THERE WAS A SHARP INTAKE OF BREATH BY SETH AND Megan. Myrna shook her head and clenched her daughter's hand so hard that her knuckles whitened. I glanced over at Ida Belle and Gertie, who were as shocked as I was. This story had more twists and turns than a roller coaster.

"I'm so sorry," Becca said. "I know it was wrong but it wasn't like you were getting Ashley's baby anyway. I just thought it would be safer. Another chasm between Cory and my son. That way, if he ever found out about Ashley and her baby and traced him back to you, he wouldn't be able to take him."

"And the couple that got your son?" Megan asked.

"Were buying a baby," Becca said. "We knew Abshire wasn't an upstanding sort of guy. He paid Ashley's bartender friend for her baby and that's not legal. By using Abshire, his clients got a shortcut to adoption and had to have known or at least suspected why because they were the ones putting the money up."

"And because things weren't necessarily on the up-and-up," Ida Belle said, "that meant Abshire and his clients would all keep their mouths shut if anyone came sniffing around with questions. It kept him insulated and his practice running strong."

Becca nodded. "The chart on the other baby's crib clearly stated no medical records available and closed adoption. The adoptive couple would never know more about his birth parents. They wanted a healthy baby boy and they got one."

Megan and Seth looked at each other and I could tell they didn't know how to react, what to think. I couldn't blame them. It was a lot to take in and all of it centered on the child they considered their own and who might as well have been dropped off by a stork.

Becca wiped a tear from her face. "Look. What I did was wrong but I'm not sorry I did it. I was protecting my son and if I had to do it all over again, I'd do the same thing."

"So where is your son?" Megan asked quietly.

"I don't know," Becca said. "I didn't open the envelope for the other baby. It's better this way. My son has an opportunity for the life I couldn't have given him because of Cory. If I don't know where he is, I'll never be tempted to seek him out. That keeps him safe."

Megan went over and hugged Becca, softly crying. "I am so sorry. I can't even imagine how hard that was for you. But you're an incredible person for what you did. I don't blame you. I hope I would have had the strength to do the same thing."

"One thing I don't understand is how did Cory find out about Caleb?" Megan said. "Did that man who died tell him?"

"I think I can explain that one," I said. "Some of it is speculation, but based on what we found in our investigation, I have a good idea about what happened."

Gertie put her hands up in the air. "Well, I wish you'd tell me, because I'm as confused as ever."

"When Becca told Cory their baby had died, he didn't believe her. So when she left town, Cory hired Cooke to track her down and find his son. Since you have some time to change your driver's license and other things, it took Cooke a while to track Becca to Mudbug. When he did, he broke into Becca's house—that was the first break-in—and didn't see any sign of a baby, but he found a business card or other contact information for Abshire."

Becca's eyes widened. "He gave me a card. I bet it was in my house somewhere. I didn't even think..."

"Why would you?" I asked. "The cops told you it was kids looking for things to hock and that you'd returned early and scared them off. But my guess is it was Cooke and nothing was missing because he wasn't there to rob you."

"So Cooke told Cory about Abshire's card," Ida Belle said.

I nodded. "And I'm sure Cooke filled Cory in on Abshire's reputation as well."

"So Cory assumed I'd let someone adopt our baby," Becca said. "This all makes more sense."

"Someone—I'm betting Cooke—broke into Abshire's office but couldn't find the records because my guess is they're all digitalized and the paper documents shredded," I said. "When Cooke couldn't find what he was looking for there, he paid Abshire a visit and roughed him up so badly he put him in the hospital."

Becca gasped and everyone looked shocked.

"What?" Becca asked.

"Abshire won't say who attacked him—my guess is because he knew why Cooke was after him and wasn't about to tell the police about his shady practices. But I paid him a visit in the hospital yesterday and even though he wouldn't tell me the truth, I think I got a good enough read on him to know what transpired."

"So what do you think happened?" Myrna asked.

"I think Cooke beat Abshire because he refused to tell him where Becca's baby was," I said. "But Abshire wouldn't have known because Cooke was using the wrong name. It was Ashley that he prepared an adoption for."

"Oh," Gertie said. "That makes sense. Then how did Cooke narrow it down?"

"Because Abshire wouldn't have remembered the names necessarily, but he might have remembered which towns babies were delivered to recently," I said. "We know that Cooke checked Mudbug and Sinful, but he could have been through others. Only Abshire knows how many locations he provided."

"And since I'd moved to Mudbug and my mother to Sinful," Becca said, "Cooke figured he'd hit the jackpot in one of those places."

Myrna shook her head. "So Cooke took over as Santa in Mudbug, so he could look for the baby."

I nodded. "Then he broke into Becca's studio and stole the pictures she'd taken so he could send them to Cory in order to double-check his work."

"I wonder if Cory would have even recognized his child," Ida Belle said.

"I'm sure he thought he would," Becca said. "His arrogance wouldn't have allowed him to think anything else."

"So obviously he didn't find what he was looking for in Mudbug," Seth said, "because he did a number on Rollie and took his place in Sinful."

"But if Cooke told Cory where to find Caleb, then why did he wait until today to come here?" Megan asked.

"Because Cooke was killed before he got a chance to tell Cory about Caleb," I said.

"Then how did Cory find us?" Seth asked.

"I'm afraid that's my fault," I said.

Megan's eyes widened. "What? How?"

"Because when I questioned Cory today, I used Ashley's full name and I left him my card," I said. "I also mentioned that her family was anxious to find her because she'd recently had a baby. My guess is Cooke had identified Ashley as a connection investigated but had her logged as a dead end. After I left, Cory must have realized where he'd heard the name before. It would have been a simple enough matter to track you down once he knew what he was looking for."

Seth blew out a breath. "Still. What Cory did was crazy. Showing up here and holding us at gunpoint. He couldn't be sure. Why take that kind of risk? Why not see an attorney and subpoena the DNA test?"

"My personal opinion is that Cory cracked," I said. "I don't think he's ever been mentally stable. Then his perfectly laid plans were ruined and he was committed to doing anything possible to salvage them. I think he was so obsessed that he didn't stop to think about the consequences."

"Or such a narcissist that he actually felt he was in the right," Ida Belle said. "That he was the victim."

I nodded. "And also convinced he could buy his way out of anything."

"Or have his father-in-law pull strings," Gertie said.

"All of this is so incredible," Megan said, then she stiffened. "Wait! Who killed Cooke?"

Everyone looked at Becca and her eyes widened.

"I didn't do it. I swear!" she said. "I never knew he was an imposter. I thought he was Rollie. Oh my God! The police are going to arrest me for killing him, aren't they? I mean, what else could they possibly think, especially with what Cory did today. Everything is going to come out and I'm going to go to prison."

"I don't think so," I said. "The police found an unopened bottled water in Cooke's car. It had cyanide injected into it. They also found a discarded bottle of water in the trash in the cafeteria with cyanide in it and Cooke's DNA on the rim. He had them before he ever got to Sinful."

"He was drinking bottled water while I was setting up the camera," Becca said. "Oh my God! What if he'd given someone one of those bottles? Someone else could have been killed."

I nodded. "It was a huge risk."

"But if the poison was in the water in his car as well, then who did it?" Seth asked.

"No one knows," I said. "The case has been turned over to the New Orleans police. Cooke was already under investigation and he had a lot of enemies. They might not ever figure it out."

"Given what kind of man Cooke was, I don't think I care," Megan said.

"I don't either," Gertie agreed.

"So I'm not going to get the blame?" Becca asked.

"I don't see how you could," I said. "Besides, even if you knew who Cooke was and what he was up to, you also knew Caleb wasn't Cory's son. You had no motive for killing him. All it would have taken is a DNA test to make Cory go away."

Becca's shoulders slumped with relief. "That's right."

"What about Ashley's baby?" Myrna asked. "Could Cory have the body exhumed and tested?"

Becca shook her head. "Ashley and I thought of that. He was cremated and we spread his ashes in the Mississippi River."

Myrna sniffed and hugged Becca. "So your son—my grandson—is safe."

CHAPTER TWENTY-FIVE

IT WAS A LONG, EMOTIONAL DAY, AND I CAPPED IT OFF WITH a long, emotional recap to Carter of everything that had happened and all my suspicions about what had happened. Carter thought my ideas were all completely plausible and probably close to the truth. He also agreed that we'd probably never get confirmation because all the parties in the know would remain silent. Cory had refused to speak at all other than to ask for his attorney.

Carter had informed the New Orleans police of his arrest, and the situation surrounding it, but had left out everything to do with the baby switching. He hadn't been happy with the duplicity but reporting that truth would only send psycho Cory after another set of adoptive parents and would land Becca in jail. Carter didn't like dishonesty but he hated the bad guys winning even more. So Becca's secret would remain in Sinful, hopefully never uncovered. As far as everyone else, the official story was that Megan had adopted her sister's baby and Becca's baby had died after she fled an abusive relationship.

The New Orleans police gladly agreed to take Cory on. I think, hoping to make a connection between Cory, Cooke, and

Abshire. I wasn't convinced they'd be able to, but I liked the direction they were going. At least they were going to try. I'd warned Megan and Seth before leaving that they should expect an attorney to contact them about providing a sample for DNA testing. No way was Cory going to take our word for it. But since Caleb wasn't his son, they had nothing to worry about.

After all the talking, we were both worn out. I offered for Carter to stay the night, but he still had to feed Tiny and he had to be in early the next morning to file paperwork, so it was better for him to head home. We were too tired for anything of the romantic nature anyway, and both of us were used to sprawling out in bed alone more often than not, so it was probably for the best.

I was asleep before my head hit the pillow, and for the first time in a long time, I had a completely dreamless and restful slumber. No alarms, no phone calls, no disgruntled cats. I awakened feeling refreshed and looking forward to the upcoming holiday celebration at Emmaline's.

But first, there was one more conversation I needed to have.

Myrna was sitting on her front porch drinking coffee when I pulled up. She took one look at me and waved me inside.

"I was wondering when you'd show up," she said as we sat in the kitchen.

"You knew Becca had given birth," I said, making a statement, not asking a question.

She nodded. "As many years as I spent caring for babies and women who'd had them, it would be a shame if I didn't recognize the signs in my own daughter. I knew that arm break wasn't a bicycle either, same as you. It didn't take much thinking to know what really happened."

"But you never said anything when you and Becca patched things up."

"She told me a little about Cory...enough for me to know that he was the root of her troubles. She was so careful about leaving her house and so secretive about her move that she had to give me a reason. All it took was her telling me she was scared of him and I knew the score. I never pushed her for more because I wanted her to tell me about the baby herself. When she was ready."

"You were the hospital nurse who did the exam on the babies Abshire filed adoption for."

"Yes. I didn't like the man, or his practices, but those babies and the families they were going to deserved the best care they could get. I saw Becca and Ashley outside his office that day. They were hugging each other on the sidewalk and they were both crying."

"Then you saw the babies, and you knew Nathan Vincent was your grandson."

She didn't say a word but I could see the tears forming.

"You knew Becca wouldn't give up her child without a good reason," I said. "So when you retired, you moved to Sinful where you could keep an eye on him."

She studied me for a moment, then nodded. "I was wondering if you'd figured things out that far."

"It was the birthmark on Nathan's cheek. Becca has the same one although the night Gertie commented on it, she thought it was face paint from the night before."

Myrna nodded. "I don't think Becca thinks about it anymore. Honestly, it had never bothered her. She wasn't that sort of child. And it had faded so much as she moved into adulthood. A light cover of makeup was all it took to hide it."

"Or pretty snowflakes."

Myrna was silent.

"I'm going to tell you what I think happened, and you don't have to say a word."

She gave me a single nod.

"I think you worked the Mudbug festival and Margaret Holden told you about the strange incident with the Santa. When someone broke into Becca's studio and all they stole were pictures, you were afraid Cory was looking for his baby. Then while you were preparing to leave for the Sinful event you saw Santa parked in front of your house, which made no sense. Then you realized it wasn't Rollie's car."

I shook my head. "Of all the unlucky moves for Cooke to make, parking where the only person who suspected what he was up to would see him. Later you overheard him on the phone with Cory and even though you'd rushed to paint Nathan's face, you knew you were too late. Cooke had already seen the birthmark."

"It's an interesting theory, but there's a hole in your story. Caleb doesn't have a birthmark and Cory still thought that baby was his son."

"He didn't have a birthmark, but he had a smudge from the face painting still on his cheek. Becca said the paint wasn't easy to get off. Cory might not have remembered the exact shape or size or he might have thought it had gotten smaller as the baby grew. But there was enough discoloration from him to believe, along with the other information he had, that Caleb was his son."

Myrna shrugged. "Hard to say what someone like that thinks."

"I'll tell you what *I* think. I think after you saw Cooke get out of that car, you went through it and found his case file on Becca, which you took and destroyed. That's why Carter never questioned you or Becca directly about Cooke. You were afraid

Cooke would discover Nathan at the gala and you came prepared to deal with that possibility.

"You tried to hide Nathan's identity with the face paint," I continued. "But then you overheard the phone conversation and knew you were too late. Your only chance to protect Nathan was to stop Cooke before he had a chance to give Cory the information. So you gave him a bottle of water injected with cyanide. And then when everyone was scrambling to handle things after Cooke collapsed, you hurried back home and put another poisoned bottle in his car. That way, the police wouldn't suspect someone from Sinful of poisoning him."

I studied her for a moment. "You see, one of the things that didn't fit was the fact that you'd spent years working in the ER but you never offered to render aid to Cooke. And the only two answers for why not were either that you knew he'd been poisoned and didn't want to expose yourself to it, or you weren't there."

"That's preposterous," Myrna said. "Cooke was just one man. Cory could easily hire another. What good would it do to get rid of him?"

"You knew the Vincents were moving to Abu Dhabi right after Christmas. You only needed to delay things long enough for them to get out of the country. You figured if Cooke was murdered, Cory would hold off on hiring someone else until he was sure the police couldn't connect him to Cooke in any way. Killing Cooke bought the time it would take for your grandson to leave the country."

Myrna took a sip of her coffee and stared out her back window. "That's an interesting story. You have a vivid imagination."

"Does Becca know that Nathan's her son?"

Myrna turned back to me. "No. I painted him before she

saw him that night. Zach Vincent's brother is a photographer. They never hired Becca to take photos of Nathan."

"Are you going to tell her?"

"No. I was going to, but after everything she said yesterday, I don't think she's ready to know. Might not ever be."

I nodded. Becca was the one who'd tried to ensure that her son was adopted to a good family that she'd never be able to track. If Myrna didn't want to tell her that she knew where her son was, then I couldn't argue the point. Not when Becca herself had taken drastic measures to keep herself in the dark.

I rose to leave, satisfied that I had the answers I'd come for.

"Are you going to tell her?" Myrna asked quietly.

"It's not my place to tell her. Nor to decide what she's ready to hear."

Myrna nodded. "Thank you for that. And for not offering up this information yesterday."

"Becca has suffered enough, and she'll probably feel guilty for everything that transpired for the rest of her life. I'm not interested in piling more on her. She and her son deserve some peace and the ability to live happy and fulfilled lives."

"Are you going to tell the police what you suspect?"

"What would be the point? They can't prove it. And besides, Becca isn't the only one who'll be living with guilt. Sometimes that's worse."

Myrna frowned and looked away.

I walked out of the house and took a deep breath. It was time to cleanse myself of all the negative energy that this case had presented and focus on happy things. A young woman was safe. Her baby was safe. Two couples had beautiful children. And a cruel man was going to prison.

It wasn't perfect, but things rarely were.

CHAPTER TWENTY-SIX

EMMALINE'S HOUSE WAS BEAUTIFULLY DECORATED IN traditional red, green, silver, and gold. There wasn't a surface in the room that didn't have some form of Christmas decor on top of it. She even changed out her drapes and had matching throw pillows and table linens with bright red cardinals on them and cute green-and-red plaid edging.

Everyone I cared about was there and all in excellent spirits. Emmaline and her boyfriend, Ida Belle, Gertie, Ally, Walter, and of course, Carter. We'd all done our gift opening and exchanging with one another before gathering at Emmaline's for dinner. Gertie and Ida Belle had been thrilled with the military-grade night-vision goggles I'd gotten them, and they'd pitched in and gotten me a hot tub—something I kept saying I needed but probably would have never bought for myself. And something I suspected Gertie would spend as much time in as I did.

Carter had been thrilled with the electric recliner with massage features that I'd gotten him and I was sporting a pretty bracelet with sparkly diamonds. It was delicate and girlie, and I absolutely adored it. Gertie claimed it was a starter diamond set and next up was an engagement ring. Since we still had to get Ida Belle married off, I wasn't ready to even go there. Carter had looked more than a little fearful when she'd made that statement, so I figured I wouldn't have to face that decision anytime soon. And that's the way I wanted it. Things were so good the way they were and as this was my virgin foray into regular living, I thought it was best to take my time.

I'd called Big and Little late the night before and filled them in on the approved version of the showdown. They were happy to hear that the baby was safe and that Cory was behind bars. They were also more than a little pleased that they'd been able to have a role in his capture and congratulated me over and over on my success. Even Mannie took a couple seconds to throw in his compliments. The next morning, I got a knock on my door at eight a.m. and a man wearing a tuxedo presented me with a bottle of Dom Perignon and a gift basket of the most expensive meats, cheeses, and caviar I'd ever seen. Courtesy of the Heberts. They certainly knew how to do things with class.

I'd gotten a call that morning from Megan Prejean. Ashley had appeared on their doorstep on Christmas Eve and was doing great. She'd left the 'rough' abusive boyfriend for good and moved to Baton Rouge when she left New Orleans. There, she'd started counseling at a women's center. She was taking classes to become a hairdresser and was thrilled to reconnect with Megan. Even Seth was happy to see her and had acknowledged that his sister-in-law had apparently changed for the better.

As I sat at the dinner table and held hands while Walter said grace, I marveled at how much my life had changed. If anyone had told me a year ago that I'd be living in a small town, working as a PI, dating a deputy, and with two seniors as the best friends a girl could ever have, I would have called them crazy. And compared to my previous life, it was crazy.

It was also perfect.

Later that night, as I sat with Carter in lawn chairs in my backyard, drinking Dom, I thought about how much I had to be thankful for. How blessed I'd been with all the things that Sinful had brought into my life. The moon was full and reflected on the bayou and it was beautiful—stinky bayou mud, casserole-eating alligators, and all.

My cell phone rang and Director Morrow's number came up. I stared for a second in surprise, but then figured maybe he wanted to extend holiday wishes.

"Merry Christmas, Director Morrow," I said when I answered.

"Merry Christmas, Fortune," he said. "I hope you're doing well. I've been enjoying your periodic emails. And I've found some interesting videos of your town on YouTube."

I laughed. "I'll bet."

He was silent for a moment and at first, I thought we'd been disconnected. Then he cleared his throat.

"There's something I have to tell you," he said, his tone serious. "And I don't quite know how to. This is a call I never thought I'd have to make. Never even dreamed..."

"What's wrong? Did something happen to Harrison?"

"No. He's fine. It's about your father."

"What about him?"

"He's alive."

More adventures with Fortune and the girls coming in 2020!

Sign up for Jana's newsletter to receive notification of new releases.
Janadeleon.com

MORE MISS FORTUNE FUN

Did you know that Jana created a publishing company that allows approved authors to pen their own stories in the Miss Fortune World? For a different take on Sinful and its residents, check out J&R Fan Fiction.

https://www.jrfanfiction.com

Sinful, Louisiana has its own website! If you want to escape to a bit of hilarity, check it out!

http://sinfullouisiana.com/